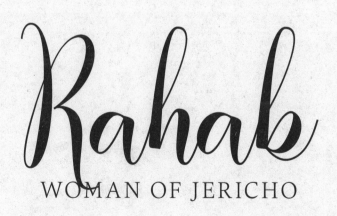

Rahab

WOMAN OF JERICHO

DIANA WALLIS TAYLOR

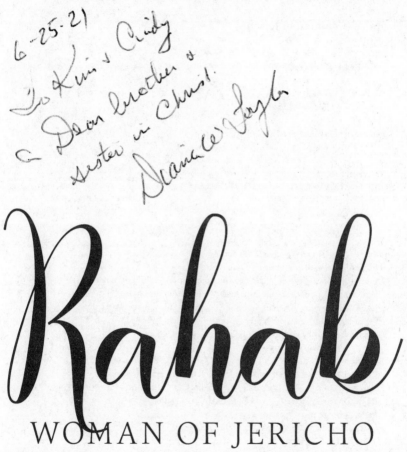

6-25-21
To Kim & Cindy
a Dear brother &
sister in Christ.
Diana W Taylor

Rahab

WOMAN OF JERICHO

WHITAKER
HOUSE

All Scripture quotations are taken from *The Complete Jewish Bible*, © 1998 by David H. Stern. Published by Jewish New Testament Publications, Inc. Used by permission. All rights reserved.

Rahab, Woman of Jericho

Diana Wallis Taylor
www.dianawallistaylor.com

ISBN: 978-1-64123-453-5
eBook ISBN: 978-1-64123-454-2

Printed in the United States of America
© 2020 by Diana Wallis Taylor

Whitaker House
1030 Hunt Valley Circle
New Kensington, PA 15068
www.whitakerhouse.com

Library of Congress Cataloging-in-Publication Data
Names: Taylor, Diana Wallis, 1938- author.
Title: Rahab : woman of Jericho / Diana Wallis Taylor.
Description: New Kensington, PA : Whitaker House, [2020] | Summary: "A
  fictional account of the biblical character Rahab from the book of
  Joshua, envisioning her as an Ephraimite whose family did not experience
  the exodus, who wed the Egyptian governor of Jericho, was widowed, and
  saved her family by saving two Israelite spies, one of whom she later
  wed"— Provided by publisher.
Identifiers: LCCN 2019058795 (print) | LCCN 2019058796 (ebook) | ISBN
  9781641234535 (trade paperback) | ISBN 9781641234542 (ebook)
Subjects: LCSH: Rahab (Biblical figure) | Bible. Old Testament—History of
  Biblical events—Fiction. | Women in the Bible—Fiction. | GSAFD: Bible
  fiction. | Biographical fiction.
Classification: LCC PS3620.A942 R34 2020 (print) | LCC PS3620.A942
  (ebook) | DDC 813/.6—dc23
LC record available at https://lccn.loc.gov/2019058795
LC ebook record available at https://lccn.loc.gov/2019058796

1 2 3 4 5 6 7 8 9 10 11 ⨆⨆ 27 26 25 24 23 22 21 20

*R*ahab stood in the garden of her home, listening to the bulbul birds chattering to one another. The weariness that had plagued her for weeks was lifting as her body slowly recovered from the strange fever that swept through their town. Her mother told her that a traveler who had lodged with a family in Upper Beth-horon became feverish and died suddenly. Afterward, the fever spread from that family until many in the town were ill and many died. Finally, with the spring rains, the fever seemed to abate, but sorrow was left in its wake.

Now, as Rahab stood quietly in the stillness of the early morning, she thanked Jehovah for sparing her. A gentle breeze brushed her cheek and she sensed His presence. While the fever racked her body, she had gone in and out of delirium, barely conscious of the cool cloths her mother had placed on her forehead or patted on her arms and chest. She heard her mother's voice, murmuring over and over, "Spare her, Lord, she is our youngest. Spare her."

During her illness, she sensed her mother's presence, but one night, in her darkest hour, she felt the presence of her God as well. In her spirit, she heard the words, *"You shall live."*

Remembering that night, Rahab breathed deeply of the fresh air and looked at the world around her with new eyes. In the distance, the morning mist was clearing; over the wall, she could see their sister town of Lower Beth-horon. A caravan route divided the towns of Upper and Lower Beth-horon, and as she watched, a caravan lumbered slowly along in the distance, the camels appearing to be the size of mice. She wondered where this one was going. Having lived in Upper Beth-horon all of her sixteen years, she knew she would probably marry and remain here. She sighed deeply. There was another world out there… but she knew she would never see it.

Maybe her restlessness came from being so ill and confined to her room for many weeks as she struggled against the illness that sapped her strength and seemed to set her body on fire. When at last it had run its course, she was left feeling weak and listless. Her mother had to feed her until she regained the strength to feed herself.

"You are better today?" Her mother, Zahava, had stepped into the garden. Rahab had not heard her footsteps.

"Yes, I feel much stronger, Imah." A tear slipped down her cheek. "I feel so sad about Tova. I will miss her." Tova, her nurse, had succumbed to the fever. She had been with their family ever since Rahab could remember and took care of all the children when they were little. No one knew her age—not even Tova herself—but from her wrinkled hands and lines on her face, they knew she was older than they could imagine.

Zahava put an arm around her daughter's shoulders. "I thought for a time we would lose you too, child. You were very ill, but you fought it." She shook her head. "Dear Tova just hadn't the strength to resist."

"Were there many others?"

As her mother told her about some of the families who had lost loved ones, including several children, and Rahab wondered aloud why she survived when others did not.

"One night, Imah, a voice whispered to me that I would live," she related pensively.

Zahava lifted her chin with one finger. "Our God knows His way, my daughter. Jehovah has spared you, but it is not for us to ask the reasons."

From the wall, they watched the distant travelers for a moment and then Zahava led Rahab to a stone bench, where they sat, each lost in thought. Finally, Rahab asked the question that had been on her mind. "Did Jonah come with his father?" Jonah belonged to one of the few Hebrew families that had not left Beth-horon. Before her illness, she'd overheard that he and his father were going to call on her father with a marriage proposal.

Zahava was silent a moment, gauging Rahab's response. "I'm sorry, child. You were so ill. Jonah's father was worried about a sickly wife if you survived. He has betrothed his son to Keren, the wine merchant's daughter."

A sense of relief washed over her, but Rahab cast her gaze to the ground to hide her reaction from her mother. She didn't like Jonah and dreaded the thought of marrying him.

Her mother patted her on the knee, her voice more hopeful than convincing. "There will be other young men, daughter. You are the most beautiful young woman in Beth-horon and when it becomes known that you are well, though you are now older, I'm sure there will be no end of suitors."

But will there be one I like? Rahab wondered. *And who will I have to choose from?*

"Imah, it is said that many of the other Israelite families are moving out of Canaan."

Zahava took her hand. "That is true. There are fewer and fewer Jewish families, not only here in Upper Beth-horon, but the lower city, and Beth-Sherah."

"Then who will be left for me to marry?"

Her mother sighed. "There will be someone. As our youngest child, your father and I were reluctant to let you go. Now, you are well and eligible, but yes, the young men are few."

It was a disappointing prospect. Rahab's shoulders sank. "I shall end up an unmarried woman and never be able to give you grandchildren."

Zahava cupped Rahab's chin with one hand and brushed a lock of hair from her daughter's forehead with the other. "We must trust Jehovah, child, and His plan for you."

"Yes, Imah."

Zahava rose, a twinkle in her eyes. "I have news to cheer you. We will be having a guest for dinner."

Rahab rolled her eyes. "Not the Egyptian governor again! He is like a peacock, so filled with his own importance."

Her mother raised an eyebrow. "I didn't know you were so opinionated! You had best watch your manners, Rahab. As the paka, our governor, he represents Pharaoh, to whom we are all required to pay tribute. It is best not to offend him."

With a knowing look at Rahab, her mother returned to the house to oversee preparations for the evening meal.

Rahab rose and went to the wall again. The caravan was now a speck in the distance.

She contemplated her mother's words. In spite of their heritage, her family was required to pay tribute to Pharaoh, just as the Canaanites did. She did not like the aging paka, with all of his pomp and posturing, but for the sake of her family, she would be respectful.

She thought about her mother's comment on her heritage and recalled one of the many times her father, Akim, had gathered his children around him and shared the story of how they came to live in Upper Beth-horon in the land of Canaan. On that particular occasion, he shared with her the origin of her name.

Rahab never tired of hearing the story. It was one of intrigue, adventure, and hope....

"Our ancestor, Joseph, was one of the younger sons of Jacob," her father had related. "He saved Egypt from a great famine and was named prime minister of Egypt. Joseph was then given Asenath, the beautiful daughter of Poti-Pherah, high priest of On, as his wife."

Isaac, always the studious one, had asked, "Was she an Israelite, Abba?"

"No, my son. She was from a high-ranking family in Egypt. Pharaoh meant to honor Joseph and perhaps tie him more to the

Egyptian culture. Joseph had no choice. He married Asenath and they had two sons, Manasseh and Ephraim. Joseph, however, brought them up to know Jehovah. Then, when Joseph's father Jacob was dying, to Joseph's surprise, he adopted Joseph's sons, giving them the same status as his own sons. But more importantly, he gave the patriarchal blessing to the younger son, Ephraim, our ancestor. He would carry the princely line. Ephraim grew up and married. He had three sons and six grandsons."

"But they died, didn't they, Abba?" Eliana had asked.

Akim had raised his eyebrows. "Now who is telling the story?" The children had all giggled and urged their Abba to continue.

"One day, these sons and grandsons of Ephraim thought that they could just ride into Canaan and do what they pleased. They saw a herd of cattle and decided to take some for themselves. Perhaps they wanted them for a sacrifice. We will never know. The men of Gath discovered what they had done and killed all of them because they entered Canaan brashly and stole the cattle. Ephraim mourned many days over the loss of his seed and the princely line."

"But there was another son, Abba," had prompted Rahab's brother Baram.

"Yes. Ephraim's wife gave birth to another son, who was given the unhappy name, Beriah, meaning, 'Because of the sadness in his house.' Beriah grew up and married, and his wife gave birth to a daughter, Sherah. She became a great leader who eventually moved to Canaan and settled here with all her household."

"She didn't become a slave, Abba," six-year-old Rahab had chimed in, remembering that part of the story.

"No, child. Her family avoided the fate of those left behind in Egypt, who suffered greatly after our ancestor Joseph died."

And Abba had smiled down at Rahab. "That is why we named you Rahab. It means 'remembering Egypt.'"

Rahab had smiled up at her father and felt so important for having a name that reminded her family of their history and how they had escaped the fate of the people in Egypt.

Her father always concluded his tale the same way: "Each generation has the honor of passing on the story of our heritage. While we live in Canaan, we will still remember Egypt."

~

Pondering that moment ten years ago, Rahab frowned. *It might be important to know their heritage, but what did it matter here in Upper Beth-horon? Would her father be able to find a good husband for her when so few Jewish men were available here?*

Her people had not intermarried with the Canaanites because they worshipped pagan gods. So, she reasoned, her husband would have come from another place. *But where?*

Her three brothers and two sisters had married when many Hebrew families still lived in Upper and Lower Beth-horon. With twelve children between them, there were now over twenty members of her family nearby. *Had her brothers' wives or her sisters' husbands any young men left in their families whom she could marry?* Rahab did not know....

The sun was arcing down toward sunset when she reluctantly left the garden to dress for the evening meal. Thinking of the aging paka, she shook her head, and had to remind herself of her mother's plea to be respectful.

2

*R*ahab descended the stone stairs from her sleeping room and walked past the storage room. She had dressed in her best tunic, tied a leather belt inset with tiny lapis lazuli stones around her small waist, and slipped on her sandals. She had lost weight with the fever, but she was thankful she was no longer so pale. The color had come back to her skin and the abundant hair that tumbled down her back had regained its shine.

Despite the growing warmth that heralded a blistering summer, thick walls made of rough-hewn blocks of stone and the multi-layered, wood-beamed roof kept the house cool even on the hottest days. The roof was covered with clay-coated branches and rolled until it was almost level. Sometimes, it had to be rerolled after a storm. Rahab was grateful her father was a wealthy landowner. Most of her friends lived in small, three-room houses. Her father's house had three sleeping rooms upstairs, a kitchen, entryway, dining room, her father's room for conducting business, a room for weaving and sewing, and a smaller room downstairs that Tova had shared with their cook, Rivka.

Guests were greeted and meals were served in the main room of the house. Just after Rahab entered, Rivka came in from the storage room with a platter of dates. Two loaves of freshly baked wheat and barley bread had already been placed on the low table in the center of the room. Stone bowls of olive oil and additional bowls of *nigella*, a mixture of ground toasted almonds, cumin seeds, sesame seeds, and peppery, nutmeg flower seeds were nearby for dipping chunks of bread. Pitchers of wine and beer stood on opposite ends of the table. Rahab's father preferred their homemade wine, but their Egyptian guest would want beer.

"I am glad you are better, mistress," Rivka said softly.

"As am I, Rivka. I am sorry about Tova. I know you were friends."

Rivka's eyes clouded for a moment and she nodded her head in response, but hurried away when Rahab's father cleared his throat.

Rahab turned to see her parents standing by the entrance with their guest. To her surprise, it was not the paka but another man, who appeared to be in his early thirties. Tall and tanned, he wore a bronze helmet and the uniform of an Egyptian soldier. His bearing was one of authority. With his firm jaw and chiseled high cheekbones, his features showed strength and determination. A jolt went through her as she realized his dark eyes were silently appraising her.

Behind him stood two soldiers of lesser rank wearing helmets of leather and carrying leather shields. Each had a bow slung over his back, along with a quiver of arrows. Gazing past them, Rahab caught a glimpse of her father's male servant, Jabari, leading the soldiers' horses to the barn.

Akim stepped forward. "My lord, may I present my daughter, Rahab. Daughter, our guest, the paka's son, Captain Radames."

Rahab inclined her head. "My lord." At a nod from their leader, the other soldiers entered the room.

Radames addressed Akim. "My father had to make an unexpected trip to Egypt. He suggested I pay a call on your family in his place on my way to Jericho." A smile tugged at the corners of Radames' mouth as he turned his eyes to Rahab. "I am surprised such a beautiful daughter has not been taken by one of your eligible young men."

Did he think she had just not had any offers? Rahab's eyes flashed. "I was…"

"Rahab was ill with the fever that swept through Canaan," her mother swiftly interjected. "We thought we would lose her at one time, but Jehovah be praised, she is strong and has recovered."

Radames' countenance changed immediately. "Forgive me. You are most fortunate. Many were lost, even in the army where I served."

Akim swept one arm toward the dining area, where ornate stools had been placed around the low table. "Come, let us partake together." He inclined his head to include the other two soldiers and they all gathered around the table.

Rivka poured the wine in pottery cups for the family, but at a nod from Akim, served him and Radames cups of beer. Jabari placed a platter of roasted lamb in the center of the table. Near Rahab stood a tureen filled with one of her favorite dishes: brown lentil pottage with onions, garlic, pearl barley, leeks, lamb broth, mustard greens, and olive oil, topped with fresh mint leaves. The aroma made Rahab realize how hungry she was and she eagerly used the large wooden serving spoon to fill her bowl. Savoring the delightful dish, she well understood how her ancestor Jacob could trick his hungry brother Esau out of his birthright with a lentil pottage such as this.

As she dipped a piece of bread in the olive oil and then into the *nigella*, she glanced at Radames and blushed with embarrassment as her eyes met his. She looked quickly down at her plate, her heart beating a little faster. *What was he thinking?*

"How long have you been in the army?" Akim asked, addressing the two soldiers who had come with Radames.

"About six years, sir," said one. Both men were in their twenties and while they were respectful, they also cast appreciative eyes on Rahab.

Radames smiled. "Hanbal and Karim are brothers and good soldiers. They are to join the garrison at Jericho."

The men were silent but obviously pleased at their captain's words.

Rahab and her mother listened politely as the men discussed mundane matters such as crops and cattle. Radames spoke a little about his time in the army, but did not go into detail concerning battles he'd been engaged in.

Then Radames told them something that surprised them. "Perhaps my father did not inform you that I have been named the new paka for Jericho."

Akim frowned. "Forgive me, but are you not young for such a post? Overseeing the tribute from the Canaanites to Egypt cannot be an easy task."

Radames gave a slight shrug. "I have spent fifteen years in the army, since I was eighteen, and led soldiers into battle. In return for my service, Pharaoh has assigned me to Jericho. I served there earlier as captain of a contingency of soldiers, so I am familiar with the city and its people. Being paka there will seem tame compared to engaging in war."

There seemed to be a note of regret in his answer and Akim merely nodded, his heavy brows knit in thought.

When his head was turned toward her father, Rahab unobtrusively observed their guest, noting a small scar on Radames' cheek. *Was he wounded in battle? What other scars did he have?* She blushed inwardly at where her thoughts were going and concentrated on the men's conversation.

Their talk returned to the weather, the crops around Bethhoron, the size of this year's sheep herds, the last caravan that had passed through the area—the usual talk of men. Rahab listened in silence, while many questions ran through her head. Radames intrigued her.

While their guest had played down his exploits in battle, Rahab decided that there could be no doubt that he had been awarded the post in Jericho for his successes, both in battle and with his men.

His comment confirmed he was indeed in his early thirties, but with his deep tan from days in the desert, she could not be sure. She glanced up at her father to see he was also watching Radames with a thoughtful expression on his face.

Ignoring her father's warning glance, Rahab broke into their conversation. "What is the city of Jericho like? I have been most curious from what little I have heard."

Radames smiled. "The city is very large, surrounded by a massive wall that is nearly six cubits thick and twice as high. The Canaanites consider it impregnable and there are watch-towers placed at intervals. I'm told the marketplace in the center of the city is the best in Canaan, with plenty of produce from the surrounding fields and a little bit of everything else. There are perhaps two thousand inhabitants, maybe more. We have a garrison of soldiers stationed at the citadel. That's the biggest building in the city, although the king's palace is a fair size, too."

"What are the people like?" she persisted.

"The population is somewhat diverse, but it's mostly Canaanites."

"Will you live in a palace like the king?"

He laughed. "No, I will live in a house that is part of the city wall, adjoining the citadel. It is the official embassy for Egypt."

Radames turned back to Akim. "My father tells me that one of your great-grandmothers was Egyptian."

Akim nodded. "Yes, Asenath, the daughter of Poti-Pherah, the high priest of On. Pharaoh married her to our ancestor, Joseph, who was the prime minister of Egypt." Akim told the captain about their family background and the daughter of Ephraim, Sherah, who had founded the towns of Beth-horon and Beth-Sherah, where she had settled.

Radames listened quietly, his gaze intent on Rahab's father as he spoke.

Then he nodded. "It is an honor to be hosted by so prominent a family. As you know, I grew up in a military family. My father was commander of Pharaoh's army before being assigned as paka to this area." He seemed to hesitate, as if thinking over his next words. "It was fortunate that your ancestor Sherah moved to Canaan when she did. Your people did not fare well in the years that followed."

Her father remained silent, waiting to see if Radames would say more.

The Egyptian captain went on. "I am sorry for the decisions of the pharaohs who followed. Fortunately, Ramses chose to let your people leave Egypt. Many witnesses came back to the city to tell stories about them crossing the Red Sea. It is said that the sea opened up, the waters piled on either side, and the people walked over the sea bed and onto dry land."

Akim leaned forward. "Have you been told why Ramses finally released the people of Israel?"

Radames looked embarrassed. "Yes, I have heard, but it is hard to believe. Frogs? Darkness? Hail?"

"The final blow was the death of Egypt's firstborn, including the crown prince of Egypt, which convinced Pharaoh to let our people leave."

The captain contemplated Akim for a moment. "Yes, that is what I've been told."

Rahab wondered at his reason for mentioning this sad part of her people's history.

Akim's eyes narrowed. "And now?"

Radames met his gaze. "They have been in the desert many years and number in the thousands. We have wondered why and how they remained there. It is a barren place."

Her father nodded. "We have not understood that either. But there is word that our God, Jehovah, ordained it. When it is time, they will come out of the desert."

The officer appeared to consider his words and Rahab could see he wanted more information. Finally, Radames asked, "And then? It is a matter of speculation and somewhat disturbing. If and when they come out of the desert, where will they go?"

Akim stroked his beard, considering his words. "They will enter Canaan."

"Canaan? Why?"

"It is our promised land, where Jehovah told our people to go more than thirty-seven years ago. For some reason, the men refused and the Lord God ordained that they remain in the desert all these years."

The captain leaned forward, his forearm on the table. "Many Egyptians left with the Israelites when Pharaoh let them go many years ago. Some have returned with stories of this Moses who leads them. He is a powerful leader. They say he speaks directly to your God. There is a large enclosure in the middle of their encampment that they call 'the tabernacle.' Does your God dwell there?"

Akim shrugged. "I do not know, captain. Our God dwells with His people. Perhaps that is why they built the tabernacle."

"I am somewhat familiar with your God, but I must admit, He is puzzling to my people, since we worship many gods. Who is Jehovah?"

Rahab glanced at her mother, who appeared to be engrossed in their conversation, although her eyes remained serene. Rahab wondered what she was thinking.

Akim, evidently pleased with their guest's interest, took a sip of beer, cleared his throat, and began.

"Hundreds of years ago, our first ancestor, Abraham, was called by the Lord God to leave Ur where he lived. The Lord told him he would have a child and his offspring would be as numerous as the sand on the seashore. This puzzled Abraham as he was old and his wife, Sarai, was past childbearing age. Yet he believed the Lord and left Ur to go to the land where the Lord would lead them. When many years had passed, there was still no sign of the promised child. Sarai, in an effort to produce the promised child, gave her handmaiden, Hagar, to Abraham. A son was born and they named him Ishmael. Abraham felt this son was to be his heir, but instead, when Sarai was ninety years old and Abraham was nearly a hundred, Sarai gave birth miraculously to the promised child, Isaac. At Sarai's request, Ishmael and Hagar were sent away. Ishmael became the father of twelve eastern tribes. Isaac grew, married, and had two sons, Esau and Jacob. Jacob had twelve sons, one of whom, Joseph, became prime minister of Egypt."

Radames rubbed his chin. "A child birthed by a woman who was ninety? That is hard to imagine. I'm sure there is more to the story, but that clarifies a few things."

Akim glanced at his wife and gave a slight nod. There were other things the men wished to discuss.

Rahab followed her mother obediently out of the room, although she wished she could remain. Radames intrigued her and every time she looked at him, her heart beat a little faster.

Zahava led the way into the weaving room. Rahab usually enjoyed making clothing, rugs, wall hangings, and the like, but this night…how could she concentrate on her work? She sat on a stool in front of the loom, its vertical warp threads suspended from the ceiling and weighted by stones, and passed the thread or weft in and out of the warp threads. While she wove, Zahava took some wool from her basket and expertly twined it into a long, even strand on her spindle. Rahab was puzzled by her mother's mood. They usually talked amiably as they worked, but Zahava was silent and shook her head when Rahab opened her mouth to speak. From time to time, her mother glanced toward the dining area.

What were the men talking about? Did it concern her? Is that why her father excused her and Imah? Rahab listened to the rumbling of the men's voices, straining to try to make out the words, but her father and Radames were speaking too quietly. *Was the captain truly interested in learning about Jehovah, or was he just trying to be polite? What news of Egypt did he bring? Was there fighting that might affect them?* At the table, she had been full of questions she wanted to ask Radames, but it would have been considered improper for a woman to dominate the conversation. Abba had finally silenced her questions about Jericho with a stern look.

Rahab supposed she was fortunate that her father had allowed her to join him and his guests for dinner. With the exception of the paka, she and her mother usually had to wait until after Akim's male visitors departed before they could have their meal.

Suddenly, her father called out for Zahava and her mother rose quickly, indicating with a nod of her head that Rahab was to come as well. She followed her mother to the dining room and was puzzled to see her father and Radames standing there alone.

Akim waved a hand toward the captain. "Our guest is ready to depart and wished to say good night to you, wife. His men have already gone to their quarters."

Radames gave Zahava a warm smile. "I wish to thank you for such a fine meal, my lady. I cannot remember when I have enjoyed such food." Radames' eyes twinkled as he spoke.

Then he turned to Rahab. "My father spoke of you and it has been my pleasure to finally meet you. I am glad to hear you have recovered from the fever and will share this good news with my father."

The captain bowed to her Abba, her Imah, and lastly to Rahab. Jabari stood at the doorway with a lantern and the captain followed him from the room.

After watching him leave, Rahab joined her mother as she went up the stairs to their sleeping rooms.

"A nice young man, is he not?" Zahava murmured. "I believe he will come again and soon. We must keep in mind that there are few Hebrews left in Upper or Lower Beth-horon." With a smile, she turned and went into the room she shared with her husband.

Back in her own room, Rahab puzzled at her mother's words. *What was she implying? Would her parents allow her to marry an Egyptian man? Surely not! Handsome he was, yes, but...*

An owl hooted as Rahab lay on her bed, her mind too full of questions and thoughts about the Egyptian captain and soon-to-be paka to sleep.

3

At dawn, Rahab said her morning prayers and dressed quickly, for she thought she heard Radames' voice. She brushed her hair and then hurried down the steps to their main room, hoping to see the handsome Egyptian officer.

Her father stood in the entry looking toward the road.

"Captain Radames?"

"He has gone, daughter. He has much to do to prepare for his new assignment."

She swallowed her disappointment.

"He, ah, looks forward to returning to us in the near future."

Rahab felt a bit cheered by this…and wondered about the strange feelings he inspired in her that left her so unsettled. *Why did she suddenly feel shy when he looked at her last night before he left? Yes, she would like him to come again—and soon.*

Her father turned to her and echoed her mother's words. "A fine young man, is he not?"

And handsome. "Yes, Abba, but he is not of our people."

Akim studied her face. "That is true. But do you like him?"

She gave him a guarded look. "Does it matter if I like him or not?"

"We have Egyptian blood from our ancestor, the princess of On," he reminded her. He shrugged. "Besides, you are past the age most young women marry." He paused, gauging her response. "And he *is* interested."

Rahab felt her heart begin to thump in her chest. "He *is*?"

"On his father's recommendation, he came here specifically to meet you."

She raised her eyebrows and gave him a mischievous smile. "Are you wanting to marry me off, Abba?"

His booming laugh echoed in the hallway. "Is it not time? As your father, it is my duty to arrange a suitable marriage for you. I must admit I am pleased at his interest."

He put an arm around her shoulders. "I was not in any hurry to part with the last of my daughters and Jonah was not the one for you. I refused him, citing your illness. Also, I did not want my youngest child to live so far away that I'd never see her again."

Now it was Rahab's turn to laugh. "I thought he just didn't want a sickly wife."

"I believe that is what he let people think to hide his embarrassment at being turned down."

She leaned her head against his chest. "Dear Abba, I confess I am not disappointed."

"And what of Captain Radames?"

She felt herself blush and blurted out, "I would not be unhappy if he comes again."

He chuckled. "I had a feeling as I watched the two of you."

She stepped back and searched his face. "Then you would accept him, Abba? An Egyptian?"

He stroked his beard. "As I said, we have Egyptian blood. If he makes an offer, which I believe he will, then yes."

"When will he come again?"

Akim shrugged and then gave her a teasing grin. "I'm not sure, but judging from his interest last night, I would venture to say soon." He hugged her then and left to take care of other matters.

She found her mother sitting in her upstairs room and Zahava greeted her with a wide smile. "I believe your father has spoken to you about Captain Radames?"

"Yes, Abba said he is interested in me."

Her mother's eyes twinkled. "I believe *interested* is not the word. He was infatuated with you. He did not hide it well."

Suddenly, Rahab felt uneasy. Radames must surely worship the Egyptian gods of his people. As for her and her family, they served the Lord, Jehovah. *How could a marriage work between her and Radames?*

"Imah, I would not want to take up foreign gods."

"Of course not. You have been brought up to worship the God of the Hebrews. But daughter, you have no other prospects for marriage and a family. Your father knows this. You will have to trust him." Zahava became thoughtful. "We must pray and trust our God for His will in this."

"I will pray, Imah. I like Radames, but—"

"We must not get ahead of ourselves, daughter. The man has not made an offer yet and it is up to your father."

She rose. "Rahab, you are my youngest and with your family doting on you, I believe I have been remiss in teaching you matters of keeping a household. Perhaps it is time I gave you more responsibilities. Let us go down and see what Rivka is preparing for our supper."

Taking her mother's arm, they headed for the kitchen, where good smells were wafting throughout the house.

She knew her mother was right. She had been treated indulgently as the youngest of six children, born later in her parents' life. She didn't know as much about running a household as she should. Then a thought came to her and her apprehension grew. *What if Radames learned of her inexperience and changed his mind?*

4

*R*ahab watched the road for weeks, hoping to see the captain heading toward their home. Finally, one day, nearly a month later, she heard the horses and looked out her window. It was Captain Radames—now Governor Radames, the new paka—and four of his men. She started to race down the stairs, but stopped and forced herself to walk slowly to the hall, where her parents waited to receive their guests. They bowed their heads as he approached.

Akim smiled. "Welcome, governor. It is good to see you again."

Radames smiled and inclined his head in return, but then his gaze turned to Rahab. "I am most happy to be back."

She blushed and lowered her eyes, her heart beating erratically.

"I pray you are also glad to see me, Rahab?"

She looked up into Radames' eyes then and almost swayed toward him. "Yes, my lord." She caught herself and forced herself to stand still. *What were these strange emotions that ran through her body at the sight of him?*

"That is good news," he said softly.

She met his gaze unflinchingly despite her pounding heart. Zahava clasped her hands in front of her chest, watching them with evident delight.

Radames seemed to sigh with relief as he turned to Akim. "It is a pleasure to see you again."

"Likewise, governor. Come, let us sit and talk for a while." Akim led the way to the dining room and signaled to Rivka to bring out some beer for their guest. Radames' soldiers stationed themselves along the wall by the entryway.

Zahava went with Rivka, speaking to her in low tones. Rivka returned with a pitcher of beer and cups. After setting them down on the table before the men, she quickly left again for the kitchen.

Should she sit or remain standing? Rahab wasn't sure. Then, her Imah came back with a pleased smile on her face. She nodded to Rahab and they took stools at the table.

Radames entertained them with stories of some of the battles he had been in and tales about Jericho. He seemed to be preoccupied, however, glancing at Rahab from time to time as she and Zahava listened quietly. After a brief lull in his conversation with Akim, Radames cleared his throat. "About the matter we discussed last time I was here..."

Akim nodded his head. "The answer is favorable."

Relief crossed Radames' face briefly and his men grinned as they glanced from their captain to Rahab.

Radames rose and faced Akim. "Then it is my pleasure to extend an offer of marriage to your daughter, Rahab." He turned to her. "I am hopeful that you will give me a positive answer."

With her heart pounding, she looked at her father. He raised his eyebrows and then nodded slightly. She turned to Radames. "I will be your wife."

Akim got up, went to a cupboard, and took out a document. "I had a marriage agreement drawn up for this occasion," he explained with a smile.

Rahab wondered how long ago her Abba had the document prepared. *Was it stored in there from the time she was a little girl... or had he gone to a scribe after Radames' last visit?*

Akim read the document aloud for the couple. It stipulated that after the wedding, Radames would be responsible for Rahab's care and well-being. If he died, she would inherit half of his worldly goods, the other half going to any male offspring they might have—or, if they had none, remaining with Radames' family. Should the marriage end in divorce, Rahab would keep whatever possessions she brought to the marriage. With a stylus, first Akim and then Radames made their marks on the document. Rahab's fingers tingled as she touched Radames' fingers briefly while taking the stylus from him to make her own mark.

When all was signed, Radames brought out a fine, soft leather pouch from his tunic and opened it before them. "I was prepared, hoping that your answer would be favorable."

Rahab's eyes widened at the sight of his gift: a sparkling gold and ruby pendant with matching earrings. "Thank you, my lord," she said softly.

Radames then pulled out a gold ring and slipped it on her finger. "May this ring serve as a token of my commitment to you as your husband and yours to me as my wife."

The touch of his hand caused Rahab to tremble slightly. This man was to be her husband...but she knew little about him. Many of her friends had married under similar circumstances, however, their parents assuming that the new couple would become better acquainted once they lived together as husband and wife.

The formalities concluded, Akim beamed. "My wife has prepared a fine meal as a celebration. Of course, your men are most welcome to join us."

His four companions, who had remained quietly in the background, brightened at the mention of a meal and, with their leader's approval, joined the family at the table.

Rivka and Jabari brought in platters containing fish cooked in garlic and onions, green vegetables, dilled cucumbers with olives and goat cheese, and fried fava beans. There were also loaves of bread sweetened with honey and dates. When everyone had eaten their fill, Rivka brought out *basbousa*, a dessert cake cut in diamond shapes with almonds in the center of each diamond. Sugar syrup had been poured on the hot cake, making each piece moist and sweet. The men almost groaned from all the food they had eaten.

Rahab and her mother had helped Rivka serve the men and while they were serving, Rahab exchanged looks with the man who was now her husband, even though they were only betrothed. The marriage would be consummated only after the wedding itself. It seemed so simple. An agreement between her husband and her father, her willingness to become his wife, and now she was married. *May he be all he seems,* she prayed.

Later, as Radames and his soldiers stood by their horses and prepared to leave, he turned to Akim. "I have matters I must take care of in Egypt in regard to my orders and must also speak to my father. As I understand it, your people are used to a year of betrothal and your daughter shall need time to prepare for Jericho before I return. However, the former paka is leaving in a little over three months due to ill health and I shall officially take his place. I wish to have my wife at my side on that occasion."

"Three months...?" Zahava glanced at her husband briefly and bowed her head. "We shall be ready."

"Very well. I shall return for my bride at the time of the grape harvest." He gave Rahab a warm smile, his eyes dark with promise. Then he turned and mounted his horse. In moments, Radames and his men were gone.

Zahava shook her head. "Three months? Is this all not happening too quickly, my husband?"

He gave her a sideways glance. "Wife, you are a most capable woman. I have no doubt you will have our daughter ready for her husband."

Zahava sighed. "Of course." She turned to Rahab. "Daughter, we shall need to hone your skills in preparing foods that are highly regarded by the Egyptians. You are certain to have a cook—your husband is the governor, after all—but you will need to oversee the meal preparations. We will begin with a review of the spices they favor. Come."

Her mother strode quickly toward the kitchen and Rahab followed behind her. Not for the first time since meeting Radames, she wished her parents had not treated her so indulgently. *How would she ever learn all she needed to know about running a household—in three months' time?*

Rahab listened attentively as her mother showed her the different herbs used in Egyptian dishes. For weeks afterward, she watched Rivka prepare each meal and listened as Imah talked about how to select ingredients, which cuts of meat were the tenderest, textures of grain for different baked goods, and other culinary matters.

Zahava insisted that Rahab learn how to prepare some foods on her own, particularly desserts. "The way to a man's heart is through his stomach," she said sagely, "and a wife can increase her husband's love for her when he knows she has prepared something just for him, with her own two hands."

Rahab learned how to slowly pour hot syrup over cooled *basbousa* so that it seeped in, making the cake extra moist. Rivka was a patient teacher and never tired of Rahab's questions about preparing meals.

One day, Rahab's mother took her to the house where the servants made beer. "It is called *tenemu* in Egyptian. Your husband will expect you to be able to serve your guests and you must oversee the servants as they prepare each batch."

Two of their servants took a rich, yeasty dough that had been prepared ahead of time, lightly baked and mixed with yeast and malt. The bread was crumbled into small pieces and then strained through a sieve with water. After dates were added for flavoring, the mixture was placed in a large stone vat to ferment.

As they returned to the main house, Zahava turned to her daughter. "The beer is sweet and thick, nutritious almost, but don't be fooled. It can be very intoxicating." Three days later, when the fermentation process was completed, they returned to the beer house and watched the servants pour the beverage into large stone jars, which were then sealed.

Zahava had her son-in-law, Aziel, the local carpenter, make an ornate wooden wedding chest that was decorated with abundant carvings of birds and flowers. She filled the beautiful chest with soft, almost sheer linen shifts for undergarments, several white linen tunics, and leather and cloth belts. She also ordered new sandals from the leather merchant and helped her daughter weave several shawls.

Rahab counted the days and weeks until, finally, the end of the third month came. She watched out her window for Radames, experiencing a longing that sometimes overwhelmed her. That evening, her Imah came to her room and indicated Rahab was to sit on the bed beside her.

"Your husband will be here to claim you shortly," Zahava said gently. "As your mother, it is my duty to impart what you must know when you go to him the first time."

Zahava was thorough and when she was finished, Rahab at last understood the mystery that happened between a man and a woman as they came to the marriage bed. Her mother embraced her and quietly left, giving Rahab the opportunity to contemplate all that her mother had shared.

Word had gone out that a wedding celebration was imminent and Rahab's siblings expressed eagerness to see their little sister finally wed. A few days later, when she heard hoof beats outside the house, Rahab suddenly felt shy. Even so, she raced down the stairs to greet Radames. Her new husband had come for her at last, accompanied by his ever-present retinue of four Egyptian soldiers. She was at the door to meet him and blushed as she watched him jump off of his horse with a barely-contained eagerness.

"You are here." She could feel her cheeks grow hotter.

"Yes, I am here." He smiled down at her, his dark eyes shining, and Rahab's heart beat a little faster.

Akim and Zahava hurried to meet him. "Welcome, Radames. Welcome as our son."

Akim studied Radames' face. "You spoke with your father?"

"Yes. I told him what you shared with me about your family and he was impressed. He was surprised that I selected a Hebrew maiden for my bride, but he was glad that I was happy, and so gave me his blessing." Radames grinned. "I'm afraid it was after the fact. What could he say?"

He turned to Rahab. "We must leave by tomorrow and travel to Jericho. I have sent word ahead and the house will be prepared for you. It is a large house, since it is an embassy."

Aware that the groom had arrived, people started streaming to Akim's house. Among them were Rahab's brothers, Isaac, Baram, and Josiah, with their wives, Keren, Ayala, and Hannah, and her sisters, Jael and Eliana, with their husbands, Aziel and Jaheem, as well as all of their children, some of them still babes in arms. Everyone brought food to share. In no time, the courtyard by their home and the nearby street echoed with the sound of merriment.

After meeting Radames, Jael embraced her sister and whispered in her ear. "He is very handsome, Rahab, and a paka at that. It will be a very advantageous marriage."

But her other sister took Rahab aside, her brow furrowed with concern. "He does not follow our God," Eliana told her in hushed tones. "How do you feel about that?"

Rahab didn't like feeling as though she had to defend her husband. "He has told me that I am to continue to worship my own God," she told Eliana. "And, sister, don't forget, Abba approved of the marriage. I'm sure he would have forbidden it if he had concerns about Radames being an Egyptian."

Her brothers, too, seemed to be watching Radames with wary eyes, although their words were friendly and pleasant.

Rahab overheard two neighbor women mutter something about her marrying a tax collector, yet every time she had doubts, all Radames had to do was catch her eye and smile at her and all other thoughts flew out of her head.

It seemed the whole town of Upper Beth-horon had come out for the wedding celebration, bringing so much food that the tables nearly bowed from the weight of all the pots, bowls, and platters. Rahab's mother had wisely spent the prior month planning for the feast, gathering ingredients, and preparing foods that could keep ahead of time, including goat cheese, olives, date cakes, and shelled walnuts. She and the cook prepared millet with saffron, raisins and walnuts; goat stew with squash and olives; grilled fish; roast lamb seasoned with cumin; melon slices; and many loaves of fresh bread.

Their Canaanite neighbors' reserve over the fact that Radames was an official for Pharaoh, to whom they were forced to pay taxes, soon dissipated. It *was* a wedding after all, a time of celebration. Wine and beer flowed freely as the men clapped Radames on the back and shared good-natured jokes and advice.

Some women brought their tambourines and began to dance, accompanied by two flute players. Rahab's brothers stomped their feet and joined in a line dance. Radames declined to join in, although he clapped his hands in time with the music, smiling broadly, Rahab sitting by his side.

Wedding gifts were laid at the couple's feet—candlesticks, pottery, weavings, pillows, and many more household items. Rahab wondered how they would transport all of these to Jericho.

Radames was especially interested in the pillows. "You put these on your beds?"

Rahab thought the question was a little strange. "Yes, my lord. They are for resting your head when you go to sleep. Do you not use something similar in Egypt?"

He shook his head. "Our women use a small wooden stand that supports their head and neck." Seeing her puzzlement, he added hastily, "But we will bring these to Jericho, of course. I want you to have the comforts you are used to."

Rahab nodded and turned back to watch the festivities. *What other customs did the Egyptians have that she knew nothing about?*

5

The moon was high in the sky when Zahava approached Rahab and Radames. "It is time," she announced.

Time for them to retire to the bridal chamber. Rahab was both excited and apprehensive. She wanted to be a good wife. *What if she didn't please him?* They would have one night under her parents' roof; in the morning, they would begin their journey to Jericho.

The celebrants cheered and lifted their cups of wine to the newly-wed couple, calling out toasts and good wishes. Radames waited patiently as Rahab embraced every member of her family, from her parents to her siblings and, finally, her nieces and nephews. Then, taking her by the hand, the groom led his bride up the stairs to the sleeping rooms. Because Rahab's bed was narrow, designed for just one person, her parents gave up their room for the night.

As they entered, Rahab was delighted to see that the room was decorated with flowers and her parents' bed was draped with fresh, fine linen. But then, she suddenly felt self-conscious. *How strange it was to think that she would soon be lying on her parents' bed with Radames!*

She turned to him, her eyes questioning. *What should she do?*

He took her in his arms and began with soft kisses that quickly increased in passion. When she found herself returning his ardor, he led her to the bed, where in the succeeding hours, he gently but expertly made her truly his wife.

The next morning, there was a tap on the door. Without hesitation, Radames removed the bloodstained bed covering that affirmed Rahab had been a virgin before entering the marriage bed. He opened the door and handed the linen to Akim, whose lips turned up in a slight smile as he nodded his acceptance and quietly closed the door. Then Radames went over to the bed, leaned down, and kissed the still sleepy Rahab. "Prepare for the journey, beloved," he murmured. He dressed quickly and left the room, closing the door behind him.

Rahab was grateful to discover a bowl of water and some cloths on the bedroom table that she hadn't noticed last night. She hurriedly washed and went to her room to dress and gather a basket of personal things to take on her journey to Jericho. Then she made her way down the stairs.

The morning meal was simple and eaten swiftly as Radames was anxious for them to be on their way. His escort had been fed earlier and the soldiers were already mounted, waiting patiently

in the courtyard, which was already a flurry of activity. Four
of Akim's donkeys were being loaded with baskets of wedding
gifts, Rahab's wedding chest, her personal belongings, and a
small wooden box that Zahava had filled with all of the herbs
and spices she felt Rahab would need in her new home.

Her mother held out a covered basket. "Daughter, here are
some seeds and small seedlings for your garden. Plant them as
soon as you can."

Rahab struggled to hold back her tears. "Oh, Imah, you have
thought of everything. Thank you." She embraced her mother
and then gave the basket to a servant, instructing him to carefully
place it on one of the pack animals in such a way that it would not
be jostled.

Radames talked to Akim about having two of his men
return the donkeys after they arrived in Jericho.

"No rush, my son," Akim said benevolently with a wave of
his hand. "Let them rest and recover a couple of days in Jericho."

Rivka stood watching them, her eyes moist. Rahab was the
last of Akim and Zahava's children to leave the home.

Seeing the tears in Rivka's eyes, Rahab hurried over to give
her a hug. "I will miss you, Rivka."

"And I you, mistress. The house will seem quiet without
you."

Rahab laughed. "Oh, there will be plenty of noise when my
brothers and sisters visit with their energetic children. Then you
will enjoy the quiet after they leave."

It was over thirty miles to Jericho. While the horses could
easily make that distance in a day, the company would have to
travel at the pace of their donkeys, which were laden with goods.
Since Rahab had never ridden before, Radames procured a slow,

steady donkey for her, with blankets of soft fleece upon its back for her comfort. He planned for their party to camp that night and then arrive in Jericho the following day.

Zahava's eyes were moist as she embraced her daughter. "Do all in your power to be a good wife and give him sons."

Akim held her a long moment. "I will miss you so, Rahab. You are the child of my heart, born at a difficult time in our lives."

Rahab's eyes misted. "Shall I not see you both again, Abba?"

"You shall see us in time. We shall come for a visit, when you are well settled into your new home and duties."

Rahab nodded, relieved. "I shall look forward to that."

Akim put a hand on Radames shoulder. "We have entrusted her to you. Keep her safe."

"I will." Radames nodded to both of them. Then, with waves and bright smiles, her family and the servants sent them on their way.

⁓

The brief coolness of the morning gave way to oppressive warmth as the sun rose on the small caravan. Rahab had placed a heavy linen cloth over her head to protect her from the sun as the company moved slowly forward in the heat. The road was rocky and the animals had to pick their way along. It did not make the ride easier.

The four soldiers rode tall in their saddles, their eyes scanning the countryside for any sign of danger. Rahab knew with a sudden sobering thought that should they encounter bandits or some other foe, these men would give their lives to protect her and Radames.

They traveled for hours, stopping only at a copse of trees to refresh themselves and partake of some diluted wine, cheese, bread, and fresh grapes. As soon as possible, they were on their way again. Rahab would not complain, but she was weary from the constant movement and still feeling sore from the night before. She had ridden for several hours when she began to feel dizzy. Radames rode up beside her, his brows creased in concern.

Rahab looked up at him, seeing only a blur. As she slipped off the donkey, she was aware of strong arms catching her before she lost consciousness. When she awakened, they were under the shade of a small tree along the mountain trail and she was leaning up against her husband's chest.

"You are better?" Radames' voice was anxious.

"What happened?"

"You fainted from the heat. We are close to Jericho so you will ride with me until we near the city. Can you manage the donkey then for a mile or two?"

She looked up at him, holding back the tears. "I am sorry to be so much trouble to you."

"Beloved, you will never be trouble to me. You have done well; we will rest this night and enter Jericho tomorrow."

She leaned against him, feeling his strength. She would not faint again and embarrass him in front of his men.

They resumed travel and Radames held her in front of him as he rode. After a few miles, she looked up at him. "I will be able to ride the donkey again."

He signaled to one of his men, who helped her down off of Radames' horse and made sure she was comfortable back atop the donkey. After they resumed travel, Radames glanced back at her from time to time and she smiled bravely to let him know she was fine.

She was relieved almost to the point of tears when Radames called a halt and ordered his men to prepare a tent for them for the night. The soldiers would sleep on the ground a short distance from the tent, taking turns keeping watch for their protection.

One of the donkeys that carried the tent and rugs was unloaded first. The tent was quickly set up and prepared with the rugs and cushions. The men removed the baskets and other burdens from the animals so they could rest. Rahab laughed as she watched the donkeys roll on the ground, kicking up their hooves and scratching their tired backs.

After a quick meal of wine, bread, and cheese, Rahab gladly lay down in their tent and promptly fell into an exhausted sleep. She was barely aware of Radames' body as he slipped in beside her and drew her to him with one arm.

❧

When Rahab awakened, Radames was gone. She peeked out from the tent and saw the men loading the donkeys. Two soldiers eyed her expectantly and she hastily stepped out so they could fold up the tent and rugs to pack them up once more. She wondered how long they waited for her to wake up.

They ate small amounts of bread and cheese as well as some grapes that had been wrapped in moist leaves and packed in a small basket to keep them from breaking open and spoiling.

The brief coolness of the morning once again gave way to blistering heat. Radames and his men pushed the donkeys as much as possible, but the burdened animals picked their way slowly along the rough road.

One of the soldiers scouted ahead and came back shortly. "Sir, the city lies ahead of us just over the hill."

As they came through the mountains, Rahab almost gasped at the beauty before her. Jericho was like a huge oasis in the middle of the desert, for surrounding the city were fertile fields and a variety of palm and fruit trees. After the harsh land they had come through, the air seemed cooler and a slight breeze refreshed her.

Radames leaned down from his horse to speak to her. "There is an underground spring that comes from the mountains. It feeds the plains around the city and is funneled into the city itself. It is called Ayn El Sulta'n."

Jericho sat upon a massive hill. Radames told her the current city had been built upon the ruins of former cities dating back thousands of years. She looked at the city itself as they approached. The walls were impressive and seemed larger than Radames had described. To Rahab's eyes, they did indeed look impregnable. She noted the lookout towers, spaced along the wall.

A horn sounded and the huge wooden gates began to slowly open. Radames rode ahead of his escort as another group of soldiers rode out of the city to meet them. The lead officer saluted Radames.

"Welcome back to the city, sir. We are ready for you."

As their small caravan entered the city, people lined the sides of the street, cheering and waving small banners. Despite the welcome, Rahab could not help but notice the wariness and mistrust in many of the people's faces. *Radames is the Egyptian tax collector, after all,* she reminded herself ruefully.

As she looked ahead, she saw that the main square was surrounded with what appeared to be public buildings with various radial streets that fanned off the main square like spokes on a wheel. Her excitement grew as she looked forward to exploring the city after she was settled.

A royal greeting committee approached and Radames raised a hand to halt his band.

"It is Hammurabi, the king of Jericho, and his court," he told Rahab quietly. "Be on your guard. He likes beautiful women, married or not."

Radames dismounted and helped Rahab from her donkey, leading her by the hand to the king.

King Hammurabi smiled broadly...but his smile did not reach his eyes. "We welcome you, governor. We have been waiting for your arrival."

Another man, obviously Egyptian, stepped from the group. Radames bowed his head. "Greetings, Governor Nephi."

Rahab sought to place the age of the departing governor. *Perhaps in his late fifties?* His skin was pale instead of the brown tones of the Egyptians. Her first impression was that the man was indeed unwell, as Radames had told her father. This man seemed to need all of his energy just to stand.

Indicating the king and the governor, Radames bowed his head. "My wife, Rahab."

Rahab also bowed her head to the king and then to the governor.

Hammurabi's eyes glittered a moment. "A most beautiful bride. Welcome to our city." His eyes perused her almost indolently from head to toe.

Rahab, uncomfortable with his attention, and overcome by the presence of so many dignitaries, gave a tentative smile, acknowledging his words. "Thank you for your kind welcome, your majesty."

The king waved a hand at Nephi. "Perhaps you will be able to regain your health once you return to Egypt, governor." And he turned his face to Radames with a bold sneer. "I do hope, for your sake, that Jericho does not age you as it has your predecessor."

The old governor drew himself up. "I am confident that my replacement will be satisfactory. He is well regarded by Pharaoh."

Rahab saw King Hammurabi grimace for a brief moment before his features and demeanor turned amiable. "Yes, I'm sure he will be quite satisfactory," he declared.

Rahab was sure he did not appreciate the subtle reminder that Egypt ruled Canaan and even the king of Jericho was required to pay tribute to Pharaoh.

Radames took her hand and Rahab smiled gratefully up at him.

"My wife has had a difficult journey. If I may take leave of the king, I would like to get her settled in her new home." He looked at Nephi. "I'm sure we have many things to discuss."

The king put up a hand. "A banquet shall be prepared in your honor. Tomorrow evening?"

Radames bowed his head. "We shall be there."

Governor Nephi indicated Radames and Rahab were to follow him as he led the way to the embassy. He couldn't seem to get away from the king fast enough.

6

*R*ahab's new home was set in a wall of the city near the citadel, which housed a contingent of Egyptian soldiers. The embassy appeared huge from the outside and as Nephi approached the front door, an Egyptian servant opened it.

Nephi indicated the man with a wave of his hand. "This is Donkor, my faithful manservant. He will return to Egypt with me." This last comment was spoken firmly, almost challenging Radames to dispute him.

But Radames merely nodded. "It is well that you travel with a known companion."

Nephi let a small sigh of relief.

Two more servants appeared, a man and a woman. Nephi smiled at them. "This is Hameda, the chief steward, and your cook, Bahiti. They are both quite capable and have requested that they be permitted to stay on with you."

Both servants bowed. Bahiti's dark, almost black, eyes contemplated her new mistress calmly. Rahab felt a sense of relief that the pair were Egyptian, not Canaanite.

Radames smiled at them. "I am certain that we will come to value your skills as Nephi has."

A handful of other servants appeared behind Hameda and Bahiti. Seeing their bright red and yellow garments, Rahab knew they were Canaanite. Their eyes were cast downward and Nephi did not introduce them.

The old paka turned to Rahab. "My lady, your husband is familiar with this place, having been here many times. Perhaps Donkor could show you the house and your quarters." He waved at the unnamed servants. "See that the lady's things are taken to her quarters." They hurried out the door to gather the goods from the burdened donkeys.

Radames turned to two soldiers who had accompanied them into the embassy. "Oversee the work and turn the donkeys over to the stable hands. They must be well cared for—brushed, fed, and watered. See to it that two men are available to return them two days' hence to Akim, my wife's father, in Upper Beth-horon."

The men saluted and went outside to supervise the moving of Rahab's things.

Donkor bowed to Rahab. "If you will accompany me, my lady, I will show you around your new home."

Despite being built into the wall, the house included a small central courtyard with some flowering plants and a stone bench. *It seems like a cool, quiet place to meditate, but there's no room for a garden here*, Rahab realized. *Where would she plant the seeds and tender young herbs and vegetables her Imah had given her?*

Bahiti showed her some features of the kitchen. A stone oven was built into the wall and two large water pots stood in one corner. The center of the room held a wooden table for mixing and preparing food. A smaller table in another corner held a hand mill for grinding grain, its volcanic stones well-worn.

Built into one wall were a half dozen shelves holding pottery plates, cups, wine goblets, bowls, and platters. Some were plain but others featured delicate, fanciful, painted decorations of birds, flowers, and animals. Rahab noticed a wine strainer and other utensils as well.

"And see this, my lady," Bahiti said with evident pride. Rahab turned as Bahiti opened a large wooden door in one wall of the kitchen to reveal a narrow storage room filled with baskets of lentils, pottery jars of wine, crates of grain, and a plethora of herbs, spices, and other foods. Rahab didn't think it appeared to be as well-stocked as her mother's storeroom, but it still was more than she had anticipated.

"A good kitchen, Bahiti," she said kindly, and the cook beamed with pleasure. Rahab smiled. "We will discuss meals later. For now, I will leave the preparation in your very capable hands."

"Very well. Thank you, my lady."

Donkor led her down a hallway and Rahab could smell the beer before they even entered the room. There were eight large, stone barrels along one wall and a varied assortment of items for its manufacture along the opposite wall. Rahab sighed. The taste of beer had never appealed to her, but it was a staple in the

Egyptian diet and she would have to oversee its production. She was glad to leave that room.

Further down the hallway, Donkor showed her a room that contained a loom much like her mother's, hanging from the ceiling with stone weights to hold the vertical threads. Nearby were baskets of yarn, dyed in various colors, and a bundle of flax to weave linen for garments. Sunshine poured in through a window. Rahab realized that if she moved the small stool in front of the loom to the window and stood on it, she would be able to observe the street below.

"This room looks like it has not been used in some time," she remarked.

"That is true. The governor's wife died two years ago and no one has used this room since then."

As they ascended the steep stairs to the upper sleeping quarters, Rahab noticed the figures of Egyptian deities placed in small niches in the walls. Not wishing to offend Donkor, she tried to hide her distaste when they passed by, but he had obviously seen the look on her face.

"They watch over the house, my lady," he muttered.

Rahab decided that her daily prayers would include an earnest request for the Lord God to bring the day when these idols could be discarded. Small clay pots of incense burned near each one and while they gave a pleasant aroma to the house, Rahab feared that the burning incense was meant as a way to worship the Egyptian gods and goddesses. She would have to minimize the use of these pots. She hoped to be able to share knowledge of Jehovah with Radames and prayed the Lord God would create an opportune time.

"The master's room," Donkor announced, interrupting her thoughts. He opened the door to a large room dominated by a bed with a dark wood frame and straw-stuffed mattress supported by leather straps. Some of Rahab's pillows were piled precariously on a bench. Evidently, the servants had not known what to do with them. A funny wooden stand placed beside the bed looked like Radames' description of Egyptian women's headrests for sleeping.

How uncomfortable that must be, Rahab thought. *How could anyone sleep on it?*

Donkor led her to a small room hidden away from the main sleeping quarters. There was a stone bench with a hole in it, a pot underneath, and a large-mouthed water jar with a ladle nearby. Rahab understood its use immediately as well as the convenience. An alcove had a small drain hole and she understood this area was for bathing. A basin caught the water underneath and could be removed to use the water for the flowers in the courtyard.

"Are these innovations Canaanite, or due to Egyptian influence?"

Donkor smiled. "The previous governor made many changes to the house, I believe, installing some of the conveniences used in Egypt."

"The bath?"

"Yes, my lady."

He led her up a narrow flight of stairs to an open storage area on the roof, where extra bundles of flax were stored.

"Where does the flax come from, Donkor? Does the governor have his own fields?"

"No, it is procured in the marketplace. It is supplied as you need it as part of the payment to the governor."

As Rahab surveyed the area, an idea formed in her head. *If she could find some large pottery containers, she could have a garden up here.* Feeling encouraged, she followed Donkor back down the stairs to the sleeping quarters.

"The previous governor used this room for guests. It can be your room, my lady."

Would she and Radames live in separate rooms? Servants had placed her wedding chest and other belongings in this small room. The bed was narrow, but the furnishings were lighter and had beautiful carvings on them. And a window let sunlight in.

"Do you wish a maidservant, my lady?"

She thought for a moment. "Yes, a young woman." It would be good to have someone near her age to help her.

"I will speak to the governor immediately."

"You have found everything to your liking, beloved?" The familiar voice behind her made her turn and she found herself in her husband's arms.

Donkor discreetly bowed himself out of the room.

Radames smiled down at her, his dark eyes gleaming. "I'm glad you have your own room for the times you wish to be by yourself. But you *will* share the main sleeping room with me."

The tone of his voice was firm and Rahab felt relieved. They were of one accord and he understood that she would need to be alone at certain times.

"Come," he urged. "The cook has prepared a fine meal for us, which we will share with Governor Nephi. He leaves in the morning with Donkor to return to Egypt."

She frowned. "He was to obtain a maidservant for me. Will he have time to do that?"

"I already anticipated that need. Her name is Donatiya and she will join us shortly."

"She is Egyptian?"

"No, she is Canaanite." He gave her a wry smile. "Unfortunately, there are no young Egyptian maidens in Jericho, bondservant or otherwise."

And no Israelites, Rahab thought to herself. In the excitement of marrying Radames, she had not considered how alone she would be in a strange city. She would send word to her parents and her sisters, asking them to visit her as soon as possible!

They descended the steps to the dining area, where fabric-covered stools had been placed around a long wooden table polished to a fine sheen. There were baskets of flat bread, plates of figs, grapes, and dates, and a large tureen filled with fragrant, goat meat stew. It was heavily seasoned and Rahab savored it as she tried to identify the herbs she tasted. *Too much garlic*, she decided, and wondered if she could convince Bahiti not to use so many cloves the next time she prepared the dish.

"This stew is delicious," Radames commented. "Just the right mix of ingredients."

So much for modifying the recipe, Rahab thought wistfully.

Bahiti brought out a clay pitcher of beer that she poured into goblets for Radames and Nephi. She came over to Rahab to pour some for her, but Rahab put a hand over her cup.

"I would prefer wine, thank you, Bahiti."

The cook registered surprise. "No beer, mistress?"

Rahab smiled up at the older woman. "I did not develop a taste for it. I'm sure that will mean more for the men."

Radames raised an eyebrow and his mouth twitched with a slight smile. The former governor also raised his eyebrows, but merely shrugged as they went on with their meal.

Bahiti hastened to the pantry and returned with a cup of wine for Rahab. As she sipped the homemade beverage, she realized that unlike the wines of her people, this had been enhanced with flavorings. She recognized honey, but what was the other? Terebinth resin? She would have to adapt to some new tastes— or, better still, vary the household's wine recipe.

After the meal, Nephi rose and bowed to Rahab. "I wish you well, lady, in your new position. Jericho is an interesting city and I trust you will find time to explore it."

Realizing that Nephi and Radames might have more to discuss and preparations to make for the former governor's departure the next morning, Rahab wished him well on his journey and excused herself to go to her quarters. To her surprise, a young woman awaited her there.

"I am Donatiya, mistress. The master chose me to assist you. Shall we prepare to bathe?" The girl deferred to her and seemed friendly enough at first, but Rahab caught a momentary glimpse of some deep emotion in her eyes. *Anger perhaps?* But the girl quickly hid whatever emotions she had as she waited with three large jugs of water.

It was then that Rahab realized that Donatiya had had to get water downstairs in the kitchen, add hot rocks to heat it, and then make at least three trips up the steps to the bathing area. Rahab took a deep breath and removed her garments before standing in the small alcove. Donatiya poured part of a jug of water as Rahab washed with soap made of ash and oil. When she was finished, Donatiya poured the remaining jugs of the warm water over her and brought a linen cloth to dry her off.

She stood at a pottery basin holding some water, moistened one of the chew sticks standing upright in a jar beside it, and then dipped it in the bowl of powder that tasted of rock salt, mint, dried flowers, and pepper grains. She rubbed the stick over her teeth, removing food particles from the evening meal.

After Donatiya helped her into a sheer sleeping garment, Rahab dismissed the maid and walked barefoot to Radames' bedroom. *Her bedroom*, she corrected herself. She placed a number of pillows on the bed, lay down, and was as comfortable as she had ever been in her bed at her parents' home.

She was awakened from a deep sleep by a soft voice whispering in her ear.

"You are beautiful when you are sleeping, beloved."

She opened her eyes slowly to find her husband lying next to her. "Radames," she murmured and with a soft sigh, she went into his arms.

$\mathcal{W}$hen she woke the next morning and stretched luxuriously, she caught sight of Radames dressing and beckoned to him.

He gazed at her with warmth in his eyes. "You tempt me, beloved, but we must bid the governor goodbye. Join us as quickly as you can."

When he had gone, Rahab sat on her bed and whispered her morning prayers. Suddenly, she heard another voice.

"May I help you, mistress?" Donatiya stood quietly in the doorway, a slight frown on her face.

Rahab remembered how Tova used to help her dress when she was a small child until she was old enough to dress herself. She would have to get used to having a maidservant.

"I shall be glad to have your help, Donatiya. I must dress quickly for the former governor's farewell."

Donatiya regarded her with a puzzled expression. "To which god do you pray in the morning, mistress?"

"Which God? Why to our one true God, Jehovah."

"You have only one God? Surely he cannot deal with all matters. We have many gods for many purposes." The girl's tone bordered on distain and Rahab wondered if she would be comfortable around this Canaanite.

"Let us be about our day, Donatiya."

After quickly washing her face, she put on a sheer shift as an undergarment, while Donatiya laid out appropriate clothes for the day: a white linen sheath with shoulder straps that came just below her breasts and a cloth of azure blue that Donatiya wound around her upper body. Rahab put on the earrings that Radames had given her as a betrothal gift and the maidservant fastened the necklace for her. Rahab slipped her feet into a pair of soft leather sandals and Donatiya walked around her with an appraising eye. Satisfied that her mistress was ready, she opened the door to the room.

"One more thing, Donatiya. There is a small basket of seeds and plants with my belongings. Please take it up to the roof and give the plants a little water."

With that, Rahab hurried down the stairs and into the dining hall.

Looking up from his conversation with Governor Nephi, Radames' eyes shone with pride and admiration.

"You are a most fortunate man, Radames," Nephi said. "You have a beautiful wife by your side. May you have many children…" His speech was interrupted by a fit of coughing.

As Rahab watched with concern, Radames patted the old paka on the back, his eyes closed and his head shaking. She noticed then that Nephi was wearing a lot of kohl around his eyes. It occurred to her that she had never seen Radames wearing it, although most Egyptian men did. She didn't feel comfortable with the idea of darkening the area around her eyes with kohl and was glad it was not required of her. *It's fortunate that we are in an Egyptian embassy and not Egypt itself, for surely it would be socially unacceptable there to go without,* she thought. The Canaanites did not use kohl either.

After Nephi's coughing subsided, he and Radames resumed their conversation and Rahab joined them at the table. Bahiti served her a small cup of date wine, a loaf of fresh bread, and some grapes and dates. Rahab realized then how hungry she was, but since the men had already finished their meal, she ate as quickly as decorum permitted.

When it came time to leave, they gathered outside, where six soldiers waited on horseback. Nephi had another coughing spell and nearly doubled over. When he had recovered, Donkor helped him up on his horse. It seemed to take some effort and Rahab wondered if he would make the long journey to Egypt without any mishaps. Finally, with a wave of his hand, the former governor left them and rode out of the city.

Radames and Rahab silently watched them until they disappeared around a bend in the road. Then they reentered the house and he took her aside.

"There is much involved in overseeing a city that resents paying tribute to Pharaoh," he said, his eyes probing hers. "Nephi said he knew of no unrest, but he was advanced in years and not a trained soldier." Radames sighed. "There is a fine line between my duties and usurping the duties of the king. And as my wife, you must be on your guard. When you are in the city, or the marketplace, or when we are guests of one of the officials, you must be cordial, of course, but must say as little as possible."

Radames then took Rahab by the upper arms and held on as if for dear life. Her eyes widened in alarm and he let go.

"Beware of the king," he whispered urgently. "As I told you before, he likes beautiful women. He has a queen and many concubines, but still casts his eyes and desires wherever he will."

Rahab put her arms around his waist. "Yes, my husband. I will remember."

He leaned down and kissed her. "Explore the house and make any changes you wish. Perhaps there are items you need that Bahiti can purchase for you in the marketplace. Most payment in Jericho is by barter. Bahiti will visit the merchants, they will come here to present their bills, and we will pay them in goods."

He then excused himself. A stack of papyrus papers was waiting for his review.

Rahab decided to take another look in the pantry to gauge its supplies. The herbs and spices that her Imah had given her would help, but those were meager amounts meant just to get her started in her new life, managing her own household. As she went to find Bahiti, her husband's words ran through her head. *Beware of the king....* Was she in danger?

8

*B*ahiti was making bread for the next day, kneading the lump of dough with her hands. Rahab watched quietly from the doorway. When Bahiti became aware of her, she looked up, her manner deferent, but curiosity in her eyes.

"Can I help you, mistress?"

Rahab had to remind herself that she was the governor's wife and this was her household. She straightened her shoulders. "I wish to take inventory of our supplies and then perhaps you could show me the marketplace."

Bahiti covered the dough with a piece of cloth to let it rise and led Rahab to the pantry.

"We are low on coriander, anise, and rosemary, mistress. And also garlic."

"Ah, garlic. I know my husband loves a good amount of garlic in his food, but I was wondering if we could use a little less."

"He will not be angry with me?"

"He can be angry with *me*. I prefer less garlic."

Bahiti smiled hesitantly. "As you wish, mistress. And you wish to explore the marketplace?"

"Yes."

Bahiti's eyebrows furrowed. "As you wish, mistress, but…"

"It will be fine. I wish to see the marketplace."

Bahiti shook her head, but said no more.

They slowly went through the pantry and Bahiti took out a small scroll so they could make a list of items to purchase. Donatiya fetched a head covering for Rahab and deftly wrapped it around her head and neck. Rahab then followed Bahiti out of the house toward the heart of the city.

As they walked, Rahab took in all of the sights and sounds—people shouting, arguing, or laughing in groups; vendors bartering with customers or wheedling passersby as they hawked their wares, open-ended canvas canopies shielding them from the sun; lamb shanks hanging on hooks; ducks in cages, flapping their wings and quacking loudly.… And the overpowering smell of fish! Several fish stalls offered a wide assortment from the nearby Jordan River, laid out atop straw-covered tables for the perusal of Canaanite wives and servants.

The raucous atmosphere filled Rahab with a rush of adrenaline. She stopped to watch a scene that other bystanders also seemed to find amusing: a donkey had planted its hooves, refusing to move, and was placidly enduring a barrage of angry words from its owner, who pulled on the bridle to no avail.

Following closely behind Bahiti, Rahab was aware of people's glances as she passed them by. Some of their looks were curious, but others were hostile. Rahab had to remind herself that she was not in Upper Beth-horon, walking through her hometown's familiar marketplace. Yes, there were Canaanites there, too, but she grew up with them; they knew her and her family. Here, she was not only a foreigner and a Jew, but also the wife of the Egyptian governor, whose job it was to collect taxes for Pharaoh. These people of Jericho were free with their words, heedless of whether she heard them or not.

"There she is, the new governor's wife."

"No doubt our taxes keep her well-fed!"

"She does not look Egyptian to me."

"Where is she from then?"

Another voice spoke with authority. "My sister's daughter is a maidservant in their house. We will know more about her shortly."

"There are rumors she is Hebrew."

"The governor married a Hebrew?"

"Hush, she might hear you. They just arrived. Do you want to anger the new governor?"

She tried to ignore the comments and smile at those who at least appeared to be friendly. Bahiti glared at a few people who had scowled at Rahab and urged her mistress to keep walking.

Rahab realized Radames might be angry with her for going to the marketplace accompanied only by the cook. *In all likelihood, he would have assigned a soldier to come*, she thought. *And yet, a soldier would have hindered them from speaking their minds.*

Vendors in the spice section had tall, tightly-woven baskets filled with ground spices and many bundles of dried herbs hanging from strings above their heads. They stopped one stall and Bahiti seemed to be on good terms with the merchant there, for they argued good-naturedly while he wrapped up herbs and spices for them in small squares of cloth, which Bahiti then placed in her wicker basket.

As they walked on to another area, they bought some melons from another stall. Then Rahab spotted several baskets of watercress and arugula leaves that looked crisp and tasty. Learning that these greens were not always available, she purchased a few bunches. She missed having fresh vegetables from her mother's kitchen garden. She selected some dates, walnuts, and several bunches of grapes, thinking about making her favorite salad for her husband. She mentioned to Bahiti the germ of an idea she had about having a garden somehow, perhaps on the roof. The cook welcomed the idea of having fresh produce practically at their fingertips. Rahab hoped she could get her garden started before the plants her mother gave her wilted and died.

The city was near the Jordan River, so fish were plentiful and available year-round, but since they had eaten fish the night before, Rahab decided against purchasing any. Instead, she added some squash and capers to Bahiti's basket.

Rahab was beginning to feel uncomfortable with the stares and whispered comments. One man had accidentally—or perhaps purposefully—bumped into her in the marketplace, increasing her discomfort and fear.

"Bahiti, let us return home."

The cook nodded. "I thought you might wish to do so."

Heading home from the marketplace, Rahab decided to let Bahiti do the shopping for the household henceforth—after they consulted on meal planning, of course. She did want to see the city, but that would have to wait until Radames was able to take her. She suspected that no untoward comments would be made in his presence.

Once back at the embassy, Bahiti checked the bread dough; it had risen sufficiently, so she formed it and placed it in the oven. While she put their purchases away, Rahab told her what she wanted in the salad for their mid-day meal: the just-purchased watercress and arugula, chopped into bite-sized pieces and topped with dates and walnuts. For the dressing, Rahab shared one of her favorite recipes: equal parts of olive oil and vinegar, a spoonful of honey, a clove of finely-chopped garlic, a pinch of salt, and some mustard seeds. Rahab was pleased with how quickly and efficiently the cook worked as she cleaned the greens and began to assemble the salad. Satisfied that Bahiti had the meal well in hand, Rahab thanked her and wandered upstairs.

Donatiya was sitting on a stool in her room, waiting for her, and immediately jumped up when Rahab entered. The maidservant had straightened the bed and piled pillows against the wall behind it. Atop the chest were two small stone jars filled with oil, their burning wicks causing the pleasant aroma of cedar to waft through the room.

"The burning oil keeps away insects, mistress," Donatiya explained quietly.

And gives worship to the Egyptian gods, Rahab suspected. But she decided to assume the servant's intentions were good. "Thank you, Donatiya. That was very considerate of you."

The girl seemed surprised at the praise, but once again, her face became closed and unreadable.

"Come," Rahab said. "I would like to do some weaving and you can assist me." She spent the rest of the afternoon becoming acquainted with her loom and sorting through yarn, planning to make a tunic for Radames.

His loud, heavy footsteps echoed in the hallway, announcing his arrival before he marched into the weaving room. Radames was obviously displeased.

"Why did you go into the city unescorted?"

She rose quickly and came to him, "Forgive me, my lord. I was used to shopping in the marketplace at home. You did not suggest an escort."

"Beloved, I *did* suggest that Bahiti do the shopping. If you must go again, take at least two soldiers with you as an escort. All you have to do is go to the citadel. I will leave orders with an officer there."

He drew her into his arms. "There is always a reason, beloved. An Egyptian governor is not popular in a city where we are overlords, collecting tribute for Pharaoh. Nephi told me there were incidents when his wife first went into the city. She was almost accosted by a group of rough men. Also, you must remember that this city has many temples of worship to their gods. I'm very sure you do not want to know what goes on in there. Some of their rites would offend you."

Rahab gave Radames a quizzical look, but he refused to elaborate.

He sighed. "I do not wish anything to happen to you. Do you understand?"

"Yes, husband, I understand. I will not go again without an escort."

He relaxed and kissed her before releasing her. He raised his eyebrows and a smile played about his lips. "For such a wife, I could almost skip this meal."

She smiled back provocatively. "But we have prepared such a fine midday meal for you."

He put an arm around her waist as they headed down to the dining area. "We will take that matter up later," he whispered.

Bahiti had made a puree of dried garbanzo beans, garlic, salt, vinegar, cumin seeds, and chopped cucumber. It made a fine paste to spread on wedges of fresh bread.

To Rahab's delight, Radames complimented her on the salad. "I have eaten few dishes like this before, but it's very good." He smiled and nodded his head. "You must make this again."

Bahiti came out of the kitchen with a platter of goat cheese and melon slices, which she placed on the table beside them.

"Where is the cheese from, Bahiti? We have no goats."

"I buy it in the marketplace once a week, lady, on the day the goat herder brings it." She smiled at Rahab. "I get there early in the morning, before it's all gone, wrap it in an oil cloth, and store it in a low chest in the pantry to keep it fresh." She sighed then, a wistful look on her face. "My family kept goats. How I wish we had room for a nanny or two here."

Radames laughed at the notion, causing Bahiti to blush and flee back into the kitchen.

But that's not such an absurd idea, Rahab thought. *I wonder....*

Radames turned to her. "The king has invited us to a banquet this evening. I wish I could decline, but since it's being held in my honor, that's impossible." He frowned. "As far as I can tell, there is little regard for him in this city, but we should not offend him nonetheless."

He rubbed his clean-shaven chin. It seemed strange to Rahab that Radames removed the whiskers from his face each morning. Most men she had known, including her father and brothers, wore beards.

"After the banquet, I will be occupied for some days with matters pertaining to the Pharaoh, but tomorrow, I will take you on a tour of the city." He paused. "Along with an escort."

Just then, Hameda entered with two male servants, who were straining under the weight of a large basket. "Apologies, sir," he told Radames, "but I must get this to the kitchen."

Radames nodded, but Rahab stopped him with an outstretched arm.

"What's in the basket?"

"Dried dung cakes for the oven, my lady."

"Thank you, please proceed." Rahab waved the men off as she tried not to flinch. At her parents' home, there had been wood for fuel. But as much as she found the idea of cooking with dung distasteful, Rahab knew wood for burning might be scarce in Jericho. Hameda had proven himself to be a capable and effective chief steward, seemingly anticipating the household's needs before they arose, keeping a watchful eye on the servants, overseeing the work, and making sure Radames' horse was ready whenever it was needed.

"How have you been occupying yourself, dear wife?" Radames asked, interrupting Rahab's thoughts. "Dreaming of doing more shopping, perhaps?" he teased.

Rahab laughed. "No, I've been working in the weaving room...."

Radames listened attentively as Rahab shared her delight at finding the yarns and flax. She told him that she had begun to weave a garment, but did not tell him what she was making, wanting to surprise him.

"I'm glad you have found something to do that you enjoy. I know it may be difficult to be confined to the house most of the time, but we are in a foreign city and must be vigilant."

"I do understand well, my husband. My family has lived among the Canaanites for many decades since our ancestor Sherah founded cities in this land. We were accepted as a prominent family, but never integrated with the citizens. At the time of our marriage, my family was the only Hebrew family left in Upper Beth-horon." *Now my family is surrounded by Canaanites,* she realized.

"Many of our people moved further on into Judea," she told Radames.

He nodded. "Yes, I heard that. How many are in your family?"

"Over twenty."

"Then by all means, you must invite them to visit us here when they can." He started to leave for his workroom, but then turned back. "Perhaps not all at once?" he suggested with a mischievous smile.

"Of course, my lord. I will ask them to come in small groups—no more than ten at a time." He heard the humor in her voice and rolled his eyes before disappearing down the hall.

Rahab had hoped to tell him about an idea she had, but seeing the distracted look in his eyes, she realized his mind was on other things and decided it could wait for another time.

⁓

That evening, six Egyptian soldiers waited at their door to escort them to the palace.

"I will make sure you sit near me, beloved, but if you speak to the king, say as little as possible and guard your conversation. Do not mention going into the city alone. We must make sure he knows that Egyptian guards will travel with you."

She puzzled at his words, but nodded her assent. For the occasion, she wore a white tunic with blue and silver borders. Radames drew her to himself and then surprised her by placing a gold necklace around her neck that spread out like a fan. He then brushed back her hair on either side and carefully hung gold pendant earrings on her earlobes.

"Oh, my husband! Thank you! But you have given me so much jewelry already...."

"You should have more than one set of jewelry to wear, lest I appear too poor to provide you with such gifts."

She put a hand on the necklace, which glinted in the light. "It's beautiful. Thank you."

He held out his arm and they descended the steps. Hameda opened the door for them and Radames helped Rahab into a small, ornate chariot.

Although it was twilight, torchlight at the entrances to most buildings enabled Rahab to see altars representing Canaanite gods scattered throughout the city. Offerings of flowers, food, coins, and other gifts had been placed on these—a stark reminder that she was in a pagan city. *How many gods do these Canaanites worship? Upper Beth-horon only had a few.* At one prominent place, she noticed a temple with smoke pouring out of a hole in the roof. She was about to ask Radames about it, but he shook his head, his mouth tight in disapproval.

"It is the temple of their main god, Baal." He said no more and urged their chariot horse to go faster. The six Egyptian

soldiers who accompanied them on horseback spurred their
mounts as well.

King Hammurabi's palace was set on a prominent hill at the
end of Jericho's main thoroughfare. As Radames' soldiers took
the horses to a stable to be watered and brushed, Rahab gazed
in wonderment at the palace before them. Its sheer size left her
feeling miniscule. Huge stone pillars held lintels of stone, carved
with many figures. A number of Asherah poles representing the
goddess stood in the atrium in front of the palace, along with a
huge stone bull representing Baal, the god of strength and viril-
ity, and a fearsome figure with seven twisted heads representing
Lotan, a sea god.

There were many other figures as well. Rahab looked at
Radames, questions on her lips.

"The Canaanites worship over thirty gods and goddesses,"
he whispered. Then he smiled. "I do not know why they have so
many. We Egyptians have far fewer."

*Would he be open to learning of Jehovah, the God Most High,
Creator of heaven and earth?* She must pray harder for a time
when he would be receptive.

As Rahab entered the palace itself, she felt an oppressive
heaviness settle over her. She didn't know the meanings of the
stone carvings she passed, but in several places, she had to avert
her eyes from the obvious phallic symbols that were so prevalent.

A number of Canaanite nobles were already seated at the
long table in the banquet room. Some brought wives, but most
were not accompanied. It seemed as though the women were
there for her benefit, but their glances were not friendly. All of
the men, including the king, surveyed Rahab from top to bottom
with lecherous eyes. The queen sat to the king's right, her face

stony cold as she watched Rahab's approach. She seemed to be weighted down with gold jewelry: heavy earrings, a large necklace, and many bracelets.

King Hammurabi heaved himself from his seat at the head of the table. "Welcome, Governor Radames and Lady Rahab." He indicated a seat next to the queen for Radames and another seat to his left, on the opposite side of the table, for Rahab to sit. She didn't like the idea of not sitting beside her husband, but what could she do? A strange odor emanated from the king's body, some sort of fragrance, but it was not pleasant. She made a point to keep her eyes on Radames.

The food was lavish: lamb stewed with green beans, garlic, and onions; bowls filled with a variety of nuts, olives, dates, pomegranates, and figs; and plates of flat bread with goat cheese. Servants made sure their wine cups were kept full. At a warning glance from Radames, she sipped her wine slowly and covered the cup with her hand when a servant would have poured more.

Noting this, the king frowned. "You do not like our wine?" His eyes narrowed and she fought against the revulsion that filled her under his gaze.

She smiled politely. "I find myself still weary from the travel and getting settled in my new home. I do not wish to offend your majesty by falling asleep at his table."

He seemed to find this amusing and laughed heartily, joined by the other officials at the table.

Radames also seemed to be limiting the amount of wine he drank. He kept glancing at her from time to time to ascertain how she was doing.

The king clapped his hands and a small group of young women appeared in sheer garments. From behind a curtain, the sound of flutes filled the air and the women began to dance. Their movements were so suggestive that Rahab wanted to shield her eyes. She glanced up politely from time to time, but mostly looked down, nibbling on some food, more for a distraction than any need of further nourishment. Whenever she looked up at the dancers, she could feel the heat of embarrassment creep up her neck. She peeked over at the king and saw him leaning forward, watching their movements with leering eyes. At any moment, Rahab was certain, his tongue was sure to hang out, drooling.

Hammurabi called one of the servants over and nodded toward one of the young women. As the dancers finished and bowed to the king, the one whom the king had indicated was escorted in another direction. It did not take much imagination to understand where she had been taken. Rahab took a fleeting look at the queen, but she merely watched with a bland countenance as the girl was led out of sight.

The queen had obviously been beautiful once, but the lines around her mouth and eyes spoke of pain and sadness. Suddenly, Rahab felt sorry for her.

The king leaned toward her, chewing a piece of lamb. A rivulet of juice trickled into his beard. "How do you find our city?"

She wished he would not speak with food in his mouth like that. "I have not had a chance to see much of the city yet, your majesty."

Anticipating Hammurabi's response, Radames spoke up quickly. "I plan to show the city to my wife tomorrow."

The king's eyes narrowed again. "I would be most happy to show such a beautiful woman my city, governor."

Was that a challenge? Rahab felt a sudden chill run up her spine.

Radames was firm. "It is most gracious of you to offer, your majesty, but I was looking forward to spending the day with my bride."

"Ah, yes. Newly married. You have been most fortunate, governor. She no doubt delights you with her charms." His words were followed by another appraising glance.

Rahab was more than ready to leave, the banquet having lasted far longer than she would have liked. It took all of her strength to be polite and demure, hiding her revulsion for this pagan king. She knew now why Radames had warned her to beware of him.

When at last the king bid them goodbye and they headed home, flanked by Radames' soldiers, she almost sighed with relief.

Once within the embassy, Radames took her by the shoulders and looked into her eyes. "You did well, beloved. I know it was difficult for you." He leaned down and kissed her. "Go ahead up to our chambers. I will join you shortly."

Donatiya was waiting at the top of the stairs. She helped Rahab remove her jewelry and clothing and prepare for bed. Rahab cleaned her teeth vigorously, as if that could erase the lamb stew she had eaten...which might have been part of a sacrifice to one of Canaan's idols. She hadn't dared to ask, but she prayed it wasn't so.

She felt safe and secure later in Radames' arms, her head buried in his chest, but her uneasiness over the banquet kept spilling into her thoughts.

"I am frightened of the king," she confided, her voice soft. "I don't like the way he looks at me, like I am wearing nothing. I pray we do not have to go there often."

Radames pulled her back a little so he could look into her eyes. "I did warn you, beloved. He has several concubines besides his wife, who put in a rare appearance this evening. Yet he seems to lust after every beautiful woman he sees. Now, perhaps, you can understand why you must not go out without an escort." He drew her close again and she snuggled back against him.

"Rest now," he said. "I will take you on a tour of Jericho tomorrow. With an escort, of course."

Rahab sighed and let herself drift off to sleep, pushing the images of the king from her mind.

9

The next morning, Rahab and Radames rode in a chariot as he took her on a tour of the city, accompanied by two armed Egyptian soldiers on horseback. The houses were made of mud, straw, and stone, similar to the residences in Upper Beth-horon. Unlike the marketplace, which mainly offered different foods, the shopkeepers along the main thoroughfare offered a plethora of different goods—everything from linen cloth, dyes, and bundles of flax to jewelry, pottery, and leather. The voices of the merchants and the high-pitched bargaining of potential customers created a cacophony of sound.

At Rahab's request, they stopped at a potter's stall and she looked among his wares for the largest bowl she could find. Not seeing what she sought, she spread out her hands and asked the merchant, "Can you make a container this big?"

He scratched his head. "Perhaps. It would take time."

She wanted to speak to him further, but Radames was ready to move on. Her idea would have to wait.

They stopped at a jewelry merchant and Radames encouraged her peruse the display. When she admired a set of gold earrings, he indicated he wished to have them, along with some gold bracelets. The merchant sullenly wrapped them in a small square of cloth and handed them to Radames. He took Rahab's arm and helped her back into the chariot.

"He did not appear to be happy, husband," she remarked. "And I did not see you pay him."

"Oh, he will be around for his beer," Radames replied. "Most of the merchants want to be paid in beer."

"No other goods?"

"They trade goods among themselves, but they want the embassy's beer. Bahiti has crafted a brew that's considered among the best."

As they continued their tour of Jericho, Rahab saw temples and evidence of the many gods that the Canaanites worshipped. It occurred to her to ask Radames about the gods of the Egyptians. Perhaps it would create an opening for her to talk to him about Jehovah and why her people only worshipped one God. She once again sent a silent prayer that there would come a time when he would be ready to listen.

At one large, ornate building that was obviously a temple, young women wearing flimsy garments, much jewelry, and elaborate make-up were lounging on the steps.

"Who are they, Radames?"

"Temple priestesses."

"Women priests? They do not look like priests."

He took a deep breath. "They are temple prostitutes who serve their god. By laying with a worshipper, they believe they assist him or her to honor their god."

She put her hand on his arm. "I cannot judge others, but my people worship one God, Jehovah, who does not require that sort of worship."

Radames seemed thoughtful and made no reply.

Her family had lived among the Canaanites for years, but she had never seen such a temple before. Beth-horon was so small—wouldn't she have seen one if it was there? Perhaps her parents and their parents had endeavored to shield their children from the worst pagan practices.

Just before they returned home, she looked back at the palace, looming over the city like some evil monster. It sent a chill through her.

When they were safely in the embassy again, they sat in the dining hall and ate their mid-day meal: fresh bread, goat cheese, figs, and pomegranates, with a cup of beer for Radames and wine for Rahab.

Rahab turned to Radames. "My lord, the Canaanites have so many gods. You said you worshipped a fewer number. I am not familiar with Egyptian gods and would like to hear about them."

He looked at her thoughtfully and took her hand in his. "Amon is the main one; he is considered the king of the gods and goddesses, and we believe he is father to the Pharaohs. His female counterpart is Amunet, called the Female Hidden One. They had a son, Khonsu, the moon god. Mut, which means 'mother' in Egyptian, is a deity who wears two crowns on her head. Osiris is considered the oldest child of the earth god, Zeb, and the sky goddess, Nut. He is the god of the afterlife. That is why many things are buried with the body when an Egyptian dies, so that he has what he needs in the life after death."

She remained silent, listening, her thoughts twirling round about. She had married Radames out of love and her father had assured her that marrying an Egyptian was not forbidden because of their family heritage. *But how was she to deal with a husband who worshipped idols?* She smiled at him. "Tell me more."

He sliced a piece of cheese and playfully fed it to her before continuing.

"Anubis is the divine embalmer. Before Osiris, Anubis patrolled the underworld. He is known for mummifying the dead and guiding their souls toward the afterlife. Horus is the god of vengeance and is the child of Osiris and Isis. He avenged his father's death and ruled Egypt. Thoth is the god of knowledge and wisdom, who settles disputes between good and evil. He maintains the universe by his mastery of calculations. We believe him to be the author of science, philosophy, and magic. He is also the one who created our calendar. Sekhmet is the goddess of war and healing. She can destroy the enemies of her allies. Geb is the god of earth, who represents crops and healing. We believe he retains the souls of the wicked."

It was a lot to digest. "Those are all your gods?"

He shook his head. "Only some of them, the most important ones."

"And you worship all these gods?"

"When I am home with my family or with my soldiers, I profess to worship them. My father would be insulted and perhaps disown me if I even hinted that I did not."

She stared at him, realizing what he had just revealed. Hope rose in her heart. "You say that as if there is something else you believe."

Radames hesitated, as if uncertain how to proceed. "I don't know," he said finally. "I have grown up with all our gods, but prayers to them are not answered. I have not mentioned this before, beloved, but I was married years ago, at the age of eighteen. My wife was only fifteen. Both she and our infant son died in childbirth a year later. I made offering after offering to the gods, praying for her to live, but there was no answer—and no comfort. So I do not put my faith in any god."

Rahab reached out to touch his arm. "Oh, Radames. I am so sorry about your wife and child. That must have been so hard to bear. Did my father know of this?"

"I told him that first night I came."

"And what did he say?"

"He said that I may someday wish to speak to you about your God...when I am ready to do so."

He took her hand. "I heard from my father how beautiful you were and I wanted to see for myself. I wasn't sure, knowing you were Hebrew, but when I saw you, I knew at once in my heart that you were the one I had been searching for all these years." He looked down at their hands and rubbed his thumb over the back of hers thoughtfully. "I was amazed he allowed you to marry me under the circumstances."

Thinking back, Rahab smiled a little wistfully. "My father wanted me to be happy, but as you must know, there were few young Hebrew men left for him to choose from." She shook her head and grinned. "But then, of course, he saw that we were attracted to each other—"

"And he gave his consent."

She squeezed his arm affectionately. "Yes, but only on the grounds that I decided to accept you."

He pulled her into his arms for a kiss. "And I am grateful you did."

Basking in their love, but feeling it might be the right moment, Rahab bit her bottom lip and then smiled up at him.

"I have an idea about planting some vegetables in big pots up on the roof."

He raised his eyebrows. "A garden on the roof? Here? Is there even room up there?"

"Enough for a small garden in pots," Rahab assured him. She searched Radames' face, hoping he would agree. She would need his permission to acquire the containers and plants.

He chuckled and shook his head. "Beloved, if this would make you happy and give you something to occupy your time, then do as you wish."

She threw her arms around him and smothered his face with kisses. "Oh, Radames! Thank you!"

He laughed. "If this is the response I'll get, plant several gardens!"

⁓

The next day, Rahab sent Hameda out to see the potter and arrange for the types of containers she wanted. "If he questions this request, just tell him they are needed for storage," she instructed the chief steward. She wished she could go, but she didn't know how quickly an escort could be arranged. Then, too, Radames wanted her to avoid going into the city as much as possible.

Upon his return, Hameda told her that he did not know when the pots would be ready. "The potter has never had to make anything like that before."

Five days later, the sound of a donkey cart and voices brought her to the door. The cart held her hoped-for pottery: two huge, deep clay pots. Rahab nearly clapped her hands with joy. The man driving the cart shook his head as several servants carefully carried the pots into the house.

As the cart drove away, Hameda came to her with a pleased smile. "He had only two ready, but will make four more and deliver them when they are finished."

Servants had taken the pots up to the roof, but Rahab did not think they were positioned correctly, so she enlisted Radames and Hameda to wrestle them into better spots. The two men exchanged a look, shrugged their shoulders, and maneuvered the pots where Rahab indicated.

After they returned to the main floor and Radames left for the citadel, Rahab approached Hameda again.

"Where I can get the soil for the rooftop pots?"

He sighed and eyed her woefully. "Mistress, one would have to go outside the city to one of the fields and collect soil with a cart and a donkey."

She continued to look at him expectantly. He flung up his hands and bowed his head. "I will take care of it. However, whatever farmer I visit will wish to be paid in beer."

"In beer?"

"At least several jars. It is a common trade item, mistress."

"I didn't know those outside the city would want beer as well. I will see to it that you have several jars of beer. I wish to have the soil as soon as possible."

"Yes, mistress." Hameda hurried away before Rahab could think of something else for him to do.

When he had gone, Rahab hurried to the kitchen to see Bahiti.

"Do we have much beer?" she asked anxiously. "I need some for the potter and for a farmer who's going to give us soil for the garden."

"Do not worry, mistress. I made a batch of beer a week ago. There may be enough, but we should start another batch. The paka does enjoy beer with his meals and often trades with our brew."

Bahiti gathered some recently baked bread containing yeast and carried it to the brewing room. She crumbled the bread into small pieces in a bowl, then picked up a large sieve from the corner of the room and placed the bread pieces in it.

"As I hold the sieve, mistress, will you pour the water over the bread?"

Rahab took the lid off a large stone jar and did as directed, pouring cup after cup over the bread. The two women then poured the bread mixture into a large vat nearby. Bahiti went to the storeroom and quickly returned with a bowl of dates, which she broke in pieces with her fingers and added to the beer mixture.

"After it ferments for a few days, we will be able to pour it into small jars for trading."

"But if we have to make more beer, Bahiti?"

"I will purchase more jars in the marketplace, mistress. I have done this many, many times for Governor Nephi."

Rahab smiled. "Of course, I am very sure of your expertise in this matter. In fact, Radames was telling me how your beer is prized throughout the city."

At that, Bahiti smiled with pleasure.

Rahab sighed. "I wish I could get used to the taste of beer. At home, we drank partially diluted wine. Our water wasn't very drinkable."

Bahiti nodded. "For that same reason, Egyptians and Canaanites drink beer. It is safer than the water. Besides, it is very nourishing."

Rahab could only nod. The cook had a point. She departed then for the weaving room and as she worked, she dreamily contemplated the garden project. She was amazed that her small container garden was coming together. She wondered where the idea had come from. She was anxious to complete it, but for the life of her, she didn't understand why.

~

It was almost three days before the hired man with the cart returned with the required soil.

He shook his head as he wiped perspiration off his brow. "The farmers were reluctant to part with some of their fields. My reason did not make sense to them. However, you are the governor's wife and they finally agreed."

No doubt the farmers thought Rahab was not in her right mind, although the cart driver didn't say so. No matter what he himself might have thought, he helped Hameda carry the sacks of soil up to the roof. Still, he raised one eyebrow at Rahab and shook his head. Then he lumbered down the steps after Hameda to get his beer.

After they left, Rahab began scooping the dirt from the sacks and pouring it into the large, shallow clay containers. When Hameda returned a few minutes later, he quickly strode over to her and snatched the scoop out of her hand.

"This is not the task of the mistress of the house!" he scolded her. Hameda then seemed to recover his manners, for he turned red and bowed. "Apologies, my lady, but you must leave this to me. Simply tell me what you want and I will do it."

And so Rahab supervised Hameda as he spread the soil into the two containers, taking care that there was enough left over to fill the four additional containers when they arrived. Each container had to be placed in such a way that there was room to walk between them and still provide space to dry the flax that was essential for weaving linen.

Rahab had been diligent about watering the seedlings her mother gave her, but a few of them were beginning to wilt, so she was glad to finally be able to plant them as well as some seeds. With carefully nurturing, they took root and grew big. When the other four containers arrived, Rahab planted the remaining seeds. In no time at all, she would have plenty of fresh herbs and vegetables—arugula, watercress, mint, leeks, coriander, oregano, dill, cumin, mustard, sage…and garlic, of course, particularly since Radames was so fond of it.

Donatiya discovered the joys of gardening and eagerly helped Rahab, who showed her which plants were weeds and how to carefully harvest so that the plants would continue to produce.

"I told my mother about this garden, mistress," she said one afternoon, her eyes shining. "We have a small courtyard where I could grow things."

It was as enthusiastic as Donatiya could get. Rahab was pleased that the maidservant's reserve was slowly melting as they worked in the garden together.

But their rapport was not to last. An incident occurred that, as Rahab looked back on it, she realized she could have handled better.

The next time Donatiya returned from visiting her family, Rahab went to her room to look for her and found small figures of several Canaanite idols on the table next to the bed.

"You were looking for me, mistress?" Donatiya stood in the doorway, her mouth tight.

Rahab turned. "Why are these here?"

"They are the gods my family worships. My mother gave these to me as a reminder that they watch over us."

Rahab realized anger would not serve any purpose; the statues were part of the girl's beliefs. She considered her words and spoke kindly, but firmly. "You are welcome to worship your gods at your home or privately, Donatiya, but I do not wish these images to be in my house. You must remove them and not bring them again."

"Your Egyptian gods decorate the house," Donatiya muttered.

"Those belong to my husband and I do not have the right to remove them as yet."

The girl gathered the small idols up, her face sullen. She marched down the stairs and out of the house. Rahab sensed the affinity she had been hoping to build with the girl was broken. When her maidservant finally returned, she did not have the statues with her, but her acrimony remained.

⁓

After Rahab had been in Jericho for over six months, her parents traveled to the city for a visit. She was overjoyed to see them and Radames welcomed them warmly. After servants placed their belongings in a chamber that had been prepared for them, Rahab excitedly led her mother up to the roof to show her the garden.

Zahava expressed amazement over her daughter's ingenuity. "You have done so well, daughter!" she exclaimed. "To think of such a thing in this small space!"

Rahab warmed at her mother's praise. "Oh, Imah, it's been such a blessing to have fresh greens and herbs for our table. Wait until you taste the meal we've prepared for you and Abba."

Bahiti had baked fresh bread and a lamb shank with millet, saffron, fresh coriander, and leeks. She also made a goat milk yogurt with honey, walnuts, and raisins. Rahab put together a bitter herb salad with wine vinegar, olive oil, honey, garlic, watercress, mint, arugula, grapes, walnuts, and fresh dill.

Both Akim and Zahava declared that the meal was as delicious as any Rahab's mother could make.

Radames put his arm around Rahab. "Your daughter is truly a wonder," he told them. "I believe there is nothing she cannot do."

After dinner, Akim and Radames talked quietly in another room, while Rahab showed her mother the weaving room as well as the beer-making room. Zahava nodded, evidently pleased, and yet regarded her daughter keenly.

"There is no sign of a child?"

"No, Imah. I have prayed in earnest, but Jehovah doesn't seem to hear me. Radames wants a son, but he is kind and patient. He does not make me feel guilty by expressing his disappointment when I am *niddah* each month."

Zahava sighed. "Our God has a purpose in everything He does, Rahab. You must trust Him, as we all must. He will answer in His time."

Rahab's parents had only been visiting for five days when, suddenly, after a trip into the city with Radames, Akim announced that they must return home. His face was thoughtful, although he did not say he had seen anything that made him feel uncomfortable. Rahab had suggested to her husband that he try to steer clear of the temples while he showed Akim around.

Early the next day, their belongings packed on donkeys and their horses ready for the return to Upper Beth-horon, Akim held Rahab in a tight embrace and whispered in her ear. "Be watchful, daughter. There are those in this city who are resentful of you."

"I go out only with an armed escort, Abba."

"That is good." He drew back and studied her. "You do not have an easy life here. I regret I did not consider that your circumstances would be so difficult. I almost wish you were home again with us."

She patted his arm. "I am fine, Abba. Radames watches over me and is a good husband."

Zahava had been listening and came over to embrace her. "I am glad for that."

When they were gone, Rahab felt a sense of melancholy steal over her. She didn't wish to trouble her husband, but her heart was heavy. She was grateful for her parents' brief visit, but she missed her whole family—her sisters, brothers, nieces, and nephews—as well as her dear old friends from Upper Beth-horon. No one came to visit, however, despite her invitations.

Rahab longed for someone her age to talk to. Bahiti was friendly, but she was older. And after the incident with the idols, Donatiya remained sour and close-mouthed. *Was there no one in this great city who could be Rahab's friend? And how could she even find such a person with armed Egyptian soldiers by her side during her rare visits to the marketplace?*

A few days later, tired of remaining in the house yet having no reason to venture into the city, Rahab opened the front door and stood in the doorway just to watch people go to and fro about their business. She was lost in thought when she realized a young woman holding a market basket was speaking to her.

"You are the paka's wife?"

Rahab smiled at her. "Yes. My name is Rahab."

Her friendly response appeared to encourage the woman, for she drew nearer. "I am Anat. I live quite close by. I have seen you in the marketplace with soldiers. Can you not go there alone?"

Rahab shook her head. "My husband's instructions. So you've just come from there?"

"Yes. I was getting some food for our meal. My father is ill and I like to make him soups and soft foods he can eat."

Rahab stepped down from the doorway. "What ails your father?"

"Something in his stomach. We don't know what it is. He used to be very strong, but now, he has lost weight."

"I am sorry. That must be difficult for your family."

Anat hung her head. "I have no other family, just my father. My mother died long ago and my husband died of a fever without giving me any children."

Rahab sighed. "I desire a child, but I have not been blessed with one yet."

Anat's face became hopeful. "Then we have something in common. Are you by yourself a lot?"

"Yes, too much. Would you like to come in or do you need to return to your father?"

"I could come in for a moment. I've never been inside the embassy."

Rahab opened the door wider. "Come."

Anat hesitated, but then entered the house. "It is larger than most of the homes around here."

"Yes, there is much to do and my husband entertains visiting officials."

Rahab, delighted to have someone to talk to, waved a hand toward the rest of the house and took Anat on a tour. She did not show her the main bedroom, feeling that was too private.

Anat was fascinated with the room where they made beer and Rahab gave her a brief overview of the process. She then showed Anat the weaving room.

Anat's eyes grew round as she studied the loom. "I was young when my mother died so she did not teach me how to make weave. I must buy fabric from the marketplace when my father or I need new clothes."

"Would you like me to teach you how to use the loom?"

Anat's eyes lit up. "Would you?"

"When can you come?"

"I could come when my father is asleep. Late in the afternoon, for an hour or so."

Rahab was delighted. "Come tomorrow then. I will enjoy having you."

After Anat left, Donatiya appeared, seemingly out of nowhere. *Strange that she wasn't around when we went from room to room*, Rahab thought. *Was she hiding?* She frowned.

"I have not seen you. I was showing a neighbor the house."

"Yes, mistress." She looked at the closed front door and then back at Rahab. "However, that girl is poor. If she comes again, I would watch your valuables."

Rahab raised her eyebrows, waiting for Donatiya to say more, but the maidservant only lowered her eyes and hurried away.

When she was a child, Rahab had confided in her nurse, Tova, who treated her like a granddaughter and showered her with love, always ready to listen, calm her, and banish her fears. As she grew older, she made friends with several girls her own age, sharing dreams and secrets with them. She had hoped Donatiya would be someone she could talk to, but the maidservant often made her feel uneasy...and she wasn't sure why. It was more than the incident with the Canaanite idols. Although Donatiya was respectful, Rahab sensed that there was something behind her subservient attitude.

10

*I*ncreasingly, Radames' duties took him out of the city and into the surrounding countryside to quell disputes and collect the tribute to send to Pharaoh. Rahab remained at home, counting the hours—and sometimes the days—until his return.

The king had invited them to the palace on several occasions, yet he always seemed to choose the times when Radames was not home. Rahab politely declined, telling the messenger she and her husband would come when he was available.

One day, she and Bahiti were in the marketplace with two armed Egyptian soldiers close by, keeping watch over them, when Hammurabi and a few of his men appeared on horseback. He stopped and greeted her.

"Ah, the most beautiful Rahab. Why have you been such a stranger? You must come to the palace. The queen would be most happy to entertain you."

Rahab doubted that the queen would be the one welcoming her. She bowed her head. "You are gracious, your majesty." When she made no further comment, but continued to regard him with what she hoped was a respectful expression, he glanced at the guards standing behind her. Then with a frown and a curt nod to his escort, Hammurabi rode away.

"A lecherous devil, my lady, and a poor excuse for a king," Bahiti grumbled under her breath as she watched him leave.

Rahab looked quickly around them, but no one else appeared to have heard…except for their soldiers, who wore tight smiles. She was very glad Bahiti was Egyptian and not Canaanite, for the cook's remarks would have been considered treasonous.

They hurried home, Rahab eager for Anat's visit that afternoon. Their friendship had blossomed and she finally told the young Canaanite woman to call her Rahab instead of "my lady." Anat was becoming proficient on the loom and Rahab taught her how to spin wool into a fine yarn, ready to be woven into cloth. As part of Radames' pay as paka, clean, soft wool arrived at the embassy in a large bundle every two months and was stored in a large basket in the weaving room. Rahab and Anat experimented with dying the yarn various colors, using different plants to get the shades they wanted.

As the two women talked and laughed, Rahab couldn't remember being so happy. Radames noticed the change in her. She no longer seemed melancholy when he had to leave on business.

"You have found a friend," he remarked.

"Yes. Anat is Canaanite, but there are no other Hebrew women in the city and she is pleasant and good-natured."

He leaned down and kissed her. "I am most happy you have found a friend. I have not been unaware of how lonely you were."

One day, Anat arrived for a visit and was obviously flustered.

"Anat! What troubles you?" Rahab asked.

Anat hesitated, clasping and unclasping her hands. Finally, she blurted, "In the marketplace, the women said I should not be friends with you because the Egyptians are our overlords. They said I am trying to curry favor with the governor's wife."

Rahab remained calm. "And how do you feel about what they are saying?"

"I told them even a governor's wife needs a friend and I'm helping you to understand our people."

Rahab took Anat's hands in hers. "That was wise and kind of you, Anat. I *do* need a friend and I consider you a dear one. I have enjoyed your company very much." She bit her lip. "I hope their comments don't prevent you from coming to see me anymore."

Anat drew herself up. "No, I am not one to just drop a friend because someone tells me to, especially those gossips in the marketplace. I needed a friend too and no one else has helped me with my father. You have sent food and provisions and even come to see if you could help him."

"I regret I have not a physician's knowledge. He is very ill, perhaps…" Rahab left the rest go unsaid.

"Dying? Yes, I know that in my heart, but if he dies, I will be alone and my uncle will make me live with him and his family. He is my mother's brother, but he is not a pleasant man. I would be no more than a servant in their home." She began to weep softly.

Rahab put an arm around her shoulders. "You will not be alone. As long as I am here, you will have me."

The two friends quickly put the matter behind them and went up to the roof to work in the garden. Rahab laughed as Anat told her about a vendor in the marketplace whose ducks had somehow escaped their cage and created havoc as they flew round about, managing to avoid capture.

After they had harvested some herbs and vegetables for both kitchens, Anat gave Rahab a warm embrace as she prepared to leave.

"You have a good heart, Rahab. The gods will surely smile on you and grant you a son."

Rahab could only smile in response. *When would she be able to tell her friend about the one true God, Jehovah?*

It became obvious that Donatiya was jealous of Anat. The servant disappeared whenever Rahab's friend came to visit and always professed that she had another errand to run when they worked in the garden. Rahab grew concerned about the girl's attitude. *Would Donatiya do something to hurt Anat?* She would have to be watched closely.

One day, Rahab discovered her favorite gold earrings were missing when she went to put them on. "Donatiya, have you seen them?" she asked. "Did I leave them somewhere else?"

The maidservant appeared to be agitated. "I saw that woman come out of your room when you went to speak to the cook. Perhaps she took them. I told you not to trust her."

Rahab was astonished. She had come to know Anat very well and although she was poor, her friend didn't seem like the type to steal things. She sent Hameda out to ask Anat to come over quickly. Her friend arrived at once, her brows furrowed in puzzlement.

"Hameda said it was urgent. What's wrong?"

"Anat, my gold earrings are missing and Donatiya says she saw you come out of my room when I went to talk to the cook yesterday."

Anat's eyes widened. "And you think I took them? I have never been in your room without you and I have never stolen anything in my life!" Her eyes flashed with righteous indignation. "How could you even think that I would do that?"

Recalling the almost smug look on Donatiya's face when she accused Anat of theft, Rahab had a sudden realization. She put a hand on Anat's shoulder. "I believe you, friend. Forgive me for a moment's misunderstanding. I think I know who took the earrings."

Rahab thought back to several occasions when she caught Donatiya looking at her with resentful, angry eyes, which would quickly turn into a vacant, far-off gaze when she realized Rahab was watching her. Ever since the matter of the Canaanite idols in her room, Donatiya had been respectful but guarded, almost wary.

"Come, Anat. I want to check something." Rahab led the way to Donatiya's room.

The servant had disappeared, as was her usual habit whenever Anat was there, but now she suddenly appeared and stood indignantly in the doorway.

Rahab spoke sharply. "Remain where you are!" She began to systematically search the room and was about to give up when, on a hunch, she went over and lifted up the straw mattress. And there was the small linen packet that held her gold earrings. She opened it briefly to confirm they were in there.

Anger blazed in Donatiya's eyes and she glared at Anat. "*She* has taken all my joy away! I wanted to tend the garden pots and now *she* is doing that!"

Rahab sighed. "We could have worked together. Why did you not speak to me? There are six garden pots—plenty for all three of us to tend, if only you were not so bitter." She sighed again and shook her head. "I cannot have someone I do not trust working for me. You are dismissed. Take your belongings and go."

She and Anat stepped to one side as Donatiya stormed into the room, snatched up the sack that held her few belongings, and raced out of the house, slamming the front door on her way out.

"I am so sorry to cause you all this trouble," said Anat.

Rahab embraced her friend. "Oh, Anat, *you* did not cause the trouble—she did. And I'm worried that if she sees you ever again, she might try to hurt you. Promise me you will be on your guard."

Anat shook her head sadly. "I will try. I think I had best return home now."

It was several days before Anat returned to visit. During her absence, Rahab had time to think about a way she could help her friend.

"If you could come a few hours each day and help me as Donatiya did, I could pay you," she suggested. "You could still live with your father, as I know he needs you."

Anat's face lit up. "The gods have been merciful, my lady. It would be a great help."

Rahab smiled. "But you must still call me Rahab!" she insisted. "We are still friends."

And so, Rahab had a companion she trusted and was not so lonely when Radames was away.

⌒

But the pleasant times were not to last. Two months later, Anat's father died. Her uncle came for her and the family packed up her things. The uncle obviously did not have time to see to his brother when he was alive, but was happy to claim the few valuables left in the house after his death. Rahab urged her friend to let her or Radames speak to him to ask his permission for Anat to stay as a member of their household, but the notion appeared to shock Anat and she shook her head violently. Rahab still tried to talk to the man, but he ignored her, as if she was a piece of furniture, and carried on a heated, whispered conversation with Anat. His face was like a thundercloud and Anat seemed to be trying to pacify him.

Although he barely knew Anat, in deference to Rahab, Radames attended her father's funeral, bringing the customary offerings of food and grain. Anat's father was buried in an old family tomb that had not been cared for in some time. None of the neighbors came, which angered Rahab. Two of Radames' guards carried the body on a bier, placed it in the tomb, and then resealed the opening.

In a brief moment in which they were alone, Rahab put her arms around her friend to comfort her. "I still do not understand why you must go," she whispered.

Anat sniffed, struggling to maintain a brave face. "My uncle says it is not fitting for me to live alone, now that my father is dead. And the idea of me being a servant in the Egyptian embassy fills him with wrath. I must go and live with them."

"He has a wife?"

"Yes, but she is very sickly and with having to tend my father, I have not been able to visit." Anat lowered her voice. "I did not mind. She too is very unpleasant. Forever complaining."

Rahab watched her friend go, her head down in despair. The uncle lived somewhere on the other side of the city, but she did not know where. Rahab had begun talking to Anat a little bit about Jehovah and her friend seemed to show some interest. *Now, how would they ever see each other again?* A weight seemed to lodge in Rahab's chest.

⁓

It was a warm day, but with a gentle breeze blowing, it seemed like a good day to go to the marketplace. She sent Hameda to the citadel for an escort and when two soldiers returned with him, she and Bahiti set off.

As Rahab paused to look at some sandals, Bahiti spoke with some women she knew. Their conversation was whispered and the noise of the marketplace drowned it out. When Bahiti returned to her side, Rahab noted the look of concern on her cook's face.

"Is something wrong?"

"My lady…" Bahiti looked around cautiously, but only the guards were close by. "There are rumors that the Israelites are coming up out of the desert with thousands of soldiers. It is said they are headed for Jericho."

"For Jericho? Why? How? The Jordan is running high because of all of the rain we have had. How would they get across?"

"I don't know, my lady. No one could ford the Jordan now."

"Perhaps they are just rumors, Bahiti. You know how some women love to gossip."

"Perhaps," the cook responded, but she still appeared to be worried.

"Let us go home. My husband would know if such rumors are true." She turned and started back to the embassy at a brisk pace, Bahiti and the soldiers right behind her.

Rahab was delighted to find Radames at home, hours before she expected him. Her welcoming smile faded at the sight of his grave and troubled face.

"Husband, what is wrong?"

He held an opened scroll in his hand and was silent for so long that Rahab was afraid he was not going to tell her.

He took a deep breath and let it out slowly. "Come." They entered his private room, where papers were spread out across the table. He closed the door. "We are being recalled to Egypt."

She put a hand on his arm. "Who? You and me?"

"Us and the entire contingent at the citadel. The Israelites have finally come out of the desert and my sources say they will be marching toward Jericho. Their army numbers in the thousands and the only thing standing between them and the city is the Jordan River. Pharaoh has ordered all troops and pakas in every city in Canaan to return to Egypt immediately."

Rahab bit her lip. "Bahiti said there were rumors in the marketplace that an Israelite army was heading for Jericho. So that's true?"

"I'm afraid so."

"So why is Pharaoh removing his soldiers?"

Radames shrugged. "We have no quarrel with the Israelites. Pharaoh chooses to not be involved."

Rahab's mind raced. *She would be traveling to Egypt? Far from her family and once again alone among strangers! And what of Anat? How could she ever see her friend again?*

Radames interrupted her thoughts. "Bahiti and Hameda will be traveling to Egypt with us, but no one else must know anything about this. No one! The king's spies are everywhere. Hammurabi must be made to believe we are traveling to Egypt to convince Pharaoh to send more troops to defend Jericho. No Canaanite can know that we are leaving permanently. It is imperative that this be done in secret. Do you understand?"

"Yes, my husband."

"I'm still concerned that the king might be suspicious since our Egyptian retainers are accompanying us. Ordinarily, they would remain and tend the house while we are gone. However, perhaps he will believe they have served out their bonds and wish to return to our homeland. You and Bahiti must pack only a few things, just what you absolutely need. Remember, no one must know that we are not returning, least of all Hammurabi."

"Have you spoken to him yet?"

"No, I go there this afternoon. He is aware of the Israelite army on the other side of the Jordan and wants to see me at once—no doubt to find out why the extra troops he asked Pharaoh for have not arrived. I hope to convince Hammurabi that we are going in person to plead with Pharaoh and make him realize the severity of the situation. I can only hope he believes me. We must leave in the morning, at first light. It would look too suspicious if we were to depart tonight."

Radames shook his head. "The king has written to Pharaoh several times, pleading for help against the Israelite invaders. It is a futile effort, but I must somehow assure him that we are returning with more troops." He sighed heavily. "It is a terrible business. I have word through the last messenger that the Israelites plan to destroy this city and all of its inhabitants."

Rahab gasped. "All?"

"Yes, all. If they find a way to cross the Jordan, they may be here sooner than we think."

As Rahab mounted the stairs to begin packing, a thought came to her with deadly force. *Anat!* There was no way she could warn her friend without letting the uncle's family know…and she didn't even know where they lived. She fell on her knees beside the bed and wept for her friend, pleading with Jehovah to somehow spare her. Yet even as she prayed, she sensed it was futile. Anat was a Canaanite and she would perish with the rest of the city.

With a heavy heart and tears running down her cheeks, she stood and began sorting through her belongings. *If only she could save Anat without jeopardizing Radames and his soldiers.* Then another thought struck her. *Her parents! Her brothers and sisters and their families in Upper Beth-horon! They would be in the path of the Israelites. Would her father be able to get word to the leader of the army that they are not Canaanites?* She dropped the clothes in her hand and hurried back down the stairs to speak with Radames, but she was too late. He had already gone to the palace.

Hameda and Bahiti were speaking in low, urgent tones in the kitchen when she entered.

"Have you both packed?" she whispered.

"Yes, my lady," Hameda told her.

"Bahiti, can you to go to the marketplace and gather some provisions for our journey? Any foods that can keep a long time—dates, figs, some honey, olive oil, and barley. We have plenty in our stores here, I know, but we must leave some for the Canaanite servants, lest they suspect anything. It must seem like you are doing the normal shopping. You must take your time, not show a sign of anxiety."

Bahiti glanced at Hameda, nodded, and then left quietly wearing a cloak in an effort to be as inconspicuous as possible.

"Hameda, is there anything I should do after I've packed?"

"There is nothing to do but wait for your husband's return, my lady," he told her. "You cannot leave the house. The city trembles at the thought of the Israelite army and all know that is your people. Harm could come to you." Hameda looked thoughtful. "I've allowed the house servants to go to their temples to pray to their gods and have watched several depart but a few may be lurking about. Be on guard."

"When will my husband return?"

"As soon as he can get away from the king." Hameda shook his head. "I just hope Hammurabi believes his story."

It was late afternoon when Radames finally returned. His face was pale and he sank onto a stool in the dining room. "The king is suspicious. He accused us of deserting Jericho, although I repeatedly told him I was only going to see Pharaoh to personally make sure he sent more soldiers to defend the city. I even tried flattery, telling Hammurabi that Jericho seemed almost impregnable to me and I'm a seasoned soldier. I told him he could easily withstand a siege, if it came to that." Radames rubbed his brow. "I even suggested he send envoys to make peace with the leader of the Israelite army."

"He would not do that?"

"No, he is too proud to ask for peace and yet the city is in an uproar. People are panicked."

Rahab shivered. "Radames, I am afraid."

Perspiration was beading on his forehead and his eyes became glassy. He swayed slightly and Rahab quickly ran over and supported him before he fell over. She shouted for Hameda, who came at once and hurried over to Radames' side.

"We must get him to bed," she said. "He's taken ill."

"Something's wrong…something's wrong," Radames kept moaning as they helped him up the stairs and into bed. "Oh, the pain!" He nearly doubled over from stomach cramps.

Rahab's heart beat faster as she tried not to panic. *What was wrong? He had been fine when he left the house. Did he eat something at the palace that made him sick?*

"Did you drink or eat anything with the king?"

"Only a cup of wine." He groaned and clutched his stomach.

Hameda ran to the citadel to summon the captain of the Egyptian troops.

Rahab got a basin of cool water and laid damp cloths on Radames' forehead. He was feverish, his forehead beaded with sweat, and he kept moaning and tossing his head back and forth.

When the captain arrived with two soldiers, Rahab looked to him for answers. "What should we do?" she asked, wringing her hands. "He was fine when he left to see the king."

The captain started to speak but then pursed his lips.

"What is it you are not saying, captain?" Rahab pleaded with him.

He glanced at Radames and then faced her. "I've seen these signs before, my lady. I believe the governor has been poisoned." He grimaced.

"He said he only drank a cup of wine with the king!" Rahab cried out in anguish and fell on her knees beside the bed.

Radames seemed to rally and reached for her hand. His voice cracked. "Beloved, if something happens to me, go to Egypt with my troops. You cannot remain here."

"Nothing must happen to you!" she cried. "You must get well. I'm not going anywhere without you. You must fight this!"

"Cannot stay here…" Radames groaned, his face contorted with pain. "The king…beware."

With a sense of horror, she understood. She had avoided the king at every turn. Now, in his anger at Radames' planned departure, Hammurabi had gotten even and poisoned her husband.

Rahab looked in shock at the captain and Hameda. "There must be something we can give him to counter the poison!" she exclaimed.

The captain looked down at Radames, his face echoing the fear she felt. "Without knowing what was in the wine, it will be difficult to find an antidote, my lady. Some draughts that counteract one poison can worsen the effects of another one."

Radames moaned. "Beloved." His hand dropped to his side and he lay still.

The captain came over and placed his hand on Radames' chest to see if there was a heartbeat. Then he bent over the governor, close to his mouth, checking for any sign of breathing. He stood up then and shook his head.

"Nooooo!" Rahab flung herself on his body, but Hameda pulled her away. "Come, my lady, we do not have much time." He turned to the captain. "Are the men ready to go?"

"They can leave in an instant," he reassured the chief steward. He nodded to two soldiers stationed outside the door, then turned to Rahab. "I am sorry, my lady, but we must be off immediately. We need to return to Egypt and must take your husband's body with us. His family will want him embalmed, as is our custom. We will ride hard, day and night, without stopping. Can you make such a trip?"

Tears ran down her cheeks as she frantically tried to decide what to do. "I don't know. My family is in Upper Beth-horon. Can someone ride to give them a message? My brothers will come for me."

"My lady, my soldiers must depart now and we may have to fight Hammurabi's troops on our way out." His lips turned up in a sneer. "Not that they are a match for us. And we will flank your horse to protect you, of course." The captain's voice softened then. "I am truly sorry, but if you cannot travel with us, you will have to find a messenger to reach your family."

He gave an order and the two soldiers who had accompanied him to the embassy entered, carrying sheets of linen. After wrapping up Radames' body, they carried him downstairs.

Dazed with grief, Rahab could only follow them with Hameda holding her arm. Her body trembled as she watched helplessly. There was a small group of soldiers outside who watched in all directions as their two comrades loaded Radames' body on one of the horses and secured it. *Only hours ago he had been alive! Why had he gone to the king? This couldn't be happening! This morning, he was strong and healthy. Only last night, he had held her in his arms.* Her mind played the agonizing thoughts over and over.

The captain turned to her. "Your husband was a fine soldier, madam. This is not the way we planned to leave for Egypt, but we have no time to grieve. We must reach the Egyptian border as soon as possible. Will you not come?"

Rahab could only shake her head silently, tears streaming down her cheeks.

The captain nodded. "I hope you are able to send a messenger to your family." With that, he gave a signal and the soldiers headed for the citadel, where the remainder of their company was waiting, ready to move out.

Bahiti returned from the marketplace just in time to see the soldiers loading Radames' body onto a horse. Her face registered shock as she took in the scene and she immediately went to Rahab, put her arm around her, and led her back into the house. While Rahab sat in dazed shock, Hameda told Bahiti what had happened. He went back outside then and Bahiti helped Rahab up the stairs and into her small bedroom. She removed Rahab's slippers, covered her with a blanket, and sat on a stool beside her.

"I will stay here with you, my lady," she said, and began to hum a childhood lullaby.

As Rahab succumbed to grief, she slipped into unconsciousness.

⌒

She awoke slowly, her vision fuzzy as she looked slowly around the room, wondering where she was. Then she became aware of her surroundings. She was in her small room and Bahiti was sitting by her side.

"Mistress, you are awake." She took a cool cloth and patted Rahab's forehead with it.

"How long have I been sleeping?"

"Over a day."

"Radames is dead."

"Yes, my lady, he is gone and the soldiers have taken his body to Egypt."

Rahab struggled to make her mind work. "You and Hameda were supposed to go with them."

Bahiti smiled sadly. "Hameda did go with them. He was afraid and fear does things sometimes even to the kindest man. He promised to get word to your family if he was able." She patted Rahab's hand. "I could not leave you, mistress. You are young and would be at the mercy of the king."

The king. Anger boiled up within her till she nearly choked. Hammurabi had poisoned her husband! "He is an evil monster!" She almost screamed the words.

"Yes, that he is. He sent a messenger yesterday wanting you to come to the palace so he could express his sorrow at the loss of your husband."

Rahab tried to sit up. "He wanted me to come to the palace? After what he's done? Never! I will kill myself first."

Bahiti gently pushed her back down on the bed. "Mistress, I told the messenger you were deathly ill with grief and in no state to leave the house."

"What are we to do, Bahiti?" Tears rolled down her cheeks. "The Israelite army is coming and the city is doomed. We will all perish."

Bahiti lifted her chin. "We will face it together, my lady."

Rahab began to cry again. "Radames.... I loved him."

Bahiti patted her shoulder. "It is good to weep. You have endured a terrible, sudden sorrow."

Rahab lay back down then and slept for several hours. She dreamt that she once again heard the voice that spoke to her years ago when she had the fever. The words were clear: *"You shall not die."*

She awoke as shadows began to fill the room.

11

*R*ahab had hoped that by now, Hammurabi had more important things to do than bother her. He needed to prepare the city for siege by bringing in produce and grain from the fields, livestock, and any other necessities he could from outside the city. Rahab's despair was almost tangible. *What was she to do?* She could only pray to Jehovah for His protection.

Bahiti shook her head sadly. "The people feel they are safe for now, mistress. The Israelites cannot cross the Jordan until the waters go down. By that time, I believe the king hopes the city will be prepared."

Rahab's mouth tightened. "He prepares in vain."

Thanks to Bahiti's careful shopping, they had enough food for many days. Rahab didn't want to think about what they would do when the food ran out, but by then, perhaps, it would not matter.

She prayed day and night, beseeching Jehovah to save her and brave Bahiti. She remembered her dream, but had no idea what her God would do.

About a week after Radames' death, someone pounded on the front door. When Bahiti opened it, two of the king's soldiers were there. "We wish a word with the lady Rahab," one said.

Hesitantly, she came to the door. "What do you want?"

"You are to come with us. The king wants news of Egypt's plans. We know your husband must have said something to you. Come peacefully or we will take you by force."

Terror filled her being. *What could she do?* Before she could react, one of the soldiers grabbed her arm and pulled her from the house.

The soldiers almost dragged her through the streets. When they reached the palace, to her dismay, Rahab found she was being taken to the king's chamber. One soldier, younger than the other guard at the door, gave her what seemed like a glance of sympathy, but the soldiers who brought her pushed her into the room and slammed the door shut.

Hammurabi saw her fear and smiled wickedly. "So, you have finally come to visit me! Perhaps now we can get better acquainted." He came closer and tilted her chin with his finger. Then he grabbed her with both hands and ran his fingers over her body. She struggled against him but he was surprisingly strong. He pulled her toward the bed.

Sending a silent prayer to God for courage, Rahab tried to consider her options. Surely this vile man planned to take her against her will—and she had no way to protect herself. Suddenly, words came to her mind and she felt strengthened.

She jerked away from Hammurabi with a fortitude she didn't know she had. "Consider what you do, your majesty," she said scornfully. "I was the wife of the paka. When the replacement troops arrive with the new paka, you will have to answer for the death of my husband *and* for your treatment of his wife. Pharaoh thought highly of Radames and will not take kindly to such actions." She stood firm, looking him full in the face, letting him feel the force of her anger.

He paled a moment and released her. "The extra troops I asked Pharaoh for are coming?"

She raised her chin and sneered. "You requested help to defend the city, did you not? My husband was going to plead with Pharaoh on your behalf and now, you have put yourself in a dangerous position. Show me kindness in my grief and it may save your life."

His face was full of uncertainty. Just then, there was a pounding on the door. "Your majesty! I've urgent news!" someone cried. The king opened the door and a messenger burst into the room. "The Israelites!" He held a scroll out to the king.

When the king read the scroll, fear contorted his features. He spoke almost to himself. "The Israelites have defeated the kings on the other side of the Jordan and now are camped by the river." He turned to the messenger. "Do we know how many are in their army?"

The messenger swallowed. "Thousands, your majesty, thousands."

Rahab stood looking at the terrified king, unable to hide her revulsion, but he seemed to have forgotten her.

"We must continue to prepare for a siege. Send out orders for those who tend the fields and fruit trees to pluck everything off of them. Have the builders inspect the walls for any weakness. Make preparations to accommodate people from the surrounding towns. They will be coming into the city for protection."

"Yes, majesty." The messenger almost ran out the door. As the two guards stood looking at the king from the open doorway, he suddenly became aware of Rahab.

"Get her out of here!" His lower lip curled and he smiled wickedly. "I will happily let the new paka know that you have been in my chamber. In fact, I will make sure the word is spread throughout the city that you came willingly and your husband poisoned himself when he found out. There is no one to dispute my story and no one to speak up for you."

He caught her chin in his hand and gripped it until she winced. "I will destroy your reputation. The whole city will come to know you as Rahab the harlot. Take her!" He waved a hand in dismissal and the guards marched her away.

Her head held high, Rahab strode out of his presence. She would let him see her anger, not her relief and certainly not her fear. *Let him call her what he will. The whole city knew the king for what he was. When the Israelite army stormed the city, Hammurabi would be among the first men slain.*

The guards followed her to the palace entrance and stopped. The one who had sneered at her earlier nearly pushed her outside. Rahab hesitated. She wasn't sure how far it was to the embassy and prayed she could make it safely through the city on her own. She walked quickly, not looking at anyone, but her face must have betrayed her fury. To her relief, people stepped out of her way or ignored her as they rushed to and fro, their faces reflecting the fear that permeated Jericho.

Suddenly, two men stepped in front of her. One of them looked her over. "Well, well, what have we here? Coming from the palace? Did the king get tired of you?"

The other, a shorter man, put his hand behind her head and pulled her to him. "How about a kiss?"

His companion looked at her closely. "It's the paka's wife. I heard he is gone."

"Well, you are all alone now, aren't you? Not so high and mighty now, are you? We know what the king does with his women!"

Rahab had enough. She stomped on his foot and he howled in pain. The taller one struck her across the face. "Mind your manners! If you can accommodate the king, you can accommodate us."

She stared at him. *Had the king's lies spread that quickly?*

As the shorter man pulled her to him again, an authoritative voice rang out.

"Leave her alone!" It was the king's young soldier who had been outside Hammurabi's chamber. He must have followed her. "You'll answer to the king if you touch her!"

The two men stood uncertainly for a moment and then shrugged and backed off. "We meant no harm. Just having a little fun." They turned and hurried away.

Rahab pushed her hair back from her face and stood glaring at the soldier. *Did he mean to have her for himself?* "Why did you save me?"

He raised his hands and shrugged. "You remind me of my sister. I know how the king treated you and overheard what he said about spreading lies about you. I could not let those men hurt you. Come. I will escort you home."

She had to walk rapidly to keep pace with him. He wore a scowl on his face, but he spoke in a low undertone to her. "Do not look at me or react to what I am going to tell you. I don't want word to get back to the king. His spies are everywhere." He paused and glanced around, but no one seemed to want to have anything to do with them. "I know you are an Israelite. I believe in your God and wish to join your people."

She struggled to keep looking ahead. "You believe in Jehovah?"

"Yes. I know the city will be destroyed and I will die, but I will die in peace."

Rahab glanced up at his face, which remained unyielding. "You are very brave. I would like to help you, but I don't know how. I still have to get word to my family to come for me. There is no one I can send."

"Jehovah will make a way," the soldier said placidly. "I would help you if I could, but if I leave the city, I will be accused of desertion and beheaded."

They reached the door to the embassy. For the soldier's benefit, in case anyone was watching and listening, she complained in a loud voice, "You need not remain here! Return to your king!" Under her breath, she whispered, "Thank you. I shall forever be grateful to you. May Jehovah watch over you and save you."

He didn't answer, but nodded his head in acknowledgement and went away.

As she bolted the door behind her, Bahiti ran to her and embraced her.

"Oh, my lady, you are safe! I was so afraid for you and thought I would be here all alone when the army besieged the city!" She put a hand to her mouth, "Your face. The king, did he…?"

Bahiti listened as Rahab told her what happened, her eyes wide with disbelief. "The king let you go? And one of his soldiers saved you from those men?"

"My God was watching over me, Bahiti. I prayed and He rescued me."

Bahiti took her hands. "I prayed also. I prayed to your God, Jehovah, to save you."

"Oh, Bahiti! He heard your prayer."

"He is indeed a mighty God." Bahiti's lips tightened in thought for a few moments, but then she lifted her chin and looked at Rahab. "I have seen your faith in this Jehovah and how He has helped you. Would He allow me to believe in Him also?"

"Are you willing to renounce the gods of the Egyptians, Bahiti, and vow to believe in Jehovah as your one true God?"

Tears trickled down the older woman's face as she slowly nodded her head.

"I renounce the gods of Egypt and will trust only in the God of your people. I will take Jehovah for my God."

"Oh, Bahiti! You give me so much hope." The two women embraced again.

They had much to do. "Let us prepare a meal and figure out how we can get word to my family."

They lit a small lamp whose flame only brightened the kitchen. Bahiti poured wine in a cup for Rahab and added a little water as she liked it. They cut some bread and gathered a few dates from the storage room. They were determined to make their food supplies last as long as possible.

A day passed as they huddled in the house. Rahab had looked for someone to carry word to her family, but no one came near enough to speak to and she was afraid to venture outside her home. Finally, she knew she must face reality. There was no one to send. She had prayed until she could pray no more and, finally, she laid it at the feet of her God. He alone could save her and Bahiti.

As she sat working at the loom, moving the shuttle back and forth, she thought of Anat. *How could she find her dear friend and warn her of the coming danger?* She couldn't leave the house and she didn't dare ask Bahiti to go either, lest the king bring harm to her. The knowledge of her helplessness was like a stone in Rahab's heart. *Anat would be killed along with every man, woman, and child in the city—and there was nothing she could do.* With tears running down her cheeks, she could only weave to try to keep the futile thoughts at bay.

That afternoon, however, a courier arrived. Rahab opened the door carefully, mistrusting anyone who might come to the embassy, but the young messenger merely bowed and recited from a scroll:

To Rahab of the Egyptian Embassy, from Anat.

I grieve with you at the loss of your husband and know you will be returning to your family. Life with my uncle's family is hard, but I am making the best of it. I will always remember your friendship and kindness.

Rahab thanked the young messenger who stood uncertainly before her. *Anat felt she was safe, but no one was safe in the city with the Israelite army on its way. But what could be done?* Rahab closed the door and slid the bolt into place.

The next evening, just as Rahab and Bahiti were ready to retire for the night, there came a soft tapping on the front door. They froze and looked at each other in fear. *The king's soldiers again?* It was not the loud pounding of a soldier, but softly persistent. Rahab thought of the young soldier. *Who else would knock on her door at this hour? Perhaps it was Anat?* She peered through a crack between two boards at the top of the door.

Two men who appeared to be in their twenties stood on her doorstep, their faces bearded. They were dressed as Canaanites, but somehow, she suspected they were not. They were glancing around cautiously. *Israelites?* Against her better judgment, Rahab opened the door and the men slipped in quickly, brushing past her.

She put on her bravest face. "Who are you and why are you here at this time of night?"

"Joshua the son of Nun sent us to Jericho and told us to seek his kinswoman Rahab."

Rahab stood tall. "I am she."

One man was silent, short, and stocky, while the other was tall and striking, with dark, curly hair that hung over one eye. He had a slight disapproving smile on his face and his manner was aloof, but there was something about him that drew Rahab. He spoke for both men. "I am Salmon and this is Phineas."

Rahab raised her eyebrows. "If the king knows you are here, you are dead men. However, this is still the Egyptian embassy, so the soldiers will not enter. Let us hope you have not been followed or seen."

Bahiti appeared, fear evident in her face. "My lady?"

"They are kinsmen, Bahiti. Please prepare something for them to eat."

She turned to the two men and raised her hands. "We have not much, but will share what we have. You will be safe here. But why have you come?"

"Joshua leads the children of Israel and we were sent into the city to gather information. We've learned that people are terrified and preparing for a siege, but that will not help them. The Lord has told Joshua to take Jericho and leave no one alive, not even the animals."

"No one?" She was puzzled. "The army of Israel is not just going to conquer Jericho?"

Salmon's features turned grim. "Surely you are aware of the evil practices and intense idolatry of the Canaanites. You live here."

Rahab shook her head. "I could not go about the city unless I had an armed escort and then only to the marketplace. My late husband did take me on a tour once and I saw temple priestesses and a temple to their god, Baal, but Radames did not explain their practices. I was mostly confined to this house."

Salmon's face softened. "That was a blessing. The Canaanites worship over fifty gods, but the priestesses you saw represent Asherah, their goddess of fertility. Their priests represent Baal, their chief god. They engage in rites and lie together as man and wife to ensure fertility and good crops. But Jehovah is condemning them for their greatest sin, which is sacrificing their children in fire. That is an abomination to the Lord God who gives us life. Their pagan practices are an evil disease that permeates the land and it could affect all Israel."

"They sacrifice their children? Are they dead before they are burned?"

Salmon sighed. "No, they are alive when they are placed in the furnace of Baal."

Rahab shuddered. "I must get out of this city. Can you help me?"

Salmon looked down at her. "Jehovah told Joshua to send us to Jericho…to you."

"Me?" She sighed with relief. "Then Jehovah has heard my prayers."

Salmon frowned. "You mentioned a husband. So how is it that you, an Israelite, are now living alone in this Canaanite city? We inquired about a room for the night, pretending to be merchants." His mouth tightened with disapproval. "We were told you were the king's woman and took *travelers* in." The emphasis he placed on the word "travelers" could not be mistaken.

Rahab felt anger rise up within her. "That rumor is the king's revenge for my refusing to warm his bed!" She almost spat at Salmon, her rage was so great. "I was married to the Egyptian governor of Jericho, the paka. He died suddenly and his soldiers took his body to Egypt for burial."

Salmon's face was skeptical. He did not believe her.

"Then why did you not choose to go with them?"

"I was planning to accompany him to Egypt, at least when he was still alive." The sorrow rose up in her again and she turned away to hide the tears that threatened to spill from her eyes. She wiped them quickly, took a breath, and turned back to face Salmon.

"When word came that the Israelites had come out of the desert and were going to attack Jericho, Pharaoh recalled his troops and his governors. He had no quarrel with our people. While I was packing, my husband went to see the king on the pretext that we were traveling to Egypt to convince Pharaoh to send more soldiers to defend Jericho. He felt if he could convince Hammurabi of this, we could safely depart the city." She paused again.

Something in her manner seemed to touch Salmon for his face softened. "Then what happened?"

This time, it wasn't sorrow Rahab fought down, but anger. She looked straight at Salmon. "When he returned from seeing the king, he fell deathly ill and...died. The captain of the Egyptian troops believed the king had poisoned him. He took his soldiers and left immediately for Egypt, taking my husband's body so he could be embalmed."

She choked up again. "The captain told me they were going to ride hard at a gallop without stopping, day and night, until they reached Egypt. I only rode a slow donkey once and that was painful enough for me."

Salmon stroked his beard, studying her. "So you, a Hebrew, were married to an Egyptian—a pagan?"

Then Phineas suddenly spoke up. "It is not forbidden in the law that Moses gave us in the desert. There were seven nations of peoples we could not marry, but Egypt was not one of them."

Salmon considered this. "I believe you are right."

Rahab sighed. "My family is descended from a great Ephraimite chieftainess named Sherah, the daughter of Beriah, who was the son of Ephraim. You know must know that Ephraim was a son of Joseph, prime minister of Egypt, and his wife, Asenath, the Egyptian daughter of Poti-Pherah, the high priest of On."

Phineas nodded. "Yes, I recall that Ephraim was given the patriarchal blessing to carry the princely line." He turned to Salmon. "Is not our leader, Joshua, of the tribe of Ephraim?"

Salmon responded thoughtfully, "True, he is."

"You are also from the tribe of Ephraim?" she asked.

He shook his head. "No, I am from the tribe of Judah."

"Then we are still kinsmen, my lord." Her tone became anxious. These men offered her hope. She looked directly at Salmon. "I wished to return to my family, but that is impossible now."

"Where are they located?"

"In Upper Beth-horon. They are only thirty miles away, but they might as well be a thousand. My family may be the only Israelites still living there. The population is Canaanite. Most of the other Hebrew families have left and gone into towns where more of our people have settled."

Salmon turned those dark eyes on her. "Why did your father and his household not do the same?"

She didn't like the seeming inquisition and answered coldly. "My father had large herds of sheep and goats and land with crops. We have always gotten along with our neighbors and perhaps he felt his age and did not want to start over. Besides, the rest of our family is still nearby."

"He may not have a choice, my lady. Those towns will be attacked and conquered. In the heat of battle, they may not discern that your family is Hebrew. If they are able to come here, they will have to leave everything and take only what they can carry."

The unwelcome tears welled up in her eyes again and she turned away.

Bahiti, who had been nearby, hurried to her. "God will make a way, my lady. They will come," she said soothingly.

Salmon was thoughtful, stroking his beard. "They may be in danger before the attack. The Canaanites fear our army and your family is Hebrew. There could be trouble for them from their own neighbors. If we can return to our camp safely, we will quickly send a messenger to them with instructions to come to you here at the embassy for safety."

Relief flooded her. "Thank you. That is an answer to prayer. There is no one here in Jericho I can send." She indicated the food Bahiti had placed on the table. "Please, eat and refresh yourselves. You are safe here if the king believes a new paka is coming with Egyptian reinforcements to help him hold the city."

The men sat quickly and made short work of the simple meal that Bahiti had prepared. Between bites, Phineas mentioned that they hadn't eaten in two days. They had had to travel cautiously.

"The city is in an uproar because of Joshua's army," Rahab said. "The king hopes to bring in enough food to withstand a siege and is counting on the walls of the city to protect its people." She paused and asked a question that had been at the back of her mind. "Two days ago, it was said that the army was at the Jordan River. How did you get across?"

"We swam across with the Lord's help. The water was swift and deep, almost up to our chests, but the Lord enabled us to cross and carry out our orders." Salmon's eyes met hers. "No river can stop the Lord our God. He will make a way."

"How many of you are there?"

Salmon studied her, his eyes narrowing suspiciously. "Why do you want to know?"

She looked him in the eye. "Not to learn anything for that horrid goat who rules Jericho, I assure you. My family left Egypt and settled in Canaan long before our people were enslaved. We did not travel in the desert with Moses, so I do not know the number of our people now. Jehovah promised father Abraham that he would have as many descendants as there were stars in the sky."

He laughed then at her boldness. "There are more than forty thousand fighting men."

Rahab caught her breath. "No wonder Hammurabi is afraid."

Phineas tore another piece of bread. "We are waiting until we have further orders from Joshua, who is waiting on God's direction."

"But how—" An insistent pounding on the door cut off Rahab's words and she gasped. "Someone must have seen you come here and told the king! His soldiers are not supposed to enter the embassy, but— Quick! No time to lose! Go up to the rooftop and hide under the bundles of flax! Quickly!"

She led them to the stairs while Bahiti swiftly removed the men's plates and cups from the table and hid them in a basket, which she covered with a cloth. While she sat down and calmly continued to eat, Rahab opened the door.

"Why are you pounding on my door at this hour?" she demanded. "Do you not know I've recently lost my husband? This house is in mourning."

Four of the king's soldiers stood there, the leader glaring at her. "The king has had word that two men came to your house. Send them out to us. They are Israelite spies!"

She raised her eyebrows, pretending to be shocked, then waved a hand dismissively. "So that's who they were! Yes, two men *did* come to my house, but they looked suspicious and were very rude so I sent them away." She stared at the soldiers, one by one. "They actually thought this was the home of a harlot!" she exclaimed indignantly. At her steady gaze, two of the men had the grace to look away.

Rahab addressed the leader with distain. "They came here and I refused them. I don't know where they went, nor do I care, but they cannot have gotten far. They might have slipped out before the gates closed. If you hurry, you should be able to overtake them."

The leader's eyes narrowed a moment, debating her words, but then he nodded to the other men and they left on a run toward the city gate.

After locking the door, Rahab hurried up to the roof and addressed the bundles of drying flax. "It is safe now. The soldiers have gone outside the city in search of you."

Two flax-covered heads appeared and the men stood up and brushed themselves off. Salmon looked toward the window in the wall. "We must leave immediately."

She shook her head. "No, the soldiers are spread out, searching for you. You would both be easily captured. You need rest. Stay the night. You will be safe."

Rahab led them to the chamber she had shared with Radames. The bed was big enough to hold both of them. "If there is any sign of the king's soldiers, I will alert you," she assured them.

Salmon nodded. "In any case, we must leave at first light."

Rahab had no thought of sleeping. She and Bahiti kept watch throughout the night, listening for any sound of the king's men returning, but they heard nothing.

～

The two Israelite spies were up well before the sun and Bahiti prepared a small meal for them.

Afterward, Rahab put her hand on Salmon's arm and spoke earnestly. "All have heard how the Lord dried up the waters of the Red Sea when our people came out of Egypt and how they somehow survived in the desert for many years. The people of Jericho melt in fear. They know the Israelite army destroyed two Amorite kings and their cities on the other side of the Jordan. Nothing will stop you from conquering Jericho."

Rahab hung her head. "I cannot go with you because the king would track us down and kill us all." Then her grip on Salmon's arm tightened. "How can I and my family be saved? Even if a messenger gets to them on time, we do not know how long the city gates will remain open. If the king believes there are enough supplies to resist a siege…"

"If you help us get away, we will make sure you and those in your house are safe," he assured her. "We will send word to your family to come in haste here to the embassy."

"Salmon, they must understand the urgency!" Rahab stressed. "The king is rabid, but he is no fool. He will close the gates as soon as he feels enough food is stored to withstand the siege."

She looked around the room and saw a large piece of crimson cloth that she had woven and dyed. She had considered placing it on her bed, but now, she had an idea. "Quick, Bahiti, bring your sharpest knife."

Bahiti ran to the kitchen to retrieve the knife and the two women quickly cut it the cloth into strips as Rahab explained her plan. "We must make a rope that will let you down from here and over the city wall!"

With their soldiers' knowledge of strong knots, Salmon and Phineas tied the ends of the cloth strips together.

Rahab glanced out the window. "You must flee before the first bare light of dawn gives you away to the sentries. This rope will not reach all the way to the ground, but it should get you close enough to jump down."

Salmon looked at the knotted cord in his hand and faced her.

"This will be the token of our word to you. When our soldiers see this crimson cord hanging from your window, they will spare all of those in your house and bring them out to safety before destroying the city. But if anyone goes out into the street, they will be killed. Your family must remain in the house until you are escorted out of the city."

Salmon looked at her sternly. "You have lived among the Canaanites all of your life. I can only pray that you are loyal to Jehovah and His people and no one else. If you keep your word and do not give us away, we will keep our word to you in return."

Frowning, Rahab stared back at him. "I believe in the one true God, Jehovah, and my loyalties lie with the children of Israel and my family. Now heed my words. The soldiers will search the roads for you. Go to the mountains and hide there for three days until your pursuers have given up and returned to the city. After three days, you should be able to go on your way and quickly return to Joshua. Thank him for his kindness in remembering me."

Salmon nodded and his dark eyes reminded her of Radames. There was no judgment there now, only warmth.

Bahiti returned to the room then. "I have gathered some food for you to take." She handed each man a linen sack.

Rahab smiled at her. "Thank you, Bahiti. They will need something to sustain them."

⟶

Rahab tied one end of the rope around her waist. "I am ready."

Salmon looked at the rope and the determined look on her face. "I am heavier. I will go first. Phineas, help her hold the rope."

He swung his feet over the window ledge. "We will see you soon." He seemed to want to say more, but instead, grasped the rope, climbed down, and dropped safely to the ground.

As Phineas prepared to climb out the window on the rope, he turned to Rahab. "Thank you for your courage, my lady. I personally promise to send a runner to your family. Make sure all of them remain in your house after they arrive."

He swung his legs over and Rahab, praying silently for strength, braced one foot against the stone wall, pulling back with all her might. Suddenly, Bahiti grabbed her about the waist and pulled back, helping her bear Phineas's weight. He quickly climbed down, dropped beside Salmon, and the two shadowy figures disappeared into the darkness.

The two women stood by the window, pulled up the crimson cord, and placed it in a basket, out of sight. It would be let down again when the army came to besiege the city.

"Mistress, you are very brave."

Rahab took Bahiti's hands. "You have been brave also. You stayed with me, not knowing our fate. And I think, dear one, that it is time for you to call me by my name."

The older woman smiled shyly. "I will try."

Rahab looked out into the darkness. "They will save us both, along with my family."

Bahiti clasped her hands. "I heard them. Let us hope they give the word to the leader of the Israelites as they promised you."

Rahab, recalling the look in Salmon's eyes, did not doubt his promise to her. "They will remember," she murmured.

12

As the three days passed, Rahab prayed earnestly that the messenger had been dispatched for her family. They must be able to enter Jericho without any problems. She stood by her bed, crossed her arms in front of her, and rocked to and fro while praying.

"Oh God Who Sees, make the seeing eyes of the king's people blind. There are others streaming into the city for what they think is safety. Let my family arrive without incident."

Late the next evening, there was a slight knocking at the door, not a pounding as soldiers would have done. Gathering her courage, Rahab resolved to stay back from the threshold if it were the king's men. With her heart pounding, she opened the door a tiny bit—and then flung it wide open with joy and flew into her father's arms. Akim held her closely, as the rest of the family poured into the house. Bahiti shut the door and bolted it when everyone was safely inside.

"Rahab! Praise be to God, you are safe!" Akim exclaimed. "We received your message and I understood the urgency at once. We gathered what food we could and came as quickly as we could travel."

"You traveled all night?"

He nodded. "I felt the Lord telling me not to stop except for necessities and we pushed on. There were Canaanite families entering the city and we just blended in with the crowd. The guards were overwhelmed and didn't seem to notice us."

He stepped aside as her mother came over to embrace her. "I have missed you and been so worried," Zahava said tearfully. "We didn't know what to do until—"

"It's all right now, Imah," Rahab said soothingly. "Everything will work out, you will see."

She spun around to look at the rest of her family, almost giddy with relief. She embraced each of them in turn: her brothers, Isaac, Baram, and Josiah; her sisters, Jael and Eliana; their spouses; and their children.

Jael hugged her again. "We are so sorry to hear of Radames's death. You were married such a short time."

Rahab looked around again, counting heads. *Who was missing?* Then the realization hit her: her parents' long-time servants, who were as close as family, were not there. "Where are Rivka and Jabari?"

Zahava shook her head. "Rivka was afraid to come to Jericho. She still has family in Damascus and she felt she would be safe with them. She could not go there alone so Jabari went with her." She rolled her eyes. "I am not a gossip, but I believe Jabari has feelings for her. I wish them well."

Rahab sighed. "What a shame! I will miss them. They have worked for you and Abba for as long as I can remember. It will seem strange without them."

Zahava put a hand on her arm. "If we did not trust you as our daughter, we would not have come to Jericho either."

It was a sobering thought. They had trusted her word for their safety...just as she had trusted the two Israelite spies. She sent a silent prayer to Jehovah that she had not trusted in vain.

Akim looked down at her, his brow furrowed. "The messenger said your husband had died and the soldiers were gone, that you were here by yourself and needed all of us to speed to Jericho both for our safety and yours."

At the look of pent-up anguish that appeared on her face, he gathered Rahab for another close embrace. "Tell us what happened."

Rahab rubbed her eyes. "Come, let us sit," she said, motioning to the floor mats and the stools around the table.

Her family sat and listened in disbelief as she related the recent events: the king's fear concerning the Israelites nearing the Jordan River...Radames's attempt to convince him that Pharaoh would send more troops...his death by poisoning...the king's soldiers dragging her to the palace....

Zahava snorted. "That evil man! To bring you such grief and you a widowed bride!"

A baby's cry brought Rahab back to the present. She looked around and counted fifteen children. Jael held her youngest, a son only a few months old, in a sling across her chest. Rahab realized that all of the children were weary and tearful. The older ones stood around, looking a little bewildered. *They must be exhausted!*

"There is more to the story, but I think the children need to rest. Come." Rahab led the children and their mothers up to the bedrooms. She and Bahiti placed pallets, pillows, and cushions on the floors for the babies and little ones, while the older children climbed into the beds. They settled down and went to sleep almost instantly, worn out from their long journey. Even the babies did not fuss.

Back on the main floor, there was controlled chaos as each family sought a place to put their personal items and sleeping mats. They handed over bundles of food for Bahiti to place in the kitchen and storage room.

While her family assured Rahab that they had eaten before entering the city, she knew they must be thirsty, so Bahiti brought out cups and jugs of wine and water for them. They gathered around the table once more.

Akim cleared his throat. "Daughter, I took you at your word when you said we would be safe here in the embassy. We were already receiving threats from people who had been our neighbors for years. When I received your message, I believed Jehovah had acted and quickly gathered our family. But if Jericho is to be destroyed, how will we survive?"

Rahab smiled. "Ah, Abba, that is the rest of my story." She told them then about the Israelite spies and their promise to her if she helped them escape.

"None of us must venture outside for any reason," she stressed. "Thanks to the provisions you brought with you and what we already had, I am certain we will have enough to eat.

We dare not go the marketplace. The city could be besieged at any moment and anyone in the streets will certainly be killed."

Rahab went over to the wicker basket that held the crimson rope and held it up to show them.

"When the Israelite soldiers see this rope hanging from the upstairs window, they will come to escort us safely out of the city. This rope, which I used to help the spies escape from Jericho, is their signal to spare us. We can only wait—and pray—until they come."

Her father frowned. "How long do we have?"

⌒

The next morning, Rahab took her father up to the roof so that they could look out at the hills outside the city. They heard muffled shouts coming from somewhere, so they ran to the weaving room, where the window looked out into the street. They peeked out, taking care not to be seen.

"The Israelites have crossed the Jordan!" the town crier shouted, terror evident in the timbre of his voice. "The waters parted and stood still!" He punctuated each sentence by banging on a small gong. "They crossed on dry ground! Thousands of them!"

"Where are they now?" someone cried out.

"They are camped at Gilgal! A few miles away!"

The Canaanites ran about like frightened rabbits. They cried out in distress, dashed into their houses, and slammed their doors shut. In no time at all, the street was eerily silent, like the lull before a storm. A deathly pall hung over the city.

With the embassy set into the city wall, Rahab and her family could hear the massive gates groan as they were shut and thick wooden beams maneuvered to bolt them closed. She sent a prayer of thanks to Jehovah for her family's safe arrival. Had they come a day later, they would not have been able to enter the city.

That afternoon, Rahab and her brother Isaac stood at an upstairs window and watched large shadows move over the hills.

"There are no clouds," he whispered. "The sky is clear. So what is casting these shadows?"

She gasped. "It's men, not shadows," she whispered excitedly.

He let his breath out slowly. "Their numbers are so vast, they cover the hills! The Israelite army is coming." He stroked his beard. "The town crier said the Jordan parted for them?"

Rahab folded her arms and looked at his puzzled face. "Did our God not part the Red Sea forty years ago, with Pharaoh in pursuit?"

He nodded. "You are right, little sister." Then they hurried down the stairs to spread the news about the approaching army.

The bolt on Rahab's door was double-checked and she admonished everyone to be as silent as possible. Few lamps burned and as the evening food was carefully parceled out, she and her family huddled together and waited, not knowing what to expect. Even the children, sensing the danger, remained quiet. They all prayed for courage and strength to withstand whatever happened.

Early the next morning, Rahab's youngest brother, Josiah, who had taken his turn at watch on the roof, hurried down the stairs and motioned to his father and Rahab. They rushed toward the stairs.

"Come quickly," he whispered. Isaac and Baram, seeing where they were going, got up and followed them, as did Eliana's husband Jaheem and Jael's husband Aziel. They feared they would spotted if they all appeared on the roof together, so they took turns peering out of an upstairs window.

Isaac shook his head in amazement. "I've never seen anything like it."

The entire army of Israel was led by a small contingency of soldiers and seven priests who carried seven trumpets. Behind them were priests carrying a large, ornate wooden box.

"It is the ark of the covenant," Akim said quietly and reverently, "from the tabernacle they built in the wilderness. I have heard stories of it."

As they watched from the window in amazement and astonishment, the priests blew their trumpets and the men marched in silence, their faces like stone. They neither shouted nor whispered. The only sounds were the blasts from the rams' horns and soldiers' feet, marching in cadence. As the priests disappeared around a corner, the army followed after them. Sometime later—Rahab couldn't say how long, for the sight was so mesmerizing, time seemed to stand still—they reappeared. They apparently had marched around the city.

And then they all marched away in the direction of Gilgal, presumably to return to their camps.

"Abba, what does it mean?" Rahab asked her father breathlessly.

He spread his hands, as puzzled as they all were. "I don't know. They should have attacked. It is like no battle I've ever heard of. There must be a reason for their actions, but only Jehovah knows it."

Rahab and the men slowly descended to the main floor, where the other women and the children were waiting, their eyes wide with fear. As Akim described what had happened, Rahab went to the kitchen to help Bahiti.

"How are our provisions holding up?" she whispered.

Bahiti smiled up at her. "Never fear," she said quietly. "We have enough to last two weeks at least. If we are careful. And I am very careful."

With their fuel supply running low and not knowing how long the siege would last, they had harvested all of the garden produce and took care to prepare meals that used up the vegetables that would not keep. Thus, for the evening meal, Rahab prepared a salad of arugula, watercress, mint, leeks, and coriander leaves, topped with a savory dressing, while Bahiti sliced their last loaf of bread and a round of cheese someone had brought.

"I will bake more loaves of bread tonight," she reassured Rahab.

They carried the meal to the table and Rahab was pleased that everyone seemed to get enough to eat. They all sat and ate in silence—even the children—as they all listened for any sound of an attack. But none came. All was quiet outside in the city, too, with none of the usual sounds of animals or people.

After eating, Rahab asked her sisters and her sisters-in-law to join her in the kitchen.

"We do not know how much time we have," she told them. "But I think we should be prepared to leave at a moment's notice. We cannot assume that the Israelite soldiers will have enough food for all of us. Therefore, I am asking for your help in packing what we can now, so that we will be ready when they come."

The women nodded their heads thoughtfully and they all got to work wrapping up foods in cloth and packing them into baskets. There were wineskins, sacks of grain, honey, figs, dates, cheeses, fava beans, lentils, muskmelons, herbs...and garlic, which made Rahab smile a little wistfully. The older foods that were wilted or overripe were left in the storage room for immediate use...for how long, no one knew. Bahiti laughed with delight when she discovered a large sack of barley hidden behind an empty crock.

To keep the younger children entertained, the women made dolls with some yarn and old pieces of cloth from the weaving room. The older ones played games with bones, sticks, and yarn. The adults told stories, too, with Rahab telling them about Jericho and the king—leaving out the unpleasant parts—while Akim related tales from his youth and their heritage. They did anything they could to keep their children occupied and not focused on the world outside the embassy. Her sisters and sisters-in-law took turns on the loom, helped out in the kitchen, or cleaned, while the men kept watch. Anything to make the time pass.

~

On the second and third days, the priests came blowing their trumpets and bearing the ark of the covenant, with the silent Israelite army marching behind them. It was unnerving—and harder to keep the children from crying out in fear. Rahab could only imagine what it was doing to the people of Jericho.

Baram, taking his turn watching from the window, pulled at his chin hairs in frustration. "Why don't they just attack and get it over with!"

Rahab put a hand on his shoulder in sympathy and then went over to the basket that held the scarlet cord, which had been moved upstairs so it was available as soon as it was needed.

She unwound the rope and brought it over to her brother. "Here, help me secure this so it can hang from the window. We couldn't hang it sooner or the king's spies would have been suspicious. But now, I think it is time."

Together, they tied the heavy cord and dropped it out of the window as Rahab had done the night she helped the spies escape.

Zahava came up and glanced out the window at the passing troops. She flung a hand up. "If it is their intent to scare us all to death, they have accomplished their goal." She went back down the stairs and her children followed. Once they reached the main room where the rest of the family had gathered, she turned to Rahab. "Daughter, tell us again what the two Israelite spies said to you."

With the eyes of her entire family on her, Rahab took a deep breath. She knew they needed her reassurance that they would be rescued, that they would not die. She understood that look on the faces of the women and children. It was the same look she must have had when the king's soldiers snatched her. While the men tried to remain stoic, the air was heavy with fear.

"They said that their leader Joshua told them he had a kinswoman in the city of Jericho and they were to go to my house. They were to find out the state of the city and find a way to rescue me. I hid them from the king's soldiers and then I helped them escape by climbing down the knotted scarlet rope that now hangs outside the window—a sign that the Israelite army is to spare all within this house and lead us to safety. The spies promised to get word to you to come to my house, which they did."

Akim nodded. "All praise and thanks to our God for that." He tilted his head and looked at Rahab with a puzzled expression. "But how did Joshua know he had a kinswoman here?"

Rahab clasped her hands in front of her. "I have thought long about that, Abba. And I believe I know. I think Radames's captain sent word to Joshua. Remember, Pharaoh decided to have no part in our people's fight against the Canaanites. And perhaps Jehovah told Joshua that I was the one person in the city who could be trusted to help his spies."

Isaac shook his head. "Let us hope they keep their word. I cannot stand much more of this. He rose. "Perhaps I can look outside and see what is happening." He got up and started for the door.

"No!" Akim stepped in front of him. "No one must go outside. Would you endanger us all?"

He then looked around at his assembled family. "Have any of you considered that the merchants have long since run out of food to sell? That those who did not prepare may be hungry? Starving people are desperate and will do things they would not ordinarily do. And these are pagans. If any suspect we have food, they could try to break down the door. We must be on our guard at all times."

Isaac sat back down reluctantly, a chagrined look on his face.

That night, Rahab could not sleep and so slipped away, up to her rooftop garden. She fell on her knees in the darkness and prayed earnestly for her family.

I do not know what is happening, Oh God Who Sees Me, but I trust You. You have promised through Your servant Joshua that we will be saved. Help me to wait on Your timing. My courage is waning, Lord. Help me be strong for my family.

Her thoughts turned to Radames. By now, his embalmed body would be lying in his family's tomb. She could not be there, nor did she wish to live in Egypt, but the sorrow rose from deep within her for the short life they'd had together…for the grief that she had not given him a child…and for the cause of his death. Bitterness covered her mind like a cloud and she struggled to let it go. She strove to remind herself that her enemy was a doomed man and it would do no good to dwell on his terrible deed.

She had gone into her husband's special room and run her fingers over the table where he worked, the scrolls he touched. She had picked up the reed pen he used to write with and touched the wooden block that still held some cakes of ink. For a few precious moments, she had felt him near.

Rahab struggled with longing for her husband, for his arms around her, and for the gentle words he would whisper in her ear. The tears began to fall and she clutched a piece of cloth to her mouth to muffle the sobs as she poured out her grief to her God.

There were soft footsteps and she was aware of someone nearby. Zahava came over, knelt beside her, and drew her daughter into her arms. Rahab sighed and put her head on her mother's shoulder.

"I could not sleep and I saw you go up the stairs," Zahava said tenderly. "I share your sorrow, Rahab. He was a fine young man. You have endured the unimaginable and I cry with you, my child."

Rahab rested in her mother's arms and the two of them sat down then beside one of the garden pots, waiting for the first rays of dawn and what it would bring.

13

The morning sent the fragile fingers of sunlight to warm their faces. Any other time, Rahab would have welcomed the coolness of dawn, a perfect time for tending her small garden. But now, the large clay pots held only soil, nothing more. They had harvested everything and carefully saved what seeds they could.

It was the seventh day since the Israelite army had gathered outside Jericho. For six days, the priests had blown their rams' horns, leading the soldiers in their silent march around the city. Rahab and Zahava peeked over the wall, their nerves frayed with uncertainty as they watched the thousands of men assemble once more. *Would the army march around the city in silence again? How many times did they intend to do this?* The two women watched secretively as the soldiers strode on. When the last of the soldiers had passed by, the first group with the priests blowing trumpets and carrying the ark appeared again. Once again, they headed around the corner. Rahab stared in bewilderment.

"Something is different today," Zahava whispered frantically. "Come!"

They raced down the stairs and urged Akim and the other men to come up to the upper window. They took turns peeking out cautiously until the army began a third march around the city, still in silence. Then the army proceeded around the city a fourth time.

Rahab sensed in her spirit that *this* day was different. She hurried down to the main floor and gathered the women together. "The army has marched around the city several times now and I think they plan to attack. We must pack up all of our food and belongings and place them by the front door. When the time comes, you will not be able to retrieve anything. Keep your children close by."

With all of their possessions and the provisions bundled, the women and children sat huddled. The men soon joined them and spoke to them in excited whispers. The air was filled with anticipation...and hope.

Akim had been watching from the roof and was the last man to come down. "They have just completed the sixth trip and are going around a seventh time," he said matter-of-factly, as if this were an everyday occurrence.

Rahab smiled in spite of herself. She realized her father was trying to keep everyone calm.

It was nearly midday when the army completed their seventh trip around Jericho. The trumpet blasts stopped. The family looked at one another as a deadly silence settled over the land. Rahab felt like her heart was caught in her throat. She could almost hear it pounding. Sensing the tension, some of the children began to cry. A few of her kinswomen wept, too.

Then came a sound that caused nearly everyone to jump up with fright: a long, almost mournful blast of the trumpets that shook the walls and the very floor under them. A mighty roar went up from the entire army of thousands: "For Jehovah and Israel!"

The walls of the embassy reverberated...but stood firm. Outside, they could hear the heavy crashing and crunching of stones and mortar, screams of terror, and continued shouts from the Israelite army: "For Jehovah and Israel!" Rahab's family huddled in terror, waiting for the walls to come tumbling down on them.

Steeling herself to be brave, Rahab ran to the window that looked down on the street. Soldiers were poured into the city, breaking down the doors of nearby homes, dragging people out into the street, and killing them without mercy. *Why must they be slaughtered like this? Can none be spared, not even children?* And she heard the Lord speak to her:

Do not make any covenant with them. Show them no mercy. Don't intermarry with them—don't give your daughter to his son, and don't take his daughter for your son. For he will turn your children away from following me in order to serve other gods.

Suddenly, there was a pounding on the door and a shout. "Lady Rahab!"

She rushed to the front door and quickly unbolted it. "I am here, with my family." Relief washed over her. "You kept your promise."

Salmon and Phineas stood outside in the road, along with four other soldiers. Salmon stepped into the house and his eyes seemed to take a quick count of the people huddled in the room behind Rahab. The men rose to their feet, helping their wives and children stand.

Salmon beckoned with one arm. "Quickly, all of you. Follow us. Do not run but walk with haste and do not stop for any reason."

Herding the young ones, the adults and older children grabbed the sacks of belongings and baskets of food and poured out of the house behind the soldiers.

Rahab slung her belongings over her back and took the hands of two of the smaller children. "Come, Bahiti," she called.

The old cook's facial expression changed from uncertainty to hope as she quickly picked up her sack of possessions and joined Rahab's family.

Scurrying as they endeavored to keep up with the soldiers, they fearfully looked around at what was left of the massive city walls. The stones that made up Jericho's seemingly impenetrable defenses had tumbled onto their faces, as if they had been thrown down by a giant. They watched as soldiers continued to walk up and over the rubble, pour into the city, and carry out their deadly task of death and destruction, their faces set like flint as they ignored the cries and screams of the city's inhabitants.

Rahab was surprised to see that they even killed the goats, chickens, and other animals.

"It must be so," Salmon told her stoically. "The Lord said nothing is to be left alive. We are only to take the gold, silver, and bronze for His treasury."

Bodies of the dead and the dying lay sprawled here and there where they had fallen and the smell of blood and death began to fill the air. Jericho's huge wooden gates were already burning as they headed toward the entrance.

"Don't look around!" Akim sharply ordered his family. "Keep your eyes straight ahead."

Yet it was a scene that would forever be etched in their memories.

Only a few feet from where Rahab walked, a woman and an infant lay dead in a pool of blood. It wrenched her heart and she felt the bile rise up in her throat. With all her willpower, she forced it down and kept walking.

As they followed the six Israelite soldiers, she wanted to plug her ears and worried about her nieces and nephews. It was impossible to ignore the screams as the soldiers carried out Jehovah's command. More armed men appeared on either side of their path, swords drawn, guarding their way.

Rahab glanced back at her house just in time to see the roof cave in and the walls crumble like the stones around it. And then she breathed a sigh of relief as she and her family passed through what was left of the city gates. They were safe.

⟞

Some distance from the city, Salmon finally called a halt at a grove of fruit trees. The family collapsed on the grass and huddled together as they looked toward the doomed city. Many of the children were sobbing quietly.

Salmon spoke to Akim. "You will be taken to the camp near Gilgal, but we must leave you here for now. You will be safe. All of the commanders know of your daughter and what she did for us." Salmon paused a moment, his eyes seeking Rahab's, and he bowed to her.

With that, he and the other five men took off at a run back toward the city.

Although they were some distance away, every now and then, the breeze carried the sounds of screaming, bleating, and crashing to them.

Bahiti tugged at her sleeve. "Perhaps we could have a little meal," she suggested.

Gratefully, she helped the older woman dig into their provisions and pass out chunks of bread, some dates, and water.

Rahab chewed slowly, lost in thought. She remembered the jealous, vengeful Donatiya, who had served her briefly as a maidservant. She cringed and shuddered as she visualized a sword plunging into the young woman's body. Then she thought of the young soldier who helped her. *Would he defend the king? He would be killed, too.* Yet she took heart when she recalled that he believed in the one true God, Jehovah. He could die in peace.

And then she thought of Anat. *Oh, Anat!* A terrible sorrow gripped her heart as she thought of the one friend she'd had in Jericho. Rahab had attempted to share stories about Jehovah with her, but Anat only smiled shyly and shook her head. She trusted in the gods she had grown up with, believing they would take care of her. Now, there was no way to save her. Grief and guilt assailed Rahab and she bowed her head, tears running down her cheeks.

Oh, Anat, I'm so sorry. I'm so sorry I didn't tell you more of Jehovah. I should have tried harder. Your gods couldn't save you, only the one true God. He would have made a way for you. When you went to your uncle's house, you didn't tell me where he lived. I didn't know where you were. Forgive me.

The pagan city was being destroyed, with all of its idols, altars, and temples. She thought briefly of the wicked, lecherous king and his aloof queen, and could feel no pity for either of them. Hammurabi would pay for the evil he had done and as for his wife…well, couldn't she have done something to rein in his passions?

For hours, the deadly conflict went on. Finally, the victorious soldiers began to pour out of the city, which burned behind them, giant flames shooting up into the late afternoon sky. No one would live in Jericho again.

⌒

Two men approached, walking slowly. One's face and clothing were covered with soot. When he drew closer, Rahab recognized Salmon and she wondered at her elation that he was alive and had survived the carnage. An older man with white hair walked by his side and, suddenly, she knew who this was.

She stood quickly and bowed her head. "Welcome, Joshua. I am Rahab. Thank you for all you have done to save me and my family. We are forever in your debt."

He smiled kindly at her. "You are a kinswoman and thanks to your service, we learned critical information about Jericho." He looked around at the group behind her. The men had risen to their feet and, for once, her father seemed to be at a loss for words. "You have quite a family, Lady Rahab. Tents have been erected near our camp for you and your family. We will return to camp and remain there three days, so the soldiers may rest and regain their strength. When the time comes, you and your family will be escorted into Judea to be settled in one of the towns there. I have put my young friend, Salmon here, in charge of your journey and settlement."

Akim approached then and bowed to Joshua, who nodded in return. "I am Akim, Rahab's father. You have my thanks for saving my family. And yet, I am wondering, is there no possibility of us returning to our homes in Upper Beth-horon?"

Joshua appeared to be considering his request. "I do not know which tribe will be allotted the land that those towns are situated in, but if it is agreeable with their leaders, you may return. When the towns have been conquered."

Rahab glanced at Salmon, who remained silent.

Joshua eyed her brothers and brothers-in-law. "You have five strong men, I see. I could use them." He turned to Isaac, seeing he was the oldest. "What was your occupation in Beth-horon?"

"Honored sir, my brother Baram and I tended my father's flocks of sheep and goats."

Joshua turned to the remaining men and addressed Josiah, Rahab's youngest brother, who was also the slightest in build. "And you?"

"My wife Hannah and I made cheese from the milk of our herds, which we sold in the marketplace, and wine from our vineyard." He hesitated. "I was a teacher before most of the other Hebrew families moved away."

The old man stroked his beard. "I see." Then he turned to Rahab's brothers-in-law.

"I was a potter," Jaheem volunteered.

Then Aziel stepped forward. "I was a carpenter."

Akim spoke up. "Sir, with all due respect, your men have been training for battle for years. My sons and my daughters'

husbands have never even picked up a sword. We left everything behind when we got word from my youngest to flee to
the embassy in Jericho. When your army storms through our
towns, knowing they are Canaanite, there is no way for us to
let the soldiers know we are Hebrew. They would think we are
merely trying to save our lives."

Joshua nodded. "That is true, especially in the heat of
the battle." He looked at the men again and shook his head.
"Unfortunately, there is no time to train you in the art of war
and you might be more of a hindrance than a help." He turned
back to Akim and gestured at Salmon. "We will obtain a scroll
and you will describe to this officer where your homes are
located in Upper Beth-horon, the location of your flocks, and
anything you can think of that would distinguish them from
the Canaanite herds. In the meantime, as we collect sheep and
goats from conquered towns, more herdsmen will be needed."
He nodded to Isaac and Baram. "You will report to the chief
herdsman and he will give you your duties."

Then Joshua addressed Josiah. "Since we have come out of
the desert, there are young boys who need to learn to read and
write Hebrew. They require a teacher. I will leave it up to you
to set this up when you are settled in the camp and notify the
families of our young boys when you will begin."

Josiah's face lit up. "I should like nothing better, sir."

Joshua then turned to Eliana's husband Jaheem. "Although
I'm sure we could use some new pots and cookware, we do
not have the means to set up a potter's wheel and kiln for you.
However, we could use your help in distributing food. My soldiers will make regular deliveries from the towns we conquer

and bring what they can to the camp. It will need to be parceled out to each family. Can you help with this?"

Jaheem nodded. "Yes, sir."

At last, Joshua turned to Jael's husband Aziel and clapped him on the shoulder. "We can always use a carpenter. There are oxen yokes to repair, tent pegs to replace, stools to fix, and things to build. I will send word through the camp that you have these skills." He smiled. "You may have as much work as you can handle."

He surveyed the family. "If these areas of service are carried out, you will earn the distribution of food for your family. All must contribute what they can to keep our camp going."

Rahab could not refrain from smiling. It was very clear why Joshua was such a great leader for their people. He was so wise!

Joshua reached out then to give Akim a brotherly embrace, then held him at arm's length. "You are an experienced leader and will serve as one of our camp elders. You will need to oversee a number of families in the area around your tent and settle any disputes among them. Greater problems may be taken to the leader who is over ten elders."

Akim nodded. "I understand. I am happy to be of service in any way I can."

Joshua turned and looked away to the distant mountains. "I know you wish to return to your home in Upper Beth-horon, but until that city is conquered and cleansed, you must be patient. Three tribes, Reuben, Gad, and half the tribe of Manasseh, already have their inheritance across the Jordan as Moses allowed. The rest of the tribes must wait for their allotments."

Rahab took a quick breath. She knew what "cleansed" meant. She thought of her former friends and neighbors in

Upper Beth-horon, people she had grown up with. On occasion, her Imah had helped to tend their sick and bring their babies into the world. As far as she knew, her parents never discussed their religion with them. When she had gone to the marketplace with Abba, he only talked to the other herdsmen about their flocks and pasture lands. *Were they all to die?* She fought down the sudden sense of heaviness and grief that filled her heart.

Salmon finally entered the conversation. "Did you mark your herds and flocks in any way?"

"Yes," Akim said slowly. "We made a mark with indigo dye on each of the ears of the sheep and goats. There was…ah…a problem. Some of the Canaanite herdsmen were claiming what was not theirs."

Joshua raised his eyebrows. "Marking your flocks' ears was an excellent solution." He turned to Salmon. "Make a note of that and pass it along to the men who attack the towns of Upper and Lower Beth-horon. The herds with the blue mark are to be set aside and kept in the pastures there."

Salmon nodded to his leader. "It will be done."

Joshua seemed to be contemplating something else. They waited until he appeared to come to a decision. "You can still be of help to the army of your people. We will need food. If we can return you to your home, what can you supply?"

Zahava, who had remained silent, stepped forward. "We can supply dried meat, flat bread, cheese, wine, and beer."

Joshua smiled. "That is good. We will re-settle you as soon as we can. I will inform the troop commanders of my decision."

Nodding to them all, he turned and walked briskly away. Rahab was amazed at the Israelite leader's display of strength, especially considering his years. He had to be in his eighties, yet he walked with the stride of a man half his age.

14

*A*s they walked to the encampment at Gilgal, Rahab noticed one of her nieces, ten-year-old Mary, stumbling along with tears running down her cheeks. Rahab went closer.

"We will be at the camp soon and there will be a tent where you and your family can rest."

The girl did not answer and when she looked up at Rahab, her eyes were full of pain. Rahab recognized the look of grief.

"What is wrong, child? You can tell me, for I have seen much in a very short time."

When the group stopped to rest, Rahab sat down under a tree and took Mary on her lap. "What troubles you?"

Mary sniffed and looked back toward Jericho. Her voice was almost a whisper and she spoke haltingly. "I…saw…the…baby."

Rahab understood then. "Oh, Mary, I would give anything if you and the other children had not seen that."

"Why did they kill the baby?"

Rahab sighed. "Your Saba is very wise. He can explain it to you." She caught her father's eye and motioned for him to join them.

Akim leaned down and patted Mary on the head. He looked at Rahab and lifted his brows in question.

"Abba, she saw the mother and child as we left the city. She doesn't understand."

Akim sat down on the grass beside them. "We are not to question the instructions of the Lord, little one, but I know it may be hard to understand His commands. I can tell you that the people of that city did terrible, unspeakable things. They worshipped many idols and rejected Jehovah. And they placed their children in a furnace as an offering to their false gods."

Mary's eyes widened. "Were they dead?"

"No, child, they were alive. And God hated what they were doing. He gave them hundreds of years to repent, but they continued to do evil. They did many other horrible things. The king even killed your aunt's husband. One day, the Lord said, 'It is enough' and they were judged. Our leader Joshua only carried out that judgment. Our God is a loving God and when we obey Him, He brings good things into our lives and protects us. We must be obedient servants of our God and do His will, even though it may not always be what we wish to do. Do you understand, Mary?"

"Yes, Saba, I think I understand. But it was so terrible to see that dead baby."

Akim rose, puffing. "Try to put it out of your mind, little one. We will be at our camp soon and we must keep our eyes on what the Lord God has planned for us. We must trust Him."

Mary nodded and wiped her nose and eyes on her mantle. She gave Rahab a hug and got up to join her parents and younger siblings.

Jael had her youngest in a sling and Rahab watched as Mary went over and kissed her baby brother on the head. That's why the Canaanite baby's death was so hard for her, Rahab realized. She was thinking of her sibling.

They were moving again and Rahab continued to walk beside her mother.

After the long trek to Gilgal, Rahab's extended family was housed in makeshift tents. Some families of the tribes of Reuben, Gad, and the half tribe of Manasseh had stayed back in the territory given to them on the other side of the Jordan, but their fighting men were taking part in the battles to conquer Canaan. Thus, there were hundreds of women and children in tents all around them, as well as soldiers recovering from their wounds.

Rahab's family had few amenities—only the things they brought with them as they sped to her in Jericho from Upper Beth-horon. But they were grateful that the children were calm at last, understanding that they finally had reached a place of safety.

That evening, while the camp slept, Rahab was restless and unable to doze off, so she stepped out into the darkness. She looked up at the twinkling stars, recognizing familiar constellations, and gazed with the wonder she always felt when she saw that each bright, glittering point of light was in the same position it always was in that season. Somewhere, perhaps above those stars, was the Lord God, Jehovah, who set them on their beautiful dance. She looked up a long time.

When her eyes grew accustomed to the night and there was enough light from dying campfires to see her way, she walked slowly away from the tents, her mind turning over the events of the past few days.

Was it an earthquake that caused the walls of Jericho to fall as they did, or was it that terrifying roar from the mouths of forty thousand soldiers? Or was it Jehovah, the One who had parted the Red Sea and the Jordan River for His people? Was He not truly a God of the impossible?

Did she really know her God? Rahab dutifully said the prayers she had been taught and believed in Him. *But was He real to her?* Radames knew his gods because he was brought up to believe in them and worship them, yet he gave them only cursory worship. *Had she done the same?*

Something in her heart longed to truly know the God of her people. He had made a way to save her when there seemed to be no way. When she had reconciled herself to the fact that she and Bahiti would perish, Jehovah had not only saved the two of them, but also her entire family. She looked up at the stars and her heart overflowed with gratitude.

As she returned to the tent she and Bahiti shared with her parents, she heard soft snores coming from Bahiti and her father. Rahab smiled to herself, thinking of the day they arrived here, when she had taken Bahiti aside.

"Without any income at present, we have no wages to give you as you received in Jericho, but my parents and I are glad to have your help."

Tears had welled up in Bahiti's eyes. "You have made a way to save my life and shown me the love of Jehovah, who is now my God. It is a debt I can never begin to repay. I am happy to serve your family the rest of the days of my life."

The rest of their days.... Whatever lay ahead for all of them was a mystery. *Would they be able to return to their homes? Had the Canaanites ransacked them after her family left? What happened to their flocks and herds, the pottery and carpenter shops? If they were allowed to return, would there be anything left of what they once had?* And yet...if they were re-settled in another town, they truly would have to start all over. The thought was overwhelming. They could only trust Jehovah and His plan for them.

The next night, Rahab ventured out of the camp again, her mind occupied with all of the events of the past month. So lost in her thoughts, she was startled to hear a masculine voice behind her, the tone of voice reproving.

"You must stay within the confines of the camp," Salmon scolded her. "Even though guards have been posted, you must stay with your family. Many men are far from their own wives. You are a beautiful woman, a temptation."

Rahab scowled at him. "If you are suggesting I am doing anything other than taking a night stroll, you need to learn some manners."

He put up both hands in response. "I was intimating no such thing! But a woman walking alone among soldiers who are battle weary and far from their wives is, as I said, a temptation."

"You are saying I am in danger?"

"No, Rahab, only a temptation. They need to keep their minds on the battles ahead of us."

She wondered if he was speaking of other men…or himself.

"You have a wife and family, Captain Salmon?"

He hesitated and then sighed heavily. He seemed reluctant to discuss his personal life. "No, I have no wife, just my mother, grandmother, and younger brother. My father died in the desert. I have been occupied with the army and preparing for the siege of Canaan." Then he moved closer to her. "How long were you married before your husband's death?"

She rubbed her eyes, brushing away the still-fresh memory. "Only a little over two years. As I told you in Jericho, we were to leave for Egypt the morning after he died." She clenched her fists then. "I will never forgive the king's treachery. He had no reason to poison my husband."

Salmon stepped closer still and peered into her eyes. "I sense there was more to his reasoning than that."

Rahab gasped and took a step backward, feeling nearly overwhelmed by Salmon's sheer masculinity. "He was a lecherous man," she told him sternly. "I am not sorry he is dead. He sought many ways to get me to the palace when my husband was away. Then after Radames died.…" A wave of sorrow overtook her suddenly and she almost swayed.

At once, Salmon closed the gap between them and gripped her shoulders. "And what happened then?"

Rahab lowered her eyes and the words tumbled out of her as she told him about how the king's soldiers had forcibly taken her to his chamber and the things Hammurabi had said to her. She still shuddered to think about it. "If he had succeeded in his evil intent, I believe I would have killed myself rather than live with that memory."

He released her shoulders and stepped back. "Forgive me, I was not thinking when I touched you."

How could she tell him what the feeling of a man's hands on her shoulders did to her? A strange feeling that she needed to think about...later. "I should return to my tent."

Salmon nodded. "Yes, you should. You need to rest while you can. The coming days are uncertain while Joshua waits on Jehovah for direction. And as he waits, we wait."

He walked her back to her tent in silence and she wondered how he knew which one was hers.

"Sleep well, Rahab of Jericho," he said genially. "You are a brave woman."

Before she could respond, he disappeared into the darkness. Bahiti and her parents still slept soundly. As Rahab slipped under the thin blanket on her pallet, she gave in to the weariness of mind and body, and slept.

Just as the sun was rising, Rahab became aware of activity in the camp. Men were stirring and her mother was looking out their tent flap. Some of the soldiers had family in this camp; she felt sorry for those whose wives and children were back across the Jordan. When the army moved forward to the next battle, the women, children, and non-fighting men would remain here. *How soon could Rahab's family return home?* Joshua had said the army would rest three days after the battle of Jericho before moving on.

Her questions were soon answered when Salmon came to their encampment the second day. He glanced at Rahab, but addressed Akim.

"For now, you and your family will stay here in Gilgal with the rest of the Israelites and other peoples who are not part of the fighting force."

Akim nodded. "Did you lose any men at Jericho?"

Salmon shook his head. "It was an easy conquest. There were no casualties among our soldiers."

"That is good. What happens now?"

"We will march against Ai tomorrow and when Ai is conquered, the Lord will tell Joshua where we should go next."

Akin nodded again. "Thank you, captain. We will make ourselves useful here."

Rahab approached them. "We have some food to share, but we couldn't carry much. What are all of us going to live on? The animals of Jericho were destroyed and we cannot eat the silver or gold destined for the Lord's treasury."

Salmon smiled at her. "Our soldiers recovered large baskets and sacks of grains and vegetables, as well as plenty of fruit from the trees outside the city. We did not take any animals from Jericho for meat, but Jehovah will supply all of our needs. After all, the Lord sustained us with His manna for forty years in the desert and when we left it and entered this land, we feasted from the fields and orchards we passed."

Rahab frowned. "Manna?"

"The food of angels, which rained down on us every morning from heaven, thanks be to the Lord our God."

Rahab and her father could only look at Salmon in astonishment. But then, she reasoned, if God could part the Red Sea and the Jordan River, He could surely shower food down on His people!

A messenger approached Salmon. He listened and quickly took his leave of them.

Akim gathered his family together. Reasoning aloud, he suggested that if the Israelite army could conquer the huge city of Jericho, Ai should be an easy battle. "Spies were sent to look over Ai and returned to tell Joshua that there was no need for the whole army to go there. It was suggested that two or three thousand would be enough to capture the town."

Listening to her Abba's words, Rahab wondered if Salmon would be among the men who attacked Ai. Then she realized with a start that she did not want anything to happen to him. She shook her head. *Do not go there,* she told herself. *You have lost a husband you loved and suffered heartbreak.* Her hands balled into fists. *I will not be that vulnerable again.*

The next morning, the contingent of soldiers assigned to take Ai left the camp. The people waited anxiously for news of the battle.

Rahab was helping her sister Jael wash her hair with water that had been carried in leather buckets from the Jordan. Her sister Eliana waited her turn. The children had been bathed with as little water as was necessary. Rahab dreamily thought back to her bathing area in the embassy and how nice it was to have warm water poured over her.... She shook the unnecessary thoughts away and began to rinse Jael's hair.

Zahava had worked with Bahiti to feed the children and then the adults ate. Finally, all retired to their tents for a midday rest and escape from the oppressive heat. Rahab and her parents lay down and talked quietly as they waited, along with the rest of the camp, for news of Ai.

At mid-afternoon, there was uproar in the camp as the soldiers returned. But there were no shouts of jubilation at another victory. Word was quickly passed through the camp for the people to gather before Joshua. Rahab, her parents, and the rest of her family obeyed, but there was an undercurrent of apprehension. What was wrong?

Joshua's countenance was dark with anger as he faced the assembled crowd. He and the elders had torn their clothing and thrown dust on their heads. People turned to their neighbors with whispered questions. It was puzzling.

"People of Israel, hear me! We have lost thirty-six valiant men today and were forced to retreat from the men of Ai. The elders of Israel and I have been on our faces before the Lord God to learn why we were not able to take the city as He commanded us to do. We have cried out to our sovereign Lord, asking why He brought us across the Jordan River only to let the Amorites kill us! When the Canaanites and all the other people living in this land hear of our defeat, they will be emboldened!"

Joshua's eyes flashed as he surveyed the crowd of people before him. "The Lord has spoken! Israel has sinned! They have transgressed the Lord's covenant and taken the accursed things and hidden their sin among their own things! This is why we could not stand against our enemies. You are accursed. Jehovah will not lead us until we destroy the accursed thing from among us."

His voice was like the roar of thunder and the entire assembly quaked with fear, including Rahab and her family. There was low chattering throughout the crowd.

"Who has done this terrible thing?"

"Why would they do that?"

"What will happen to us?"

Joshua's accusing finger pointed at them like a sword. "Consecrate yourselves in preparation for tomorrow; for here is what Adonai the God of Israel says: 'Israel, you have things under the curse of destruction among you; and you will not be able to stand before your enemies until you remove the things that were to have been destroyed from among you.'"

Joshua paused and glared at the crowd. "Therefore, tomorrow morning you are to come forward, one tribe at a time; the tribe Adonai takes is to come forward, one family at a time; the family Adonai takes is to come forward, one household at a time; and the household Adonai takes is to come forward, one person at a time. The person who is caught with things in his possession that were reserved for destruction is to be burned to ashes, he and everything he has, because he has violated the covenant of Adonai and has committed a shameful deed in Israel."

Waves of terror passed through the people and they hurried to their tents to prepare themselves for the next morning.

Akim gathered his family. "You must not fear. We took nothing of Canaan with us. This can only be the act of one soldier. May we pity the guilty man whom the Lord condemns tomorrow."

Rahab glanced at Bahiti, a question in her eyes. Bahiti shook her head. Rahab went and put a comforting hand on her shoulder. "You belong to the Lord Jehovah now. You have no need to fear."

The camp settled into an unearthly silence. Rahab sensed that families were praying. She lay awake on her pallet and glanced at her parents. She was sure they were also awake, but no one spoke. Her family had not witnessed the terrible judgments of the Lord that they had heard about from the people who came out of Egypt. She could not imagine what would happen to the soldier who had transgressed.

⟋

The next morning dawned and in the growing light, heralding sunrise, a subdued crowd left their tents and slowly made their way to the front of the camp. Rahab stood between her parents and held her mother's hand. Her brothers, sisters, and in-laws carried their children in their arms or held them by the hand and they all drew close together.

Joshua stood on a platform that had been put together so the people could see and hear him. As each tribe was named, they passed before Joshua. He took the clan of Zarhites from the tribe of Judah and then the family of Zabdi from that clan. Trembling, Zabdi's household came forward, one man at a time, and Joshua singled out Achan. And that man's face was the picture of dread.

Joshua said to him, "My son, swear to Adonai, the God of Israel, that you will tell the truth and confess to him. Tell me, now, what did you do? Don't hide anything from me."

Achan began to weep. "It is true: I have sinned against Adonai, the God of Israel. Here is exactly what I did: when I saw there with the spoil a beautiful robe from Shinar, five pounds of silver shekels and a one-and-a-quarter-pound wedge of gold, I really wanted them. So I took them. You will find them hidden in the ground inside my tent, with the silver underneath."

Joshua pointed to a couple of men nearby and ordered them to search Achan's tent. They found everything and brought them to Joshua, laying them on the ground in the presence of the Lord and all of the people.

Rahab realized that Achan's family must have been aware of his deed. Their faces were panic-stricken as they realized that they, too, would suffer the consequences.

Several men grabbed on to Achan, his wife, and their children, while others went to gather his tent and possessions and round up his cattle, donkeys, and sheep. All of Israel followed the sorrowful procession to the valley, Achan's family weeping and crying out in terror as the men pulled them along.

"Please! Have mercy! Please!" Achan's wife held her hands out pleading with Joshua as everything they owned was dumped on the ground, including the things he had stolen from Jericho.

Then Joshua said in a loud voice, "Why have you brought trouble on us? Today Adonai will bring trouble on you!"

And all of the people took their turn throwing stones at Achan and his family. Each threw a stone and then moved back for the next group. Rahab grieved for them yet she knew the Israelites had no choice. Achan's sin had led to the deaths of thirty-six men at the battle of Ai and the Lord God demanded that he be punished. If the people did not listen, wouldn't the soldiers find defeat in other cities like Ai? Fear of the Lord caused each person in the camp to step up and take his or her turn. With tears in her eyes, Rahab and her family did what the Lord God had ordered them to do. Joshua watched until all of Achan's family and their animals met their end. Then wood was brought and everything was burned. More stones formed a cairn over all of the remains.

"From this day on," Joshua cried, "this place will be called the Valley of Trouble."

As they walked back to the camp, the people were subdued and silent. Bahiti clung to Rahab. Returning to their tent, Rahab realized that the heaviness that had come over the camp was lifted. The Lord was no longer angry with them. She glanced at her father and he shook his head sadly. It was a terrible lesson learned.

15

Word was passed throughout the camp that the soldiers would attack Ai again. This time, Joshua
had been assured that the Lord had given them the king, the
people, and the city. And in contrast to Jericho, the men would
be allowed to keep the plunder for themselves, as well as any
food and livestock they found. Thirty thousand of Joshua's best
warriors were chosen and they went to attack Ai at night for an
element of surprise.

The camp waited anxiously for news of the battle.

Rahab had not seen Salmon for several days—in fact, she
hadn't even see him when Achan was punished. As she went
about her tasks, she found herself looking for the Israeli captain
and one-time spy. *Why? Was she not still a widow in mourning?*
Yet, as Rahab considered her marriage to the Egyptian officer,
she realized that although they had had a strong attraction for

one another, she did not really know her husband that well. Handsome and strong, Radames had swept her away when she was young and impressionable.... She shook her head to try to clear it of conflicting thoughts, but in spite of her efforts, she kept thinking of Salmon.

This time, when the army returned, there was jubilation in the camp. Ai had been completely destroyed and all of its inhabitants slain.

Rahab's brother-in-law, Jaheem, who helped to distribute food and water to the soldiers, came over to the family's tents once his duties were completed to share what he learned of the battle.

"Some of the army hid by night behind the city and the rest of the army was in plain sight on the hills opposite Ai. The king felt they could once again defeat us and when the king of Ai and all the men of the city came out to fight, the army seemed to flee as before. Then when they had been drawn away from the city, the soldiers in hiding attacked and set the city on fire. When the men of Ai saw the city burning, they realized they had been fooled and while they tried to fight, we were too many for them." He waved a hand, grinning, "It was a brilliant strategy. Joshua is truly a great commander."

Rahab put her hands on her hips. "Yes, he is a great commander, but do not forget who gives him his commands! Give Jehovah the glory, not a man!"

Jaheem shrugged, his palms up. "Yes, that is true, forgive me. Jehovah guides our army."

Joshua built an altar of uncut stones to the Lord, the God of Israel, on Mount Ebal. The Israelites gathered around and on that altar, the priests presented burnt offerings and peace offerings to the Lord.

The entire assembly was divided into two groups, foreigners and native-born alike, along with the elders, officials, and judges. One group—among them Rahab and her family—stood in front of Mount Gerazim. The other group stood in front of Mount Ebal. Between the groups stood the Levitical priests carrying the ark of the Lord's covenant. Joshua then read to them the blessings and curses Moses had written in the book of instruction. Every word of every command that Moses had ever received from the Lord was read to the entire assembly of Israel, even the women and children.

As she listened, Rahab realized these words had been given to the Israelites in the desert, but she and her family were hearing them for the first time. Their God was a powerful, miracle-working God, yet He was exacting in the areas that were an abomination to Him. If they obeyed His commands, her people would receive blessings instead of curses.

It took a long time to read the words of the law and the children were weary, but no mother dared to move from there and return to camp. The older children seemed to sense the seriousness of what Joshua was saying and though hours went by, they were attentive. When the little ones grew tired, parents or relatives picked them up and held them, letting them fall asleep on their shoulders. When the babies cried, their mothers somehow managed to quiet them.

At last, Joshua finished reading the Lord's instructions to them and Rahab felt like the words were burned on her heart.

Yet questions echoed in her mind. How could they remember and keep all of these laws? Could any man or woman?

⟳

Rahab's sisters had made friends with some other mothers and spent time doing chores with them as their young children played together. Zahava helped Bahiti and Rahab with the family meals from the provisions given them, but Akim seemed to have nothing to do. There were few quarrels to settle after the incident with Achan.

Rahab watched her father as he sat looking out over the camp, his countenance glum. In shock, she realized that his face looked as though he had aged years in the past few weeks. She went over to him.

"Abba, does something trouble you?"

He did not answer at first and then gave out a long sigh. "What is our lot, daughter? What shall become of us? I was a prosperous landowner, with servants, sheep, goats, and fields that provided for our family. What have I now? A tent and all of us dependent on others to provide our food? My wife toiling like a servant to take care of my family? Will we have to start over? Will we be allowed to return to our home? And if we do, what is left there?"

He shook his head sadly. "I cannot take care of my family. Of what use am I to any of you?"

Rahab put her arms around Akim's shoulders. "Beyond the strength of our God, whom we cannot touch and who speaks to us rarely, we have *you* for our strength. We look up to you for your protection, your wisdom, your patience, and your lovingkindness. We will have our home again, Abba. I feel it in my spirit."

Akim looked at her, his face thoughtful. "You have come so far, daughter. I wanted you to have a good marriage and children. How could you know it would turn out like this?"

"None of us know what lies around the bend in the road, Abba. We must put our hand in God's hand and trust Him for what we cannot see."

He chuckled. "And how did my youngest child become so wise?"

"I learned from you, Abba." She smiled. "And I think I remember Joshua saying that as long as I honor you and Imah, we will live long in the land the Lord is giving us."

He got up. "I have some people to call on. I will think on your words. When all is lost, there is always hope."

Rahab watched him walk away. Her tasks for the day were done until it came time for the evening meal. Restlessness stole over her and she walked slowly to the edge of the camp, studying the mountains in the distance and contemplating where her life was now. Her thoughts were interrupted by the voice of a woman nearby.

"You are Rahab. The woman of Jericho."

Rahab turned around to contemplate the speaker. It was an older woman with gray hair and a pleasant expression on her face. Small crinkles lined her eyes and the corners of her lips, but it appeared to Rahab that they were from smiling and laughing a lot.

"Yes, I am Rahab."

"I am Meira."

"I am glad to meet you, Meira." Rahab realized the woman was probably in her fifties and a thought came to her. "You took part in the exodus." It was a statement but also a question.

"Yes, I was twelve years old when we left Egypt. Would you like me to tell you about it?"

Rahab's heart lifted. She had not wanted to approach any of the women in camp unbidden to ask them about the exodus. At last, here was her opportunity to learn what happened.

"Yes, please."

Meira indicated a large, flat rock. "Let us seat ourselves here."

After they brushed twigs and dirt from rock, they sat down and Meira began, "When I was twelve years old, my parents worked in the fields, my mother gathering straw and my father making bricks for the cities Pharaoh was building. I, too, had to work rather than enjoy the pleasures of childhood. I was bonded to an Egyptian family to take care of their two young children, a boy and a girl."

Meira paused, looking out across the plains, remembering. "We had been told for years that Jehovah would send a deliverer to us, but after several hundred years, our people had become discouraged. It seemed like we would be slaves forever. Then, one day, a man of great age, his hair totally white, came and stood in our midst. He called the elders together and told us his name was Moses and that God had sent him to deliver us from Egypt."

"Did they believe him?"

"At first, no. Some of the elders remembered that Moses had been the adopted son of Pharaoh's daughter, raised in the palace with all of the education and privileges of the royal family. But then he had committed some crime. I believe it was the murder of an Egyptian man. In any case, he was banished from Egypt and sent into the desert, presumably to die."

"But then he appeared out of nowhere?"

"Yes. No one had heard from him or seen him in forty years and then he was in our midst claiming to be our deliverer and carrying a staff that looked like a serpent." Meira shook her head slowly. "He wasn't alone either. When he had trouble speaking, his brother Aaron spoke for him. And when Moses performed some miracles, the elders believed him and were overjoyed that Jehovah had truly sent us a deliverer. We were so full of hope. Moses and Aaron then went to Ramses, the Pharaoh then, and told him to let our people go so they could hold a festival in Jehovah's honor in the wilderness. Pharaoh just laughed at them. He did not recognize our God. Then, because he thought Moses and Aaron were preventing the people from working, he ordered the slave drivers and foremen to stop supplying straw for the brick. Now the people had to go and find straw for themselves, but still make the same number of bricks as they did before."

"Why did Pharaoh not kill him?"

"Moses and Ramses grew up together. Perhaps he felt Moses was just a mad man and no threat to his throne by then."

Rahab shook her head. "How could the people make more bricks without any straw?"

Meira's eyes were downcast. "To this day, I remember the bloody stripes on my parents from their overseers' whips. Everyone was beaten and so angry. Now their work was even harder. When they cried out against Moses, he talked to God again and then went back to Pharaoh."

She looked up at Rahab then, a satisfied smile on her face. "And the Lord God sent plagues among the Egyptians each time Pharaoh refused to let our people go. It only affected the Egyptians. In Goshen, where we lived, we did not suffer as they did."

"I heard a little bit about the plagues and am curious to hear more."

"First, there was the plague of blood. Moses turned all the water into blood. When Pharaoh's magicians did the same, Pharaoh would not listen. Each time, Moses went to him to let our people go, he refused, and each refusal was followed by another plague: frogs all over the land, gnats, flies—even a plague against the Egyptians' livestock. When Pharaoh refused again, the next morning, there were dead animals all over the area, but our animals in Goshen were not touched."

"It is an amazing story is it not?" Rahab turned to see Salmon standing behind her.

Meira smiled indulgently. "Have you not heard it a thousand times?"

"But Savta, you tell it so well."

Rahab looked from one to the other. "Meira, you are Captain Salmon's grandmother?"

Meira nodded her head, suppressing a smile. "Yes, unfortunately. He is the one who gives me all my gray hair."

Salmon took his grandmother's arm and helped her to her feet. "Mother was worried about you."

"Ah, what harm can come to me in a camp full of our people? I have enjoyed talking with this young woman."

"You will tell me more one day, Meira?" Rahab asked.

She smiled. "Yes, I am sure we will talk again."

Salmon nodded to Rahab, his dark eyes unreadable as he contemplated her for a moment. And then they walked away, the tall Israeli soldier carefully holding his grandmother's arm.

A memory came to mind of her own grandmother telling her stories when she was about four. A short time later, her Savta died. Thinking back, she suddenly had the urge to weep—for her lost grandmother, for Radames, and for all that had happened to her. Tears slipped down her cheeks and she faced the mountains, lest anyone see. Finally, gathering herself, she wiped her eyes then turned and headed back to her own encampment for the evening meal with her family. Thoughts of what Meira shared ran through her head as she imagined the plagues and their consequences. Yet if Pharaoh refused to let her people go so many times, what finally changed his mind? She hoped to talk with Meira again, and soon.

16

*T*he next day, a strange group of travelers straggled into their camp. Their clothes and saddlebags were worn; their beards and hair were long. When Joshua confronted them, they said, "We are from a distant country. We heard of your prowess at war and have come to make treaty with you."

One of the elders narrowed his eyes. "How do we know you don't live nearby? For if you do, we cannot make a treaty with you."

The leader of the travelers bowed low. "We are your servants."

"But who are you?" Joshua demanded. "Where do you come from?"

Rahab, along with her family and the rest of the people, moved closer to hear their answer.

"Your servants have come from a very distant country because of the reputation of Adonai your God. We have heard reports about him—everything he did in Egypt, and everything he did to the two kings of the Emori across the Yarden, Sichon king of Heshbon and Og king of Bashan at Ashtarot. So our leaders and all the people living in our country said to us, 'Take provisions with you for the journey, go to meet them, and say to them, "We are your servants, and now make a covenant with us."' Here is the bread which we took for our provisions. It was still warm when we took it out of our homes the day we left to come to you. Now look at it! It's dry and turned to crumbs! And these wineskins were new when we filled them, but look, now they're torn. Likewise these clothes of ours and our shoes are worn out because of the very long journey."

As the people listened in astonishment, the travelers showed them their dry, moldy bread and their old, split wineskins. Their clothes, too, were worn out.

Joshua shook his head, examining them, but did not consult the Lord. Then he and the elders made a peace treaty with the travelers, guaranteeing their safety, and they ratified the treaty with a binding oath.

Akim murmured to Rahab under his breath. "I don't trust them. It is a strange story and something doesn't seem right." He shrugged. "But Joshua has made a treaty with them. I hope he doesn't regret it."

⁓

That evening as Rahab walked in the early twilight, enjoying the cool breeze, a familiar voice said, "May I walk with you?"

Salmon.

She was not sure it was proper, since she was a lone woman and a widow, but she sensed he had something to tell her and stopped so he could come beside her.

"Living in our camp must agree with you. Are you happy here?"

"Am I happy? That is a strange question. We had homes, but are now living in tents. We have no idea where we will go or if we will be able to return to our homes. And my husband was murdered. Perhaps, though, I should be happy to be alive."

He moved closer. "I am sorry for all you went through and I realize you still grieve. I do not know if you will be able to return to your parents' home in Upper Beth-horon. We will be marching there, to conquer it, but I do not know when."

"How long will you be serving in the army?"

Salmon shrugged. "As long as Joshua leads us to take the cities in Canaan as the Lord God commanded."

"So your life is as uncertain as mine."

"Perhaps that is so. I *do* know that when we have accomplished our mission, each tribe will be given a portion of the conquered land. I do not know yet what the tribe of Judah will be given when Joshua divides up the land. It will be by lots. It may be far from Beth-horon."

"And you are concerned about that?"

"I am a soldier and it is my duty to follow our leader to conquer the land our God has given us. I do not know how long that will take. Until Joshua disbands the army, I am not free."

She looked up at him. "And why are you saying this to me?"

He swallowed. "Because you have touched me as no other woman has. When I am free from my duties, I wish to come and find you."

For once, Rahab had no words. *He was asking her to wait for him?*

"And if you find me, what then?"

He hesitated and his eyes looked deep into hers. "I would see if what is between us now is still there."

She raised her eyebrows. "What is between us?"

"It is there, Rahab, whether you wish to acknowledge it or not."

She shook her head. "Salmon, we hardly know each other. We met under difficult circumstances and most of the time now, you are off fighting with Joshua and the army."

He leaned down, his breath on her cheek...but he did not touch her. "If you tell me you have no feelings for me, I will understand and I will not bother you further. Tell me now to leave you alone and I will."

But instead, Rahab had a strong urge to lean against him and feel his heartbeat. She pulled back and looked up at him, surprised by the yearning she felt. "I do not wish you to leave me alone."

His smile was like the sunrise and it warmed her like the rays of dawn.

"Your words fill my heart with hope," Salmon said and he swallowed again.

Rahab felt a little smile come to her lips as she realized that this mighty man of valor was nervous. She felt a wild mix of sympathy, compassion, and attraction.

"In between battles, we will talk," he said huskily, "and I will tell you more of myself. Until we marched as an army and crossed the Jordan, life in the desert was all I had ever known."

"And our people remained there for forty years?"

"Yes. Our wandering there is as much part of the story as the plagues of Egypt and the exodus."

She looked up into his face. "I will look forward to talking to you again, Salmon. We do not know the plans Jehovah has for our lives, but I believe we can trust Him as they unfold."

Salmon nodded. "It is enough. Let me walk you to your tent."

Her sisters raised an eyebrow as Salmon walked away from her family's encampment and would have asked questions, but Rahab shook her head and went into her tent. She quietly slipped under the blanket on her pallet, not wanting to disturb her parents or Bahiti. She tried to let the soft snoring lull her to sleep, but Salmon's words echoed in her mind.

She was attracted to Salmon, but not in the same way she had been with Radames, whom she had wed in her youthful exuberance without really knowing him. Radames had been a good husband and she had enjoyed being his wife, but her life in Jericho had been so confining. And after his sudden death, the incident with the king, and everything else that had happened, she was not a young girl anymore.

This time, Rahab wanted to understand the will of God for her life. Salmon said she touched him as no woman had. He did not mention love. Radames had called her "beloved" and whispered words of love, but she was not sure she knew what love meant. As she said her evening prayers, she put Salmon in the hands of Jehovah. *If he survived the coming battles and Joshua disbanded the army after giving them their assigned territories, what then?* Her mind turned until she fell asleep.

17

Akim's hunch proved to be correct when it was discovered that the "travelers" were Gibeonites who lived nearby. Joshua's soldiers had set out to investigate and reached their towns in three days.

"Tricksters, all of them," Akim grumbled. "Their towns are Gibeon, Kephirah, Beeroth, and Kiriath-jearim. Our army would have attacked and destroyed them if we had not made the treaty. Joshua is furious, but there is nothing he can do. He made the treaty and must keep his oath."

The people grumbled against Joshua and the other elders, who were embarrassed that they had made the treaty without consulting the Lord. Now, they would now have to stand by their oath. The army could not attack the Gibeonites' towns because Israel had sworn in the name of the Lord.

When called to account for their deceit, the Gibeonites confessed they feared for their lives and the lives of their families.

Joshua thundered against them. "Now you have a curse on you: you will be slaves forever, supplying people to chop wood and draw water for the house of my God."

The Gibeonites returned to their towns and heeded Joshua's words, sending out groups of men to bring water from the Jordan to the camp and others to cut down trees and split wood to fuel the Israelites' fires.

⌒

Word soon came that the king of Jerusalem was angry that the Gibeonites had made a treaty with Israel. He called together four other kings to attack and destroy Gibeon.

When Joshua received a message of distress from the Gibeonites, begging him to rescue them from the Amorite kings' huge army, he called the elders together to inform them of his decision, but did not hesitate. He was a man of his word and he had no choice. Joshua gathered his entire army and left the camp. They would be marching all night to reach Gibeon.

Once again, the camp was tense as women said goodbye to their husbands. Rahab wanted to find Salmon to tell him goodbye, to tell him she would be praying for him, but the army was by now well-trained and able to muster out quickly. She had no time to find him.

She walked along the edge of the camp that afternoon, sorting out her feelings. *Did she care for Salmon? Was that enough for her, this time?* She wanted a helpmate, someone to love who loved her in return. This time, it was not enough to carry out the duties of a wife, keeping a home and raising any children she was blessed with. This time, Rahab wanted more....

"I see you are deep in thought." Meira walked over, a smile on her face.

"How did you find me out here?"

Meira's smile broadened. "Oh, I have my ways. As a matter of fact, I was looking for you. I thought you might like to hear more about the exodus from Egypt."

Rahab brightened. "Oh, yes. I was hoping to talk with you again."

They sat down in the grass.

Meira tucked her finger under her chin. "Let me see, where did I leave off?"

"I believe the Lord God sent a plague among the livestock?"

"Ah, yes. There was quite a commotion among the Egyptian farmers...." And Meira related the amazing tale of the Lord's wondrous power that He wanted His people to always remember—the plague of repulsive, running sores that made the Egyptians weep from pain...thunder, lightning, and a mighty hailstorm that killed every living thing outside...a huge, black cloud of locusts that ate every leaf, every crop, that had survived the hail...three days of darkness so thick that no fire could pierce it....

"There was light in Goshen, however, and we stayed huddled in our homes. Finally, Pharaoh called for Moses and told him he could go and make the sacrifice the Lord wanted, but we had to leave our flocks and herds behind. When Moses refused, Pharaoh threw him and his brother Aaron out of the palace and warned them that if they came again, they would die."

Rahab was stunned. The things her people endured!

Meira sighed and turned her face in the direction the army had gone. "So much has happened and so much death. I know the Lord God has given this land to us for our inheritance, but it's come at a terrible price. And I worry about Salmon. He has changed."

"In what way?"

"He was always an amiable boy, kind and helpful. When he was old enough, while we were yet in the desert, he began training with the army, preparing for the day we would enter Canaan. He was so dedicated to carrying out the Lord's commandment to take this land. After Moses and Aaron died, the Lord raised up Joshua to lead us. Salmon idolized Joshua and had his eyes only on the conquest of the land, not what it would mean."

Rahab was puzzled. "But you said Salmon has changed."

Meira took her hand and studied her face. "I know the army obeys the Lord, but killing women and children? I can see the pain in my grandson's eyes."

Both women were silent for some time and Rahab understood then the look she had seen on Salmon's face the day they left Jericho, with the cries of death all around them. One day, the battles would be over, the land would be allotted, and the soldiers could settle down. She began to wonder. *Could you just stop fighting and killing after months or years of it and put it aside to live a normal life with a family? Would Salmon be able to do that?*

Finally, Meira broke the silence. "I should not have mentioned that. It is my own grievance. Let me tell you the rest of the story and why Pharaoh at last let us go."

Rahab shook her head. "I cannot understand why he was so very stubborn and hard-hearted."

Meira patted her hand. "Ah, yes, we found out why later. The Lord told Moses that He had hardened the hearts of Pharaoh and his servants so that He could show them all of these signs and our people would forever remember His mighty deeds."

She paused and Rahab waited until she collected her thoughts and began to speak again.

"Moses warned Pharaoh that if he did not let our people go, the Lord would kill the firstborn of all the land, from the highest official to the lowest servant—even the firstborn among the livestock. Still, Pharaoh's heart was hard."

Rahab frowned. "But what of the firstborn of the Israelites?"

Meira smiled a little sadly. "The Lord told us what to do and the angel of death passed over our homes and killed the firstborn of all of the Egyptians, even Pharaoh himself...." Her voice trailed off.

With a start, Rahab realized how long Salmon's grandmother had been talking and how tired she must be. "Perhaps we can continue another day, Meira?" she asked, standing up.

Meira rose slowly with Rahab's help and sighed. "I am an old woman with too many aches and pains."

"You set a good example for all of us." Rahab took her arm and they walked slowly to Meira's encampment. She took her leave then and began to walk toward to her own family's tents.

The army had only been gone a day, but perhaps her father had news. She saw Salmon's face in her mind and realized her heart was being drawn to him. *Yet what good would it do to admit it to herself if he didn't love her in return?* She recalled his grandmother's words: "He was always an amiable boy, kind and helpful...."

As Rahab walked, she noticed people looking up at the sky. She stopped to look up, too. A day had passed, yet the sun remained high in the sky. *What strange occurrence was this?* People were murmuring—some in fear, some in wonder.

Hours passed and still the sun shown. *What happened to the night? What did it mean?* When at last, the sun began to sink into the hills and the familiar darkness settled on the camp, there was a sense of relief.

When Rahab and her family questioned Akim, looking for answers, he merely shrugged in bewilderment and waved a hand at the sky. "Only Jehovah knows His way. Who are we to question what He does with the sun, which He created?"

If she sought an explanation, there was none to be had, until the next day.

18

"Victory!" The runner from Joshua was jubilant. "We slew the men of Ai and took the armies of the Amorites by surprise. We chased them all along the road to Beth-horon and on to Azekah and Makkedah! We slew many, but the Lord God sent a mighty hailstorm down upon them and more were killed by the hail than we slew with the sword!"

As the people gathered around him, amazed at the news he brought, they began to give praise to the God of Israel for His deliverance.

The messenger raised his hand again to be heard. "That is not the only miracle. Joshua prayed to the Lord for the sun to stand still and the moon to stay in place until we had defeated our enemies!"

Rahab listened with her family, "Abba, a mere mortal asked Jehovah to cause the sun to stand still?"

He shook his head. "I have never heard of such a thing." He stroked his beard. "Did I hear the messenger say something about Beth-horon?"

"I believe he mentioned it, Abba. Perhaps when the army returns, you can speak to Joshua."

"I will certainly do that."

She could see the hope in his eyes that they might somehow be able to return to their home. Tonight, she knew he would pray, as would all of her family. Home. At last, it was a possibility.

People began talking among themselves. Some in unbelief, some giving God praise.

Then a man called out, "And the Lord God heard Joshua's prayer?"

The messenger nodded. "It was just as he prayed. The sun remained in its place in the sky until the battle ended. Surely, you must have seen the sun standing still in the sky here. Our leader is truly a man of God."

The people disbursed to their tents, but the hum of conversations could be heard all over the camp. Rahab and her family returned with a sense of awe. They had not seen the plagues of Egypt and Rahab could only contemplate the stories that Meira told her. She always prayed to the Lord faithfully in the morning and again in the evening, but this God Meira told her about was more awesome than she could ever imagine. She had not given Him the exaltation He deserved, yet all her life, she had sensed a presence in her lowest times. *When she was ill, did He not whisper in her ear that she would live? Did He not tell her again in Jericho when she feared for her life? What purpose did the Most Holy God of Israel have for her?*

The next day, she anxiously sought Meira. Salmon's mother, Deborah, was just leaving, carrying a basket of laundry and a jar of soap powder. She smiled and nodded in a friendly manner, while her youngest son walked beside her, swinging an empty jug. Rahab sat down beside Meira, who patted her on the hand.

"Now, you must understand, the Lord gave us very specific instructions about how to ensure the angel of death did not take our firstborn. We had to slay a perfect lamb or goat, spread its blood around the doors to our homes with a hyssop branch, roast the animal, and eat it with bitter herbs and unleavened bread. If there was any meat left over, it had to be completely burned. All of our people did as we were commanded and after midnight, there was horrendous wailing throughout the land. There wasn't a single house without someone dead in it."

As she described what it was like for the Israelites and the Egyptians, Rahab thought back to the carnage she had glimpsed in Jericho as they were hurried out of the city. Once again, she saw the young woman and her baby lying in a pool of blood on the street. She pushed the grisly memory from her mind and concentrated on Meira's story.

"And Pharaoh? What did he do?"

"He sent for Moses and Aaron and told them to take our people and get out of his land. Pharaoh was finally very eager to let us go."

Rahab leaned forward. "What was the exodus like?"

Meira waved a hand. "To a young girl like me, it was like nothing I'd ever seen in my life! Women wrapped their kneading boards in their cloaks and carried them on their shoulders. The Egyptians were so afraid of us, they gave us jewelry, clothing, silver, and gold. There were horses, carts with donkeys, herds of

sheep and goats, people carrying bundles and small children—
the dust was terrible and there were thousands of us. No one
knows how many women and children, but we learned later that
the men numbered six hundred thousand. I helped drive our
small herd of sheep and my father had been given a cart that he
filled with our possessions. My younger brother rode with my
mother."

She clapped her hands. "Oh, the jubilation and singing! We
were all shouting and praising the Most High God for our deliverance. After four hundred and thirty years in Egypt, at last, we
were free!"

Meira stared off into the distance for a moment. "It was a
feeling I almost couldn't believe. You must remember, we were
all slaves, even me. I was forced into labor as soon as I was able
to walk...." She told more stories about what life was like for the
Israelites who had remained in Egypt after Rahab's own family
left. Yes, they had a good reason to remember Egypt!

"I heard the story of the crossing of the Red Sea," Rahab
said. "My father heard it from a Syrian who had left the Israelite
camp."

Meira smiled, her face alight with the memory. "The Lord
led us in the desert by way of a cloud in the daytime and a pillar
of fire at night. When the cloud moved, we moved, and when it
stopped, we camped."

Rahab shook her head thoughtfully. "I cannot even imagine
what it was like back then." She was silent for a moment as she
looked out toward the mountains and the road leading to their
camp at Gilgal. "I wonder when the men will return. I pray they
have been victorious."

Meira's eyes twinkled. "Could it be that you are looking for a certain soldier to return?"

Rahab felt the heat rise in her face. *Was she looking for Salmon to return?* She rose quickly, embarrassed. "Thank you for telling me about the exodus, Meira. My family will be eager to hear this story, especially my father."

"Come again, Rahab. You are always welcome in our camp."

"Thank you." She stood and saw Deborah returning with clean, still-damp clothes in her basket, her son skipping happily beside her. He dropped a stick he was carrying, squealed, and ran to his grandmother, who laughed and embraced him.

As she walked toward her own encampment, Rahab felt a touch of melancholy. If only Radames had left her with a child, someone to love and hold and care for. She had her nieces and nephews, but that was not the same. *Would she ever have a family of her own?* She tucked her feelings away and went to help her mother and Bahiti with the evening meal. Her sisters were already spreading wooden platters on a large rug where they all ate, the men first and then the women and children.

After the meal, she told them some of the stories Meira had shared with her. Then her brother Baram played softly on his *kinnor*, the little harp he used to soothe the sheep. Rahab looked around at her family and felt a wave of gratitude. They were together—safe—and had enough food to eat. For now, as she contemplated the Lord's care of them, she knew she must be content and wait for whatever her God had planned for her life. It was in His hands.

19

From the sudden commotion in camp the next day, Rahab knew the army was returning. Women rushed to their sons and husbands; there was a sense of jubilation as loved ones were found to be alive. Rahab followed the throng, not sure why she went. Yet she knew she must look for that familiar face, to know he was safe and had not been killed. Then she saw Meira and Deborah embracing Salmon as his brother Samuel danced around them. She stood at a distance, relieved almost to the point of tears. She hoped to remain unseen and was just about to turn and go back to her family's tents when he looked up and their eyes met.

Meira saw where Salmon was looking, grinned broadly, and gave him a gentle push.

As he came toward her, she felt embarrassed. *Why had she not stayed out of sight?* In a few strides, Salmon stood before her, looking down into her face.

Although obviously weary, his eyes twinkled and a smile tugged at the corners of his mouth. "I'm glad you are here to welcome me."

She looked away. "It was the commotion. I knew the army was returning and I just followed the crowd."

"To see if I came back alive?"

Heat rose to her face and she looked up at him. "I'm glad you are alive."

"And I am glad *you* are glad I'm alive."

She tossed her head. "Are you teasing me?"

Their eyes met again and once more, she had to fight the urge to fling herself into his arms.

"Never, Rahab. I kept thinking of you, kept seeing that beautiful hair of yours, framing your face."

She lowered her eyes. She was aware of his presence, his manliness, yet she could not touch him, nor could he touch her without sending the wrong message to any who were watching them.

Then she remembered. The messenger had mentioned Beth-horon. She looked up. "You were near Upper Beth-horon. Was that town conquered also?"

She sensed he knew what she was asking, but he merely smiled. "Your father will want to talk with Joshua about that."

Rahab knew they had been talking longer than they should, so she stepped back. "I'm sure your family is very happy you are back, safe and sound, Salmon," she said, a little loudly.

"Yes, thank you," he responded. Then looking off in the distance, he softly whispered, "You will walk this evening?"

"Yes." And she knew he would come. Holding her head high, she turned and strode quickly back to her camp, neither looking to the left nor the right.

Her sister Eliana met her, smiling. "You have seen Salmon? He is well?"

"Yes, of course. I just welcomed him back."

Eliana gave her a knowing look. "Of course you did." Then she became serious. "Did he say anything about Beth-horon?"

"I did ask him about that, but he said Abba needs to talk with Joshua."

"I'm sure Abba will. He has been distracted and pacing like a caged animal ever since the messenger came! He will not rest until he finds out about our home."

Rahab nodded. "I didn't think he would. Perhaps he can give Joshua a day to rest from the battle before he rushes to question him!"

Eliana rolled her eyes. "One can hope. But I am certain that as soon as he learns Joshua has returned to camp, he will go."

The sisters embraced. "I'm glad Salmon is safe," Eliana said.

Rahab sighed heavily. "But for how long? There are other battles to fight, cities to conquer. He came through this one, but what about the next?"

"Sister, if the Lord God has a plan for him, it will be accomplished. We must trust Jehovah."

"Now you sound like our father."

In the late afternoon, the men returned from their tasks: Baram and Isaac from shepherding, Josiah from teaching the boys how to read and write, Jaheem from overseeing a group of Gibeonites, and lastly, Aziel, who complained he would never be able to keep up with all of the carpentry work for so many people. With the welcome cries of the children and the task of helping to serve the evening meal, Rahab realized that she was happy. Her family was all around her and for the first time since the siege of Jericho, there was hope that they would be able to return home.

As the evening approached, Rahab looked toward the mountains. There was something comforting in knowing they had been there long before man walked the earth. As she reached for her cloak, she felt a hand on her arm.

"You go out to walk again, daughter?"

"Yes, Imah. Would you like to walk with me?"

Her mother smiled. "I'm not sure that is what you truly want. Will you not meet Salmon?"

"He did not ask me to meet him, but I believe he will find me."

"Just be careful, Rahab. He is a soldier, a strong man. Think about how much you encourage him. I do not want anything unseemly to happen."

"Nothing has happened, Imah. He is respectful and does not touch me."

"That may be true, but being alone can be more of a temptation than you realize. You may not think anything can happen, but when two people are attracted to each other and they are alone in a secluded place, emotions can be strong."

"I understand. If he meets me, we will stay within sight of the camp."

Zahava hesitated for a moment. "That is a good idea. But, Rahab, you have been married and have experienced physical love. I know you are lonely. Once awakened, the feelings a woman can have for a man are strong. And it is plain to see that he is attracted to you."

Rahab swallowed. "I will remember your words, Imah."

Her mother embraced her briefly and then turned away. As Rahab glanced back at her family for a moment, she could see her sisters watching her. She wrapped her mantle around her and moved slowly toward the edge of the camp, contemplating her mother's words.

20

*H*er father had not gone to see Joshua yet and Rahab was filled with curiosity. *What would their leader say? Would they be able to go home again?* She could only pray and leave it in the hands of their God.

Lost in her thoughts, she was not aware of his presence and was startled when Salmon spoke.

"Am I interrupting some deep thoughts?"

She sighed. "My father wants to talk to Joshua about our home."

He moved closer. "I do not know what Joshua will say, but the town has been conquered and many of its inhabitants had already fled their homes. I pray you will be able to return. But not too soon."

She turned to look at him in the twilight. "You don't wish us to return to Beth-horon?"

He chuckled. "Your family is welcome to go, but I would miss seeing you."

She turned back to look at the mountains. "You have other cities and towns to conquer, as the Lord has commanded. How long will that take?"

He broke a small twig he'd been holding in half. "It could take years."

She looked up at the night sky. "I think of the wives and children of the tribes who have land on the other side of the Jordan. They must wait for husbands and fathers to come home, but only when the battles are over."

"Yes," he said lowly, slowly, his voice deep. "And the wives and children here who must wait out every battle for us to return." There was sadness in his voice then. "We conquer and do what we have to do, but it is a bloody business, to take the land promised to us."

"I saw, as we left Jericho. It was hard on the children."

"And you?"

She looked down. "I saw a young woman and her baby, lying dead in a pool of blood in front of their house. I still see them in my mind."

Salmon grimaced. "The soldiers won't talk about it, but I see their eyes in the firelight and when they think no one is watching. How can they tell their wives and children what they are doing? It was unfortunate that you all had to walk through the city to reach the gate."

"I can only pray that the children will forget."

"What was it like, living in Jericho?"

The sudden change of subject caused her to look up at him.

"My husband was good to me, but he was basically the tax collector for Egypt and I had to have an armed escort if I wanted to go to the marketplace. I had a young Canaanite woman as a maidservant for a while, but I caught her keeping idols in her room and then she stole from me and I had to let her go. I made friends with another Canaanite woman, Anat, who lived nearby and was taking care of her ill father. I tried to teach her about our God, but then her father died and her uncle took her to live on the other side of the city. It grieved me to think of her fate, but I didn't know where he lived. And then I was dealing with the death of my husband and that evil toad, the king...."

Rahab stopped abruptly, wondering why she had said all that. *What must Salmon think?*

"You believe the king poisoned your husband." It was a statement, not a question.

"That is what the captain of his guard told me. Perhaps he had seen the symptoms before."

Salmon was silent for a moment. "Did you ever talk to your husband about the Lord?"

"He was familiar with our customs, but while he was not diligent in worshipping the Egyptian gods, he felt that my faith was my choice and didn't involve him. There was no one there to celebrate the Sabbath with. It was then that I missed my family the most."

She didn't want to talk about her life in Jericho. Radames had been a loving husband and she grieved for him, but he was gone and she was alone. Something else was on her heart. *What would life be like if she returned to Beth-horon, while Salmon went on fighting for years, conquering the land of Canaan?*

"What is the next city Joshua has indicated you will attack?"

"We have taken Jericho, Ai, and the towns all the way to Azekah and Makkedah. We have defeated and killed the kings of Jerusalem, Lachish, Eglan, Hebron, and Jamuth." He looked out toward the mountains. "There is still so much territory to conquer."

She acknowledged his words with a slight nod. "Then there is a chance Joshua will allow my family to return to Upper Beth-horon."

"For your family's sake, I pray he will agree, but the territories have not been assigned to the different tribes yet. That will be by lot when we have completely conquered Canaan."

She looked up at him earnestly. "What happens to the widows and children of the men who have been killed? Most have no families to return to."

"In His law, the Lord God instructed us to care for widows and orphans. They will be settled in towns where there are other families to see to their care."

"But many of them will remarry?"

"Hopefully. Many have sons nearing the age to serve in the army and are being trained even now. The younger boys are learning trades to support their families."

She marveled. "I didn't know all of this was going on."

Salmon's brow creased and his gaze was resolute. "Unlike your family, Rahab, they have no homes to return to. They will be resettled when the territories are distributed."

"So they must stay here in the camp until then?"

"It would be confusing and unfair to settle them in one territory only to uproot them and place them in another later."

She sighed. "It seems so—"

He interrupted her. "Rahab, this is not what I really wish to talk to you about."

She stiffened in the darkness. *She knew what was on his mind, but was she ready to hear it?*

"I can promise no future, save what is there when Canaan has been conquered. You will more than likely return to your home and I have no doubt there are those who would also find you a beautiful and eligible woman to take to wife."

She felt heat rise in her face and she shook her head. "If the town has been cleared of Canaanites and all the other Hebrew families have gone, I don't know where he would come from."

He hesitated, then pointedly told her, "Other families may settle with you. I cannot ask you to...." He stopped speaking.

"Wait for you?"

"Yes." His voice was husky, shaky.

She had to ask. "For how many years, Salmon?"

This time, his voice was almost a whisper. "I don't know."

Rahab put a hand on his arm. "Then we must leave this with God. He alone knows our path and His plan for us. You may not survive one of your battles. It could be months before I would know if you were dead or alive. How can I promise you something on the basis of what is so unknown?"

He sighed deeply. "Yes, I understand that. It is too much to ask of any woman."

"Let us trust our God, Salmon. I can give you no other answer than that I will pray."

He bowed his head. "I can ask for nothing more."

In the darkness, they stood so close together. The urge to press up against him, to feel his arms around her, was so strong...

yet she knew they would be compromised if anyone saw them. She stepped back. "Good night, Salmon."

From his breathing, she knew he had the same reaction to her that she did to him, but he restrained himself. "Good night, Rahab."

She walked quickly back to her camp, her mind turning. He wanted her to wait for him. *He cared for her, she knew, but did he love her? Would she wait for him or would the Lord bring someone else into her life?* The rest of her family was asleep. She sat by their campfire, deep in thought until the embers faded, and then wearily sought her bed.

21

*A*kim's countenance was jubilant as he called the entire family together. "Joshua has given us permission to return home!" he exclaimed.

They all cheered, clapped and laughed for joy, and then began to ask him questions all at once.

"When can we leave?"

"Are there any families going with us?"

"Does this mean Canaan is nearly conquered?"

Akim held up his hands. "Wait, wait!" he begged them. They quieted down and looked at him expectantly.

His voice became grave. "We are the only family with homes to go back to. Everyone else has been wandering in the desert for forty years. Think of that and how blessed we are! Even so, we do not know what awaits us. Our homes may have been looted by the Canaanites after we left. The army took what grains they could glean from the fields and we may have to start over. What sheep and goats were not used for food that still have our blue mark on them will be returned to us." He turned to Isaac and Baram. "I'm trusting you to round up the flocks and shepherd them as you did before."

He then sought out his sons-in-law, Aziel and Jaheem. "You will have to see what is left of your woodshop and pottery business. That is all I can tell you. We must trust the Lord God for whatever awaits us."

More than twenty pairs of eyes gazed eagerly at Akim. "It is a thirty-mile walk, so prepare yourselves for travel. Joshua has agreed to provide us with ten men to escort us there in safety, along with some other families from the tribe of Ephraim, who will settle in Upper Beth-horon with us. There are fields to tend and homes to rebuild. There will be work for us all to do. Josiah, we will find a place for you to continue to teach Hebrew to the boys, just as you have been doing."

There was silence for a moment and then they all began to chatter. "Home. We are going home...."

Akim turned to Rahab. "Daughter, we could use your help. You will return with us?"

"I am coming, of course, Abba." She smiled, turned to Bahiti, and raised her eyebrows in question. "We will need a cook."

The woman's face lit up and she nodded with enthusiasm. Rahab turned back to her father. "And Bahiti, too, Abba."

He smiled, clasped his hands together, and nodded to the older Egyptian woman. "Wonderful! Thank you, Bahiti."

⌯

Their small bundles of possessions packed, Rahab's family prepared for travel to Upper Beth-horon. She had gone to Salmon's camp to bid goodbye to Meira, hoping to see him one last time.

Meira embraced her. "Go with our God, Rahab. I believe He has great things in store for you."

Rahab was glad she had seen the dear woman, but disappointed that Salmon was not there. As she returned to her family and they were completing their preparations for the long trek home, ten soldiers walked up to their camp—led by Salmon. Her sisters gave Rahab knowing smiles, but said nothing. Her mother raised her eyebrows and looked from Rahab to Salmon, but she too said not a word. Instead, Zahava shook her head and continued her packing.

To Rahab's surprise, Joshua himself came over to bid them goodbye.

"Your situation is unique," he told Akim, "and I felt the Lord God telling me to let you return to your former homes. May you prosper as you did before."

Akim was touched. "Thank you. You have been most generous with us and we are grateful. When we are once again able, we will send food for the army as we agreed."

Joshua nodded, stepped back, and glanced at Salmon and then at Rahab. "I believe you are all in good hands."

Salmon did not look at her and Rahab wondered if he had asked for this assignment or it had been given to him. She had a feeling that Joshua knew more than he said.

Akim acknowledged the soldiers and then waved to his family to move out toward Upper Beth-horon—and home. Salmon and three other soldiers led the way, while six soldiers rode behind them and the other Ephraimite settlers, including widows with older children and former soldiers with too many injuries to fight anymore. Rahab, her siblings, and their spouses were glad they weren't going alone. Settling with other Israelite families would give them an opportunity to make new friends and increase their capability to rebuild Upper Beth-horon.

⌒

The sun was high in the sky when Salmon finally called a halt near a copse of trees. Those who needed to relieve themselves did so and weary children sat down in the rippling grass to rest. Small babies had been carried in slings in front of their mothers and the women were glad to be able to stop and nurse their little ones.

When everyone had been refreshed and eaten a small meal, they began their walk again. The soldiers paced their horses to accommodate those walking and even took some small children up in front of them. Rahab noticed Salmon had a little boy riding with him. The expression on Salmon's face was touching as he talked to the boy. The thought occurred to her that he would probably make a good father. She shook herself. *Where did that thought come from?* He hadn't spoken to her since they left Gilgal, but she sensed he would find a time that was right.

That evening, they made camp and when everyone had finished their meal and laid down on their pallets or cloaks for the night, Rahab stood at the edge of their camp in the twilight. And he came.

"Are you faring well?"

"Yes. Tired, but well. The trip seems longer than when I made it with Radames years ago." She smiled a little. "Of course, I was riding a donkey then...."

"We shall be there tomorrow about midday."

"I find myself anxious about what we will find when we get there," Rahab admitted.

"We must trust the Lord, Jehovah Jireh, our provider." Salmon smiled kindly. "That is all we can do."

She changed the subject. "I was surprised to see you leading the soldiers who are escorting us."

He chuckled. "I don't believe Joshua was surprised at my request to lead them."

Rahab did not think he could see her smile in the darkness. "I'm sure he wasn't. He seemed to know everything that went on in camp."

"I wanted to see you safely home and know that everything is going to be all right for you and your family."

"Do you have to return right away?" she blurted out.

"Yes, we must be back as quickly as possible. As soon as I determine the town is safe and we return, the army moves out again."

She could feel her heart thumping. He would be fighting again, killing and destroying. She knew the army moved on the orders of Joshua, who did not send them forth until he heard clear direction from the Lord. She sensed Salmon tensing up, suddenly shy and nervous once more, so they bid each other good night and he returned to his men.

Rahab could see her brothers with some of the soldiers and wondered what they were talking about. Then she smiled.

Perhaps they wondered the same thing when they watched a group of women talking together.

She wrapped her cloak about her and settled down for sleep. Another long walk awaited them tomorrow, but concern for what would happen beyond that kept her mind occupied for a while.

22

As the bedraggled group of travelers neared Beth-horon, Rahab and her family were apprehensive. *What would they find?* The walls of the city were still standing, but as they approached, it was deathly silent. A hawk flew overhead and a flock of sparrows rose up at their approach.

After Salmon called for a halt at the entrance, he and his men rode ahead through the town, looking for any sign of danger. From what Rahab could see, it looked like an abandoned, ghost city, with no one in sight. The doors of many houses were missing or hanging to one side. A red fox crossed the road and looked up, startled, then trotted off between two buildings.

When the soldiers returned, Salmon nodded to Akim. The city was clear. The settlers entered slowly, looking all around at the signs of destruction. In some places, the streets bore evidence of dried blood, remnants of the casualties of war. Rahab wondered why there were no bodies lying around—but she was grateful that there weren't.

Her family walked on until they came to Jaheem's pottery shop. The door was splintered apart, but the kiln and potter's wheel had been untouched. Small pieces of broken pottery were scattered about, but Jaheem rushed to the back of the shop and returned grinning from ear to ear.

"My clay is still here!" he cried ecstatically. "I can begin again."

With a little trepidation, his wife, Rahab's sister Eliana, entered their house next door. Anything of value had been taken, including bedding, but the bed frames were intact. Her open clay oven still stood in the kitchen and her shelves still held a few dishes and some wooden platters. And God surely smiled on them, for her old broom still stood in the corner of the main room.

"Thanks be to the Lord!" Eliana cried. "I have my home again and work to do!"

To her delight, she found the cradle that her brother-in-law had made still standing in a corner. Eliana quickly brushed out the debris and placed her youngest son, still sleeping, in it. She rocked it with her foot for a few moments to be sure he stayed asleep. Then she and her older children set to work to sweep and do what they could to put the small house to rights.

Salmon turned to Akim and the rest of his family. "Come," he said. "The others are waiting for you to reclaim your homes so they can find houses of their own."

"Of course, of course," Akim said apologetically. "Come, my children." His family trooped after him, continuing further into the town. One by one, while the other families and battle-worn old soldiers who came with them rested and waited in the town square, Akim's family returned to their homes.

Jael's husband Aziel found his carpentry shop basically intact. He hurried over to a rear wall, removed a few bricks, and reached his hand inside. "They are still here!" he cried triumphantly. He had had the foresight to hide his tools before they raced to Jericho.

Rahab marveled at her brother-in-law's cunning. He had done this without even knowing if they would ever return to Upper Beth-horon.

The adjoining house was intact, although stripped of nearly everything except the heavy wooden table and the broom. Jael was nearly gleeful as she began to sweep.

"Ah, the army doesn't know how valuable brooms are, Captain Salmon!" she told him.

He grinned and shrugged his shoulders.

As each of her brothers and their wives reclaimed their homes, they broke off from the group and began their own restorations.

Joined by Salmon and two soldiers, Akim led Zahava, Rahab, and Bahiti up the hill to Rahab's childhood home. Her Imah had tears running down her cheeks and her Abba put an arm around his wife's shoulders. "We are home. Our house is still here."

Rahab was startled to hear the bleating of sheep. Two young men came to meet them, seeking Akim. "We were sent by Joshua to return what sheep and goats belong to you that were marked in the blue dye, as you described," one said. "We have them corralled outside for your family."

Turning to Salmon, the other remarked, "We will return to camp with you, sir."

Akim was speechless. Joshua had mentioned returning their flocks, but Rahab wondered at the care the army must have taken to separate them from among all of the animals taken as plunder.

Akim shook his head and addressed Salmon. "We owe you and Joshua many thanks, captain. We don't know how to repay you."

Salmon grinned. "I believe when you begin to prosper, you will be supplying the army with food?"

"Yes, of course. I promised Joshua and I will keep my word."

As the family walked from room to room, they were not surprised to discover all of the stools and extra cloaks were no longer there. The kitchen and pantry were void of any food, of course, but some of the cooking utensils and heavier pots remained. Bahiti, who had silently followed along, sighed with pleasure. "I will have a kitchen to work in again!"

Zahava was so happy to be back in her home, she could only go around clasping her hands and exclaiming over and over, "Lord God, thank you!"

Rahab went upstairs with her mother to view the sleeping rooms. Her parents had taken some bedding when they fled to Jericho, knowing they would need it, but the simple wood frames Aziel made for them remained. He had woven strips of leather to form a framework for a simple mat. Evidently, soldiers on the march were not able to carry away furniture. Zahava laughed and clapped her hands when she discovered a pair of her sandals were still in the cupboard.

Only the bed, the small wooden table next to it, and the oil lamp were left in Rahab's room—but that was enough.

Rahab went out to the garden. In their haste, the army had not found it necessary to destroy the trees and bushes, being more interested in their grisly task and what spoil they could take from the house. She walked to the wall and looked across at Lower Beth-horon. There was no sign of life, either from the town or on the road.

Two golden butterflies flew above her and rested on a nearby bush. To Rahab, they were a sign of hope. They had made the metamorphosis from creeping caterpillars to beautiful, delicate, winged creatures. She and her family would also rise above their circumstances and be restored to a brighter future.

While Rahab's family set to work making their homes livable once more, Salmon and his soldiers took the other settlers through town so they could select houses of their own. They were told they were welcome to choose any building that did not belong to Akim and his kin—the whole town was available to them. Each widow and her children seemed to have different criteria when it came to their decision. Some selected houses near Rahab's family, even if they were missing doors or needed other repairs. Others looked for houses further away that had not been damaged. A group of the wounded old soldiers decided to lodge together in one of the larger dwellings. But no matter what they decided, all seemed thrilled that after years of wandering, they would finally have a roof over their heads and a place to call home.

With smiling faces, they walked through the streets, choosing vacant houses as they went. Soon, all were hard at work making their homes habitable. Rahab learned later that some people had to brush red stains off from the earthen floors, a reminder of what had happened in the city.

It didn't seem to matter. All of these people had been born in the desert and had only lived in tents. The joy among them was palpable.

Isaac and Baram returned after taking the sheep and goats out to a nearby pasture and leaving them in the care of Isaac's twelve-year-old twin sons. Rahab's brothers would take charge of the flocks as they had done before and lead the animals out to farther pastures on the morrow.

Her youngest brother, Josiah, worked to restore the small building where the Jewish men once gathered on the Sabbath, planning to use it for his school.

Rahab was sweeping the front steps when she heard footsteps behind her and turned to see Salmon approach.

"I'm glad your family found your homes intact. I'm sorry about the things that were taken, but to the soldiers, they were the spoils of war."

"We know," she reassured him. "And much was left behind. We are grateful that we were able to return, glad to have the sheep and goats back. We can start again. My brothers are good herdsmen and my sisters' husbands will have plenty of work helping the others get settled and build new lives for themselves."

They were both quiet then. There was so much to say, yet she didn't know where to begin.

Salmon broke the silence. "We leave tomorrow morning."

Her eyes searched his. "So soon?"

"As we found no danger and you were able to return to your homes and the other families have found places to their liking here, our job is done. As soon as we return, we go to war again."

She didn't want to think about that. "You must do what Jehovah has called you to do. You will be victorious. Joshua is a great leader."

"Yes, he is. We trust him with all our hearts." He looked down at her, his eyes warm with little flecks of light. "I pray we meet again one day, Rahab."

One day, if the Lord God allows it. But then, perhaps, never again. Her thoughts tumbled about in her head, but all she could say was, "May the Lord God go with you and keep you, Salmon."

He reached in his short tunic and produced a small leather pouch. He shook a small bright red gemstone into his palm.

"It was among the spoils I picked up. I don't know what it is, but I want you to have it, to remember me by."

He returned the stone to the pouch, placed it in her hand, and closed her fingers over it. He gulped. "Goodbye, Rahab." He turned then and walked swiftly away.

"Goodbye, Salmon," she whispered after him.

A short time later, she saw him and his men ride down the road between the towns of Upper and Lower Beth-horon. She watched until they were small dots in the distance. Then she opened the leather pouch and took out the bright red gem. Its ruby depths sparkled in the sunshine.

"Oh, Salmon," she whispered, as two tears rolled slowly down her cheeks.

23

*A*ziel was hard at work building looms, first for the women of his family and then for the other women in town. After years in the desert, clothing passed down from generation to generation, they were eager to weave new garments and coverings. The older women taught the younger ones how to wash the wool, card it, spin the thread, and weave on the looms.

To Zahava's astonishment, she found she still had clean wool in the storage room. She could only conclude the soldiers didn't have time to thoroughly search the house—or, like the brooms, they didn't realize its value. The family had fled for Jericho with only the clothes on their backs and one or two extra garments. Rahab had packed a little more, along with her jewelry, which she had no occasion to wear.

All of the women took turns at the looms, working many hours a day. There was so much to replace and so many others who needed their help.

For their first Sabbath together as a new community, Akim gathered his sons, sons-in-law, and the soldiers-turned-settlers in the small meeting room where Josiah held his Hebrew school. The room was not big enough for a partition, so the women stood in the back. They had no priest, so Akim, being the oldest male, led them in prayer. He gave thanks for their deliverance from the desert and for his family's deliverance out of Jericho and return to their homes. He also gave thanks for the widows and their children who had the courage and faith to settle in Upper Beth-horon and pledged his family's continuing protection.

The dry season came and the wheat that had not been ripe enough for the soldiers to pluck was ready. They would have a harvest soon, during the month of Silvan. Although many of the fruit trees had been stripped bare, the summer figs were just beginning to ripen. By the next month, the grapes would be ready for the vintage harvest and the town would begin treading the grape presses and making wine. The date palms would not produce until the month of Av and the summer figs the following month. The women looked forward to making date cakes.

Aziel worked long hours making wooden platters and bowls for meals, repairing furniture, and overseeing reconstruction efforts. Some of the older boys who were interested in carpentry joined him in his workshop. Jaheem kept busy as well, supplying the town with water jugs, basins, and cookware. They were paid with jewelry, produce, and anything else the other families could barter. But Rahab's brothers-in-law did not insist on payment, for they knew some people had little and they remembered Joshua's counsel that the Lord instructed His people to care for widows and orphans.

At Akim's home, Rahab and Zahava were glad to let Bahiti take charge of the kitchen. They scavenged some empty houses unclaimed by the other settlers and found a sack of barley flour tucked behind some empty crates. The other families made similar discoveries. For their simple meals, Bahiti baked loaves of barley bread and prepared salads using spices from the storage room and vegetables from the kitchen garden. Each Sabbath, the whole family gathered at their father's house for their evening meal and they would have a lamb roast or goat stew. Sometimes, one of the men took the older boys to the Ayalon River, where they were often able to catch a few fish for their meals.

Word quickly spread throughout Canaan that people were living once again in Upper Beth-horon and traveling merchants arrived. The marketplace was reborn and the residents were able to trade for items they could not make themselves, such as leather belts and sandals, soft tunics, and metal cooking pots, as well as wine, ducks, spices, and many other things.

One Sabbath, after hearing a rumor that there was some squabbling and jealousy among some of the women and false swearing by a couple of the men who had had too much wine, Akim realized they needed a reminder of God's law.

"In the desert, the Lord gave us certain commandments," he began gravely. And then Akim read aloud from the scroll of the exodus, which Moses wrote down for the people of Israel:

> *I am Adonai your God, who brought you out of the land of Egypt, out of the abode of slavery. You are to have no other*

*gods before me. You are not to make for yourselves a carved
image or any kind of representation of anything in heaven
above, on the earth beneath or in the water below the shore-
line. You are not to bow down to them or serve them; for I,
Adonai your God, am a jealous God, punishing the children
for the sins of the parents to the third and fourth generation
of those who hate me, but displaying grace to the thousandth
generation of those who love me and obey my mitzvot. You
are not to use lightly the name of Adonai your God, because
Adonai will not leave unpunished someone who uses his
name lightly. Remember the day, Shabbat, to set it apart for
God. You have six days to labor and do all your work, but
the seventh day is a Shabbat for Adonai your God. On it,
you are not to do any kind of work—not you, your son or
your daughter, not your male or female slave, not your livestock, and not the foreigner staying with you inside the gates
to your property. For in six days, Adonai made heaven and
earth, the sea and everything in them; but on the seventh
day he rested. This is why Adonai blessed the day, Shabbat,
and separated it for himself. Honor your father and mother,
so that you may live long in the land which Adonai your
God is giving you. Do not murder. Do not commit adultery.
Do not steal. Do not give false evidence against your neighbor. Do not covet your neighbor's house; do not covet your
neighbor's wife, his male or female slave, his ox, his donkey
or anything that belongs to your neighbor.*

As he closed the scroll, Rahab's heart filled with pride for
him. She knew her father had studied it over and over so he
would know what to emphasize to the people of their small

Jewish congregation. She and her family—the remnants of the tribe of Ephraim descended through Sherah—had heard these commandments for the first time when Joshua read them aloud to the gathered Israelites camped near Gilgal.

One day, while Rahab worked at the loom, Akim came into the room after hearing a complaint and rendering a judgment for two neighbors. He sighed deeply.

"I pray our God will send us a priest," he confessed. "I feel so inadequate for this task."

She smiled, filled with tenderness. "Abba, all know you are doing your best. Perhaps when the lots are drawn, the tribe that receives this territory will have a Levitical priest or rabbi assigned to our town."

⌒

The months went by quickly as everyone worked together to rebuild the town. It was not too long before all of the buildings they occupied had been repaired and the floors, streets, and walkways were cleansed of any trace of the carnage that had occurred there. Young and old alike set themselves to the task with zeal.

One evening, after he and Baram had returned with the flocks after grazing them for a few days in some far-off pasture lands, Isaac looked around at his family and shook his head. "There were signs of a mass grave in the hills," he reported.

Rahab had wondered what happened to the bodies of those killed by the Israelite army. The wild animals and birds would take care of some of the carnage, but they had found no bones. *Someone had buried the remains of the Canaanite citizens, but who? The army?* She did not think they had time to do that. Then it occurred to her that perhaps some of the Canaanites who had fled the town had come back after the soldiers left to take care of their own. It was a sobering thought.

⌒

For the next two years, once a week, as the Lord God prospered them, Akim sent cheese, dates, dried figs, and other fruits to the army. At first, he would send a lamb or goat as well, but Joshua sent word back that there was plenty of wild game available for his soldiers and sheep they had plundered from various towns. The women baked bread almost continuously, keeping only what they needed for their own families and sending the rest. Since Rahab's brothers and brothers-in-law were the only able-bodied men, by turns, at least two of them took the supplies and returned with news.

The army had captured more of the southern towns and left no survivors. Libnah fell, as did Lachish, Eglon, and, eventually, Hebron and its surrounding villages. Then the Israelites attacked Debir and the whole region, including the hill country, the Negev, and the western foothills. From there, they went on to Gaza, the town of Goshen, and on up to Gibeon.

When it was time to plant or harvest the crops, everyone from the community helped in some way in order to receive a share of the grains or fruits. They grew wheat, barley, lentils, and peas. The old grape vineyards and orchards with fig, date, olive, apple, and almond trees were lovingly pruned, tended, and restored to peak health.

Harvesting the olives seemed to fill Bahiti with mirth, for she continuously chuckled and smiled as she worked beside Rahab, who had to laugh at her evident delight.

"Why do you like to pick olives so much?" she asked the old cook.

"You know, I am thinking how delicious they will taste after they've soaked in brine for a couple of months!" Bahiti declared. "And how nice it will be to press some new oil."

As the month of Tishri approached and the early rains began, Rahab once again thanked the Lord for their homes. Her brothers told her some families were still living in tents at the Gilgal camp.

When it came time to sow seed for their wheat harvest, they prayed that the rains would not be too heavy and cause the tender shoots to rot. They all seemed to be of one heart because for the last two years, the Lord had answered their prayers.

And so it was, month after month and season after season— grapes, figs, and apples in hot Elul, when harvests had to take place in the cool of the morning or late afternoon; almonds in Shevat and the joy of baking almond cakes; flax and barley in Nisan and, oh, what back-breaking work that was!...

The month of Nisan also marked the Passover. Akim, Isaac, and Baram inspected the lambs and selected ones without blemishes for the feast. Those families too small for a whole lamb shared with another family. Spits were set up around the town to roast the lambs on skewers. Greens were gathered for salads, along with bitter herbs. All of the women baked enough unleavened bread to last them for a week.

They placed rugs and stools along the main street, so people could sit, feast, and celebrate the Passover together.

Akim stood and prayed before the assembled community.

"The Lord, the God of Israel, gave us the festival of matzah to observe from generation to generation. As we gather here at this Passover, let us give thanks to our God for His provision, for leading our people out of Egypt, for safeguarding us in the desert, and for blessing us with these homes. All thanks be to our God, Jehovah Sabaoth, who has protected us from harm and made sure our children thrive. All praises be to our God, Jehovah Jireh, our provider, who has never failed to put food on our tables. May the spring rains be as dew, to protect the wheat harvest once again, and may we continue to find favor with our God as we honor Him by keeping His laws."

And after each sentence of praise spoken by Akim, the people cried, "Amen—so be it!"

The conversation flowed as the people took part in the Passover feast, passing the salad with bitter herbs and sharing the unleavened bread. The men carved pieces of roast lamb and placed the meat on platters to pass around. It was a joyous time for Rahab as she watched her people and listened to the conversations around her.

As she ate, her heart lifted. God had been gracious to them. Her father's flocks were growing and Akim now had a couple of horses and a few donkeys as well. Josiah and Hannah made so much cheese that they not only had enough for the whole family, but sold a great deal in the marketplace as well. The grape harvest produced so much wine that Akim felt it necessary to caution the men about the dangers of overindulging.

Sitting beside her sisters and their families, Rahab took note of Eliana's rounded belly and rejoiced that she was expecting another child. Yet a wave of melancholy suddenly struck her. She had no husband, no children. *Was she destined to be the maiden aunt to her siblings' children forever?* She thought back to a conversation she had with her Abba only a few days before.

He'd taken her aside. "Rahab, it is time you married again," he had said in a hushed tone.

She'd heaved a mournful sigh. "And who would you like me to marry, Abba? Of the males not related to our family, the oldest is not more than fifteen. Until the war is over—and that will evidently not be anytime soon—how can there be anyone for me to marry? The last time, you had to find an Egyptian husband for me!"

He had stroked his beard and shrugged. "That is true. I am sorry, my daughter, that this is your plight right now. I don't know what to do about it."

"Do nothing, Abba. The Lord God knows my path and will do as He wishes with my life."

He had looked down at her fondly. "You have more faith than I. You are right. We must leave this in His hands."

She had spoken bravely, but how truly brave was she inside?

24

Five years had passed since they returned to their home in Upper Beth-horon. Over the past several months, Rahab had noted that her mother appeared to tire easily much of the time. The rough, hurried flight to Jericho, their frightful time there, and all of Zahava's hard work over the years, done without complaint, had finally taken their toll. Rahab persuaded her father to hire Anna, a young girl from town, to help Bahiti in the kitchen and relieve her mother of some of her duties. Zahava still insisted on taking her turn at the loom. One day, Rahab discovered her mother hunched over it, her face twisted in pain.

"Imah, what's wrong?"

Zahava gasped. "My chest…it hurts."

Rahab rushed to the kitchen to get Zahava a cup of water. She urged her mother to drink it slowly and it seemed to help a little. "Has this happened before?" she asked.

"A few times," Zahava admitted. "You have so much to do, I didn't want to trouble you."

"Imah, you are never any trouble to me. Come; let me help you to your bed. You must rest."

"It is all right, daughter. It comes and goes."

Nevertheless, Rahab helped her to her room and into bed, staying until she was sure Zahava could rest comfortably. In moments, her Imah was asleep, her face pale against a pillow.

Rahab found her father going over accounts on a table in the corner of the main room.

"Abba, did you know that Imah has been having spells? She says her chest hurts."

Akim hung his head, shaking it slowly from side to side. "I didn't know what to do and didn't want to worry you. So much is on your shoulders already."

"She is not well, Abba, and there is no physician in town, not even a healer or midwife."

He spread his hand, tears forming in his eyes. "What can we do? I have prayed and sought the Lord on her behalf many times."

"We will care for her and she will get well, Abba," Rahab told him, determined to make it so. "I will have Bahiti prepare a fine broth for her and perhaps some stronger nourishment will help her."

Her heart pounding as she left her father, Rahab went back upstairs to check on her mother and found that she was breathing shallowly. It was only then that Rahab noticed how thin her mother had become, how the veins on her white hands stood out. In the stillness, she heard a soft voice in her head. "Gather your family. She will come to Me."

Rahab gasped and ran downstairs. "Abba, Imah needs you! She's in bed!" she called out to Akim. Without waiting for him to ask any questions, she ran to the kitchen. "Anna, run to my sisters' homes and tell them they need to come here. Also the schoolteacher, Josiah. Have them send word to my brothers out in the pastures. Tell them it's urgent."

Wide-eyed, Anna nodded and hurried off.

Rahab turned to Bahiti. "Imah is sleeping now but she will need some strong broth later. She's very weak."

"I know just what will help," Bahiti reassured her.

Rahab went back up to her parents' bedroom and knelt by her mother's side, sitting back on her heels. Soon, Akim came in, kissed Zahava on the forehead, and sat on a stool, frowning and clasping his hands as he watched his wife breathe.

Within the hour, Rahab heard footsteps and her sisters entered the room.

Jael put her fist to her mouth. "What is happening?"

Eliana rubbed her forehead as she stared at her mother. "I sent a messenger to the fields to tell Isaac and Baram to come. Josiah is closing the school for the day and will be here shortly."

Akim rose from his stool to give his daughters a quick embrace, but then he sat back down, his hands clenched between his knees and his brows knitted with worry.

Rahab sighed and motioned her sisters over to sit beside her. "It is her heart," she told them quietly. "She has been having these spells off and on, but didn't want to worry us. I found her hunched over the loom in pain this morning and got her up to her bed."

It was more than two hours before Isaac and Baram arrived from the fields and at once saw the gravity of the situation. They embraced Akim and went to either side of the bed, where they looked down in anguish at their mother, who was lying very still, her breathing slow and shallow.

They took comfort in the fact that Zahava was still breathing, still with them. Rahab considered the words she had heard in her head. *She knew the Lord had spoken to her, but should she tell her family? Wasn't there a glimmer of hope that she might recover?*

Rahab and her sisters took turns sitting beside their mother and holding her hand, occasionally wiping her forehead with a cool, damp cloth, but Zahava did not awaken or stir. They didn't know what else to do.

Finally, the entire family was at Akim's house. One of Rahab's sisters-in-law kept the children occupied while the rest of the adults gathered in the bedroom or the hallway just outside the door. They spoke in hushed, muted tones about nothing in particular—the weather, the crops, any little bits of news they knew—anything to keep their minds occupied instead of fretting about their beloved Imah. They said quiet prayers...but Zahava did not stir. Rahab would not leave her side.

Suddenly, Zahava's eyes fluttered open, startling everyone. She locked eyes with Rahab. "Wait...daughter...for what is right," she said slowly, her voice barely a whisper. Then she looked around the room at her family. "You have been my joy," she murmured and sighed deeply. Then her body shuddered and she was gone.

The family tore their clothes and wailed in anguish; Rahab's siblings fled the room and went down to tell their children, whose youthful cries for their beloved Savta soon filled the house. Rahab bent over her mother, checking for a pulse, a breath, some sign of life, but there was nothing. Akim was inconsolable, beating his chest and weeping loudly. He went down to the kitchen, threw open the oven door, grabbed some ashes, and ran outside, scattering them on his head and moaning out the sorrowful news to their neighbors.

⁓

Two old wounded soldiers and two boys who had made their *bar mitzvah* joined Rahab's brothers and brothers-in-law to form a *minyan* to sit *shiva*, the seven-day period of mourning, with Akim. He leaned heavily on Isaac's arm as he slowly made his way to a low bench in Josiah's school and their makeshift synagogue.

As the oldest son, Isaac recited a prayer for his mother: "God, full of mercy, Who dwells above, give rest on the wings of the Divine Presence, amongst the holy, pure and glorious who shine like the sky, to the soul of Zahava, daughter of Zebulon, for whom we offer this prayer in the memory of her soul. Therefore, the Merciful One will protect her soul forever and will merge her soul with eternal life. The Everlasting is her heritage and she shall rest peacefully in her lying place. And let us say amen."

⁓

By the time the seven days of *shiva* had passed, Rahab had wept until she thought she could weep no more. She had depended on her Imah and sought comfort from her all of her life, especially during these last few years. *How had she failed to see that the woman she always thought of as so strong, so reliable, had actually grown weak?* Rahab was angry at herself then and her eyes filled with tears of remorse. And then *that* made her angry, for her tears were useless.

It seemed strange to go about the house and not see her Imah coming and going, planning meals with Bahiti, laughing as she worked the loom.... Zahava was the strength of her household and Rahab felt a large void in her heart. She spent more time with Akim and her Abba slowly reconciled himself to the loss of his wife and began to take up his duties once more.

⌒

The morning was still cool as Rahab said her morning prayer, dressed, and went down to the kitchen. Bahiti was slicing fresh, warm bread.

"Have something to nourish you." She chided Rahab if she failed to eat properly. There was so much to do, it was easy for her to pass up breakfast.

The Egyptian cook had been a comfort to her when Zahava died. She had proved to be a true friend throughout the ordeal in Jericho and now Rahab went to her when she was troubled about something.

"Dear Bahiti, what a blessing you have been to me," she said, biting into a piece of bread just to appease the cook.

Bahiti waved a hand to dismiss her comment, but went back to her meal preparations with a smile.

After she'd eaten, Rahab picked up the water pot and placed it on her shoulder to go to the well. She considered calling on Josiah to see how his school was going, perhaps stay in the back shadows and listen. It occurred to her that she had been privileged to read and write their language. As the last child at home, her father had indulged her wish to learn. Perhaps there might be other girls in their small community who would like to be schooled as well. The idea began to take root and she realized with a smile that there were few men to object.

As she neared the well, she saw a man nearby talking to one of the boys. He was obviously Hebrew, perhaps in his early thirties. *Why was he not with the army?*

He turned as she approached, appearing startled, and then his eyes lit up with interest.

She debated whether to speak to him, a stranger, or not... but she was curious. Aware that her tone might be slightly reproachful, she raised her eyebrows in question. "It is rare to see a man of your age in our community. Most men are fighting in the Israelite army."

A brief look of pain crossed his face, but he merely nodded. "Yes, I know. I was there a few months ago."

She lowered her eyes. She'd judged him without knowing the truth. *Which family did he belong to?* Then it occurred to her. "You were wounded."

He sighed and nodded. "I am Micah, son of Heli." He looked down at the worn tunic that covered his legs. "I nearly lost my right leg to a spear. It became infected and almost cost me my life. With thanks to our God, the leg was saved, but I could not keep up the pace any longer, so Joshua sent me back to my family. Two of my fellow soldiers traveled here with me and then they returned to the army."

"I'm sorry. I'm sure your family was glad to see you."

"It is just my mother and two younger brothers. I hope to be of some help to them, but I'm not sure what I can do."

Micah looked towards Aziel's carpentry shop. "I'm surprised to see other men here. Everyone over twenty is in the army."

Rahab frowned. *Was he casting judgment on the men of her family?* "Our family did not wander the desert with Moses, so our men have not been trained for war. We've lived in Canaan all of our lives and I was raised here in Upper Beth-horon."

Micah considered that. "Joshua did not conscript your men?"

Rahab's frown deepened. "Can a man who's not been trained from boyhood survive a battle with a seasoned warrior? Joshua felt our men were of more use here. My older brothers tend my father's flocks and my youngest brother teaches Hebrew. One of my brothers-in-law is a skilled carpenter and the other is the local potter. We supply food to the army and my father is the town elder."

Micah looked a little sheepish. "Forgive me for my curiosity. And may I ask your name?"

"I am Rahab, daughter of Akim." She hesitated before adding, "We lost my mother several months ago."

"I am sorry. It is hard to lose a parent, mother or father."

Rahab suddenly realized she'd been having a long conversation with a man who was a total stranger. She did not think Abba would approve. Other than his too-personal questions, Micah seemed pleasant enough—but she should not have been talking to him for so long. She went to the well and began to lower the rope that held the wooden bucket for water.

Micah limped over to help her.

"Does your leg pain you?"

"All the time, but I manage." He pulled the rope hand over hand until the full bucket of water appeared. She took it and filled her water jar.

"Perhaps I shall see you again?" He looked at her with a hopeful expression.

"It is not a large town. Perhaps."

He smiled and Rahab discovered that he was rather handsome. She turned and went on her way home, still thinking of his smile. It was nice to know that the town now had an unrelated man close to her age to talk to when she had a minor disagreement with one of the men in her family and needed a listening ear. Going over their conversation in her head, she realized Micah really hadn't told her much about himself and she wanted to know more about him.

Then it occurred to her that there was one question she had not asked him, one person she had not asked about....

25

Over the next couple of weeks, Micah seemed to be every-where. If she went to Aziel's carpentry shop, he was there talking to her brother-in-law. After seeing him in the marketplace one day, she discovered him at Jaheem's pottery shop the next.

"You are getting around very well, Micah," she commented.

It was obvious from the embarrassed looks on their faces that he and Jaheem had been talking about her.

"I was just getting a storage jar for my mother. It is good to see you again." Micah picked up the jar and with a smile, nodded to her and limped away.

She watched him go, his uneven steps pronounced, and her sense of exasperation gave way to pity.

Sitting at his wheel, forming the wet clay into a pot, Jaheem spoke up. "He likes you. He thinks you are the most beautiful woman he's ever met."

She turned to see him grinning at her. "I hardly know him," she responded.

Jaheem became more serious. "You must admit, Rahab, that in spite of his leg, he is eligible—and you need a husband."

Anger rose up, causing her words to be sharp. "Are you that anxious to see me married?"

He went back to his work, setting the wheel spinning and forming the clay with his hands. Without looking up, he commented matter-of-factly, "You are single. You need a husband and children to take care of. A woman should not be alone."

"I do not need my family to find a husband for me! My father is alone and needs my help with the household." She turned to leave and glanced back over her shoulder. "I will choose my own husband, thank you!"

She fumed all the way home.

Two days later, her father casually mentioned that they were having a guest for dinner.

"A guest? I know everyone in the town, Abba. Who is it?"

"A young man who had to leave the army due to an injury. His name is Micah."

She turned on him. "Abba, if you are trying to arrange a husband for me, please do not do so. I have met Micah and he is nice, but I don't want a husband right now."

Akim looked pained. "But you are still unmarried and there are no other single men here right now. Besides, you have grieved over the loss of your husband long enough."

"I am not grieving over Radames, Abba. That is past. It is more than that."

He waved a hand. "The captain? Who knows if he is dead or alive? Have you had any word from him?"

She took a deep breath. "No," she admitted.

"Then why not consider this young man? You are still in your twenties. You can still bear children. Do you not want a husband and a home of your own?"

Rahab burst into tears, turned, and fled up the stairs to her room. Akim called after her, but she ignored him. She went to her cupboard, took out a small leather bag, and pulled out the beautiful red gemstone. It sparkled in the sunlight as she held it between her fingers.

"Oh, Salmon! Are you alive? Have I watched and waited all of these years for nothing?" She sank down on the edge of her bed and let the tears flow.

~

During dinner, although Akim was a most gracious host, he kept looking from Rahab to Micah and back again as if urging them to like each other.

Rahab listened patiently while the two men talked about Micah's time in the desert, battles he had fought, and his joy at finding his remaining family in Upper Beth-horon.

"He has come at a most auspicious time, has he not, daughter?"

Rahab took a sip of wine and smiled politely. "I am glad you found your family, Micah. They will need your help. Do you have a trade?" She lifted her eyebrows in question.

Micah glanced at Akim. "Ah, no. I have spent my last several years in the army, first training in the desert and then freeing Canaan as the Lord commanded."

"But you are not in the army now," Rahab noted. "How do you plan to help your family?"

She knew her words were impertinent and Akim frowned, his eyes sending her a warning.

Micah was silent, his gaze thoughtful.

Then she remembered what she had wanted to ask him. "Are you familiar with a Captain Salmon? He was kind enough to lead my family out of Jericho at the time of the siege there."

Micah nodded. "Yes, I know of him. He is a good officer and a hard fighter."

Rahab's heart skipped a beat. "Is Salmon is well?"

Micah's expression changed and there was a question in his eyes. He studied her face a moment and then turned deliberately to Akim, as if Rahab had not spoken. "So you and your family were in Jericho at the time of the siege?"

Akim nodded. "My daughter was married to the Egyptian paka, the governor of Jericho, and newly widowed. When word of the Israelite army invading Canaan came, my family and I went to the embassy for refuge, fearing we would not be spared when the army attacked Upper and Lower Beth-horon. Joshua knew he had a kinswoman living there and, ah, sent word we would all be led out of the city when the attack came."

It was a very short version of all they had been through. Micah only nodded thoughtfully. He looked across the table at Rahab. "I did not know you had been married to the Egyptian governor of Jericho."

Akim rose and spread one hand magnanimously. "Perhaps you and my daughter would like to walk in the garden. It is a very pleasant evening."

Seething inside, Rahab swallowed a retort and rose obediently. As she led the way to the garden, she walked slowly to accommodate Micah's injured leg.

They stood at the wall overlooking the valley and Rahab was reminded that she had stood in just that spot several years ago with Radames. Conflicting thoughts bubbled to the surface of her mind. On the one hand, she did not want to be unkind to Micah, who was obviously interested in her. On the other, she wondered if she was being foolish to continue to wait for a man she had not seen in years. Then again, if he was still alive.... Micah's next words startled her.

"There was something between you and Captain Salmon?"

She bit her lip. "There was, but it has been several years."

Micah leaned over, put his hands on the wall, and looked out at the silent, empty town of Lower Beth-horon. "Soon, Joshua will draw lots and the tribes will be given their territory. It will mean people settling in the other towns of Canaan."

She followed his gaze across the road to Lower Beth-horon, but of course, there were no lights or signs of life.

She sighed. "I'm sorry I was not agreeable at dinner, Micah. I feel so much pressure from my family to marry again and I'm not sure where my feelings are right now."

He gave a small laugh. "You are a beautiful woman, Rahab. Surely you wish for marriage and a family." She turned to look at him and his gaze became more intense. "You do not know where he is and *I* am here. I am asking you to think about it."

She dropped her eyes. "I will think about it, Micah, but we must be friends for now. Should my family insist, there would always be this matter between us."

"I am a patient man, Rahab. I will accept your terms for now, in spite of your father's obvious plans. But if you choose me, it must be with your whole heart."

Relief flooded her. He understood. He would not let her father cajole them into marriage.

"Thank you," she told him.

"I will take my leave. Do not worry about your family. I do not bend well under pressure." With that, he limped off, leaving her in the garden.

When she entered the house, Akim was waiting for her. "What did you say to him?"

"We had a pleasant conversation, Abba. I assume he did not make an offer of marriage to you?"

"I anticipated it from what Jaheem told me, but no, he did not." He looked at her accusingly. "Did you discourage him?"

"Abba, I made a promise. Until I know whether Salmon is dead and my promise void, I must keep it."

He rubbed his eyes, then pulled his hands away and gazed at her sadly. "If you made a promise, you must honor it. But if Salmon does not survive the war, you will marry someone here." His voice was firm. He would see her married somehow.

"Thank you, Abba. I'm sure other soldiers and families will come here to settle after the war."

Akim inclined his head and looked down at her. "Have you considered that if Captain Salmon does not return, Micah may choose someone else? A man who is here is worth more than one who may or may not be elsewhere."

She smiled at him. "Yes, Abba, I will consider that."

They embraced then and she went up to her room and prepared for bed. Micah was indeed handsome and his limp did not bother her. She sensed that he would make a kind and loving husband and father. But the turmoil in her mind began again and she saw Salmon's face, kept hearing conversations they had had in her head.

"*You have touched me as no other woman has. When I am free from my duties, I wish to come and find you.*"

"*And if you find me, what then?*"

"*I would see if what is between us now is still there.*"

"*What is between us?*"

"*It is there, Rahab, whether you wish to acknowledge it or not.*"

...

"*I'm glad you are alive.*"

"*And I am glad you are glad I'm alive.*"

"*Are you teasing me?*"

"*Never, Rahab. I kept thinking of you, kept seeing that beautiful hair of yours, framing your face.*"

Tears filled her eyes. *Oh, Salmon, are you alive? Will you come for me? Please, come soon.*

26

*I*t had been seven years since the battle of Jericho, seven years since Salmon and Phineas appeared at her door and she hid them under bundles of flax on the embassy roof. It seemed like a lifetime ago.

Upper Beth-horon was growing slowly. Micah did not come to dinner again, but they spoke occasionally in the marketplace. Their conversations were mundane, but the question was always in his eyes.

When Isaac and Aziel returned from their most recent trip to take food to the army, they urged the whole family to gather at Akim's house, saying they had momentous news. Rahab could barely contain her excitement and had Bahiti prepare a meal for everyone.

After Akim said the blessing, Aziel stood up and announced, "Joshua is dismissing the army! They have conquered all of the towns the Lord told them to and lots are now being drawn for the territories for each tribe."

Akim spoke up. "My son, has all of Canaan been conquered?"

"For now, from what Joshua told us. Some of our people in the remote areas may have to fight a few Canaanites, but for the most part, the land belongs to Israel."

The family buzzed with many conversations going on at once. If another tribe besides Ephraim received the region that included Upper and Lower Beth-horon, its leader could ask them to leave their homes to make way for his own tribe.

As Bahiti and Anna served the food, Rahab could see from the faces of her family that this was a heavy concern for them. After nearly seven years, Jaheem had a thriving pottery business and Aziel had all of the carpentry work he could handle. The flocks of sheep and goats had grown so large that her father and two oldest brothers were as prosperous as they had been before. Josiah had more than forty students in his school and did not ask any of their families for a stipend. He and his wife made excellent cheeses that were in great demand at the marketplace.

As the chatter grew louder, Akim suddenly hushed his family to lead them in prayer. It took a minute or two, but he finally had silence.

Bowing his head, he said, "Blessed are You, Lord our God, King of the universe. We give thanks for Your many blessings. Through every generation, You have been the rock of our lives, the shield of our salvation. O God, mighty and merciful, we place our trust in You. Accept our prayer with favor, for You are a God who hears prayers and supplications. O our King, have compassion on us and allow us to remain here, where we have built homes and raised sons and daughters to worship You as we do. Hear our plea and have pity on us. For You are our mighty Lord, God of our fathers, forever and ever. Amen."

Akim's prayer seemed to bring peace to the entire family. They all stopped worrying about the future and talking about the present.

Rahab's mind wandered. Now in her mid-twenties, she would not be considered marriage material in their former society. *Now that the war was over, would Salmon finally come? If he did not come soon, how long would Micah wait?* She could only trust her future to the Lord.

All of the families in Upper Beth-horon waited anxiously for word from Joshua. After hearing from Isaac and Aziel that the army had disbanded, no further news came because no supplies had to be sent out.

Two months later, Rahab was in the garden and started at the sound of voices on the road below. She looked over the wall and saw over a thousand people walking on the road to town, accompanied by a few men on horseback—probably soldiers, she guessed. There were men, women, and children, with flocks of sheep and goats with their shepherds bringing up the rear. The first of the settlers were coming...but which tribe were they from?

As the people streamed into town, Akim was there to meet them, along with his sons, sons-in-law, and their families. Rahab stood back with the women and children.

"Where do you think they're from?" Jael whispered.

"Shhh!" Rahab scolded her sister and then gave her a big grin.

The leader of the group, riding an old bay gelding, held up a hand to halt the crowd behind him. He dismounted and came forward to greet Akim.

Rahab's father drew himself up. "Welcome to Upper Beth-horon. I am Akim, an Ephraimite, and this is my family. You are the tribe allotted this territory?"

The leader smiled. "I am Baruch, one of the leaders of our tribe. We are Ephraimites also. Upper and Lower Beth-horon are part of our allotted territory."

Rahab could hear one of her brothers breathe out a loud sigh of relief.

Baruch came forward and stood before Akim. "Joshua has told me about you and your family, as well as the other settlers who have come here. I want to assure you that we will not displace any of you from your homes."

Rahab glanced at her family and saw the tension leave their faces. The Lord God had answered their prayers.

"Well met, Baruch," her father said graciously. "I welcome you and the other members of our tribe. I must tell you, there are some widows, children, and old soldiers here who may not be Ephraimites. Were you given orders concerning them?"

"Yes. Those who are of other tribes may join their people if they wish and will be escorted to their territory. Those who choose to remain will be welcome to stay."

Akim nodded. "That is good news. There are many houses that are not occupied here and the town of Lower Beth-horon is deserted. There should be many dwellings available for everyone you have brought with you." He looked back at the crowd behind Baruch. "This is all of our tribe?"

Baruch shook his head. "No, many have gone to the hill country of Bethel and to other towns that were allotted to us. We were chosen to come here."

Akim stepped back. "Then let your people come in and find homes for themselves. Do you have adequate food?"

"Joshua gave us provisions, but most of them were used on our journey."

"I will send word out to all of the families here. We will provide a meal for your people this evening in the center of town and I'm certain we can put together sacks of flour and other necessities for them until they are settled. We do have an active marketplace as well."

Akim smiled and waved to the hills around Upper Beth-horon. "We welcome your men's help in tending the fields and orchards and there is much grazing land for your sheep and goats; my two sons here will show your shepherds the way. I have a son-in-law who's a potter and another who's a carpenter and they are available to help anyone in need."

Baruch turned to the people behind him. "You have heard Akim. Find lodging for yourselves and your families and a communal meal will be provided at sundown. Shepherds, you know what to do. Husbands, make sure your families are settled and then report to me."

The people began to stream past Baruch, moving down the streets and choosing houses that were obviously vacant. Rahab's heart lifted as she watched them go. Yet in her delight at seeing the city filled with people again, a thought occurred to her. *Salmon was of the tribe of Judah. Where was their territory?*

27

Another month went by and Rahab finally made up her mind to accept Micah as her husband. She had not heard from Salmon in over seven years and the army had been dismissed three months ago. *If he wasn't dead, he would have come,* she thought. Perhaps there really was nothing between them and she needed to let him go and move on with her life.

She stood at the window of her room as the sun began its descent and shadows played over the patio below. She looked down at the beautiful red gemstone in the palm of her hand. *"I want you to have it, to remember me by."* Her lips tightened. *Just a memory.* She returned the ruby to its small leather pouch and laid it among her things in a cupboard. She could not bring herself to part with it.

Rahab gathered her courage and started down the stairs. She would tell her father that she had decided to marry Micah.

He would be relieved—they all would be. She was still young enough to have children and she had waited long enough.

As she descended the steps, there was a firm knock at the front door. *Had her father invited company?* They had hosted Baruch and his wife for dinner several times; the men had discussed the settlement and the people's needs that were apparent among them. Having been soldiers for so long, the men needed work, trades, to maintain their dignity—and soon.

No one else seemed to have heard the knock, so Rahab opened the door herself. With a gasp, she gripped the doorpost.

"Salmon!"

He was thinner and there was a tired look in his eyes, but he gave her a weak smile and her heart leaped at the sight of him.

When she recovered from her shock, she glared at Salmon and then her eyes filled with tears. "I have had no word from you in seven years!" All of the exasperation and indignation she felt made her whole body tremble. "I didn't know if you were alive or dead! Could you not have sent me word?"

He hung his head a moment, acknowledging her pain. "I had no way of knowing how long we would be fighting. What was the use of giving you false hope? I could only trust our God." He gulped and looked at her earnestly. "I wasn't going to come. I couldn't bear the fact that you might be married and have a family."

Then he reached out and took her hand. "I didn't know if you would still be here or not, but I felt the Lord telling me to come."

They stood looking at each other for a long moment as he still held her hand. She was silent, mixed feelings tumbling in her chest.

His eyes were almost pleading. "I prayed you would still be here," he said. "I have seen your face in my mind over the years and I thought it was better to know what you had chosen than not know. So here I am."

She took a breath then. "I am not married, Salmon."

They stood in the doorway staring at each other and both of their eyes filled with tears. There was so much she wanted to ask him, so much she wanted to say, but she had no more words. So finally, Rahab did what she had wanted to do years ago and threw herself against his chest and felt his arms go tightly around her.

"What is this?" Akim had come from another room. "Step away, daughter! Would you behave as a common woman? You are not even betrothed yet."

But still, they held each other.

Salmon's eyes searched her face. "You were to be betrothed?"

"There was someone, but no, I am not betrothed."

Then Akim recognized their visitor and raised his eyebrows in surprise. "Captain Salmon?"

He released Rahab and stepped back. But again, he reached out and held her hand.

"Yes, sir. I'm sorry it took so long to get here. I wish I had been able to send word to your daughter, but we traveled so much and all we could do between battles was catch some rest."

"Has Joshua released you?"

"Yes, sir. The officers were the last to be freed from our duties, since we had to help the tribes settle in their territories."

Akim looked from Rahab to Salmon. "I did not expect to see you again. My daughter evidently thought differently." He shook his head, then peered around Salmon. "You came alone?"

"Three other men and their families came with me. They were Ephraimites who planned to settle in Upper Beth-horon. I myself had to get my own family situated before I came."

Akim came to his senses as host. He waved a hand. "Please enter, captain, and close the door. Come, join us for dinner, and tell us what has transpired with Joshua and the army."

Anna came into the room and with a nod from Rahab, showed Salmon where he could wash his hands and face.

Once clean and presentable, Salmon lowered himself onto a stool and eyed the table's bounty with hungry eyes. Bahiti had cooked squash with capers and mint from their garden, along with lentil stew mixed with fava beans. Two loaves of fresh bread graced the table with a bowl of soft yogurt cheese to spread on it. Recognizing Salmon, Bahiti offered Rahab a knowing grin and a barely perceptible nod.

Salmon ate the meal with zeal. He paused between bites and gave Akim an apologetic glance. "It has been a while since I ate. I'm afraid I was rather in a hurry." He looked at Rahab.

Their eyes met and she felt a familiar jolt in her chest.

Akim looked across the table and leaned forward. "You say the entire army is now disbanded?"

"Yes, we accomplished what the Lord God appointed us to do and Joshua released us to our territories. Some of the tribes still have some fighting to do to claim their inheritance."

"And your commander, Joshua. Where is he now?"

Salmon, obviously controlling his emotions, looked down a moment. "Our great leader and commander gave us final instructions on possessing the territories each tribe had been given and then was gathered to his fathers. He was one hundred and ten years old. We buried him in the land he had been

allocated, at Timnatah-serah in the hill country of this territory, north of Mount Gaash, for he was also an Ephraimite.
The people mourned for him for thirty days and then the camp
broke up. Each tribe is seeking out the territory allotted them
to settle their families."

He looked at Rahab. "I then had to travel to the territory
allotted the tribe of Judah to see that my mother, grandmother,
and brother were settled in one of the towns there before leaving
them to come here."

Salmon's feelings were plain on his face. "If I could have, I
would have flown here months ago—years ago!—on the wings
of an eagle."

Rahab's heart filled with joy.

Akim looked from one to the other, stroking his beard
thoughtfully. "I have tried to marry her off, but she has been a
bit on the obstinate side. It seems she had her mind set on someone else." A smile twitched at the corners of his mouth.

Rahab laughed then, the release of pent-up emotions giving
her a freedom she hadn't felt for years. "My family thinks I
should be married and have children before I become an old
woman."

Salmon grinned. "And they are right." The implication was
clear. He turned to Akim. "Sir, I wanted to approach you for
Rahab's hand before you left the camp at Gilgal. But I couldn't
ask any woman to wait for who knows how long before I was
released from the army. We had the Lord's command to carry
out."

"Yes, that was your first duty," Akim agreed. "Tell me, where
is the territory of Judah?"

"I can show you." Salmon pulled a scroll from his tunic and spread it out on the table. On it was a crude map that showed landmarks and the tribal territories.

"Here is the Jordan River. The tribes of Reuben, Gad, and half the tribe of Manasseh were given this grazing land on the east side. The rest of the tribes are here on the west side. Judah's southern boundary begins at the Salt Sea and goes south and west to the Great Sea. The northern boundary is north of the Salt Sea and follows along the Ajalon River to the Great Sea."

Akim nodded his head thoughtfully. "That is a large territory. What town were you assigned and how far is it from Beth-horon?"

"We will live in an old Canaanite town, renamed Bethlehem, which is being rebuilt even as we speak." He thought a moment and then traced a route on his map. "From here in Upper Beth-horon to Gibeon is about a day's walk, then Gibeon to Ramah another day's walk. From Ramah, the road turns south and east, then we pass near Jerusalem and travel south to Bethlehem. All told, a journey of at least six days, into the hills of Judea. I took my family there to settle them before I came here." He turned to Rahab. "The trip was hard on my grandmother, but she is doing well now and sends her greetings. She looks forward to seeing you again."

Rahab smiled and clasped her hands together. "As do I."

Akim studied the map and then looked up at Salmon. "Tell us about your house in Bethlehem."

"It is of average size, big enough for our family. There were a few repairs to be made to make livable again, but I had help, friends I made in the army who are also of Judah. They are watching over my family and seeing to their needs while I am away."

Akim turned to his daughter. "So, Rahab, this is what you have waited for all these years?"

She met his gaze. "Yes, Abba." She sighed. "I felt the Lord God was telling me to wait and now I know why."

Salmon's broad smile then filled her with joy.

He turned to Akim. "I would like to ask for your daughter, sir, to be my wife."

Akim flung up his hands in mock surrender. "Do I have a choice here? Rahab is not a young maiden anymore and she has a mind of her own. If she agrees, you have my permission." He gave Salmon a pointed look. "And may I say, it is about time, captain."

Rahab thought her heart would burst with happiness. "Time is short, Abba, and Salmon must return to his family."

Her father nodded. "Yes, I suppose it has already been long enough. We will have the wedding the day after the Sabbath. Is that enough time to prepare?"

"Yes, Abba, that is all the time I need."

The sun was setting and the cool breeze of early evening began to waft through the gathering shadows as Salmon and Rahab walked together in the garden.

"Do you still have the red stone I gave you?"

"Of course I do."

He cocked his head and looked at her quizzically. "I was thinking it would make a nice pendant. I'd like to take it to a gold craftsman and have a necklace made for you. Of course, nothing will ever be as beautiful as you are."

Salmon caressed her cheek with his hand and Rahab gave a small involuntary shiver.

"I have longed for this moment," he whispered, his voice deep, so near she could feel his breath. "But I can wait a little longer."

28

Family, friends, and neighbors were notified and there was a flurry of activity preparing for the wedding celebration—just three days away. Rahab's sisters came to the house immediately to help her select her wedding attire. Rahab chose a simple tunic, dyed a light blue, with a silver belt and sandals. She considered the gold earrings Radames had given her, but chose some with blue stones instead. Her sisters made a wreath for her hair and found a sheer veil in a wooden chest among their mother's things. They made headband of coins for Rahab to wear on her forehead.

"You will make a beautiful bride, sister," Jael said. "We are happy for you that Salmon was able to return. He is a most worthy bridegroom!"

"And handsome," Eliana added.

Bahiti came in with tears in her eyes. "Rahab, I will miss you so much! Are you sure I cannot go with you?"

Rahab shook her head and embraced the dear old cook. "You are needed here, Bahiti. My father is going to rely on you. My brothers and sisters have families to take care of, but they are nearby and will help you in any way they can."

"That's true," Jael chimed in. "Don't worry, Bahiti. We think of you as one of the family."

"See? And of course, I will come back to visit." Rahab took Bahiti's hand then and looked into her eyes. "Anna is older now and should be given more of the workload. And I have spoken to my father about bringing in another servant."

Bahiti sighed. "Your family has been good to me." She tsked. "I should get back my kitchen. So much food to prepare!"

⌒

On the day of the wedding, some of the women helped to set food and serving plates on the tables in the courtyard, while others still worked in the kitchen. Rahab could hear the children as they chased each other around outside.

Jael came in. "The little ones are doing their best to be underfoot as much as possible. I had to ask the older children to take charge of them and keep them away from the food until it is time!" She looked a little weary as she sat on a covered bench nearby. There was a sudden silence out in the courtyard and Jael spoke up. "The men have been peppering Salmon with questions about the army and Joshua. I think he is speaking."

The women went to the window that looked down on the courtyard and listened as Salmon spoke.

"Before we were dispersed to our allotted territories, Joshua called all the people together and admonished us to fear the Lord. He reminded us that it was not our swords, bows, or slings that made us victorious, but the Lord God, who now gave us land we had not worked on and towns we did not build. He gave us vineyards and olive groves for food, though we did not plant them. Joshua called on us to remember the fate of Achan, who perished with his entire family and whose belongings were destroyed because he did not obey the Lord. He warned us that if we turn away and serve other gods, the Lord will turn against us and destroy us, even though He has been so good to us."

All who were listening were aware of the gravity of Salmon's words.

"We swore before Joshua as a people that we would honor the Lord and serve Him and obey Him alone." He looked around at those assembled before him. "We made a covenant with Joshua that day at Shechem, committing to follow the decrees and regulations of the Lord given to us by Moses in the wilderness. A huge stone was rolled beneath a terebinth tree beside the tabernacle of the Lord and Joshua told us this stone would be a witness to testify against us if we went back on our word."

The men in Rahab's family and the assembled guests murmured among themselves and Rahab saw her father put a hand on Salmon's shoulder. "It is good of you to share this with us. We will honor Joshua in our memory. He was a great man and a kinsman."

⁓

It was time. The musicians began to play and Rahab was brought from the house with her sisters in attendance. She came and stood by Salmon before her father.

Salmon's face lit up at the sight of her. Their eyes met and her heart began beating quickly.

Akim straightened and began to speak. "My family, friends, and neighbors, this day I give my daughter Rahab in marriage to Salmon, son of Nashon. As of this day, they will be as man and wife and she shall keep herself only for him for as long as she lives. Salmon, you will take care of my daughter and provide for her as long as she lives under your roof. Do you both agree?"

Rahab and Salmon both spoke at once. "I agree."

Salmon took a gold ring out of his tunic and placed it on Rahab's left hand. He looked down at her tenderly. "May this be a symbol between us of our covenant."

Akim looked out at those gathered and spread his hands in invitation.

"Then let us celebrate the coming together of my daughter and her husband, to wish them long life and many sons."

Those gathered cheered and as the couple sat on chairs, gifts were brought forward: pillows, clay lamps, bags of grain, jars of olive oil, wineskins, tunics, mantles, leather sandals, jewelry, and freshly baked bread. There were date cakes and pottery serving dishes from Eliana and Jaheem, and half a dozen beautiful olive wood platters from Aziel that Jael had painstakingly decorated with tiny painted flowers along the edges. Akim's wedding present was a wondrous loom that could be easily disassembled for transport, plus a heavy sack of coins that he dropped into Salmon's lap with a smile and a wink. Rahab's sisters-in-law Keren and Ayala gave her cloth bags filled with colorful yarns

for weaving, while Josiah and Hannah gave them a large wheel
of their very best cheese, wrapped up in oiled cloth.

Then the celebration began in earnest as everyone feasted
on grilled quail, goat cheese and olive appetizers with melon,
fig cakes, roasted lamb, pomegranates and poached apricots in
honey syrup, leavened griddle bread, and sesame-almond *nigella*
mix for dipping. The wine flowed freely and Salmon joined the
men as they formed to dance.

Rahab could hardly contain her happiness. She had waited
long for this day, hoping, praying, and seeking the Lord's
wisdom. She watched the dancing and looked all around at the
happy guests. Then she happened to glance across the courtyard
and spotted Micah leaning against the wall watching the dancing, his face downcast. He caught her eye and slowly made his
way over to her.

"I wish you well in your marriage, Rahab."

"Thank you, Micah."

He looked over at Salmon, who was laughing, shouting, and
dancing with the other men. "He is the one you were waiting
for?"

"Yes. I didn't know if I should wait any longer, but I trusted
the Lord God to lead me."

"And if he had not come? What then?"

She frowned briefly. She felt bad for him and yet…. "It was
not the Lord's plan for me, Micah." She smiled and touched his
arm. "There are many young women in town now who would be
pleased to have you for a husband."

He let out a deep breath. "It is kind of you to say so. I
pray you have a good life, Rahab. May you bear sons for your
husband."

It was a common blessing, but coming from Micah, it seemed bittersweet. Rahab watched as he turned away, made his way back across the courtyard, and left.

"You are very thoughtful, beloved."

Startled, she looked up at Salmon. "I suppose the army taught you how to walk as silent as an old cat on the prowl."

"Perhaps." Salmon nodded in the direction Micah had gone. "Did I have a rival for your favors?" He smiled, but his eyes searched hers.

Rahab raised a hand and touched his cheek, her eyes full of the love she had for him. "He would have liked that, but I refused him. I was still praying and hoping for someone else."

Salmon's eyes were warm and sparkling. "I'm glad I came in time."

The evening shadows began to slip across the courtyard and some of the families went home, carrying the young children who had grown tired from all of the feasting and excitement.

Because the weather was still warm, Rahab had chosen to make their bridal bed on the roof. She had slept up there sometimes as a young girl. She didn't want to use her parents' room as she and Radames had done. Her sisters happily set up and decorated a rooftop tent for her, scattering fresh blossoms on the low, thick pallet.

Rahab's family gathered around her and as she embraced each one, they whispered words of encouragement and blessing. Last of all, she embraced Bahiti, who had given so much of herself, protecting Rahab when she mourned for Radames and renouncing her Egyptian gods to serve Jehovah. Rahab wished the beloved cook could come with her, but Salmon already had his mother and grandmother living at his house—and Abba needed Bahiti more than Rahab did.

At last, everyone had gone but her father. He had tears in his eyes. "Once more, I give you to a husband. May you and Salmon be blessed."

She embraced him and then turned to Salmon. He took her hand and led her up the stone steps to the roof, which her sisters had bedecked with flowers and plants. In their bridal tent, a small clay lamp cast a soft glow on the fresh linen and pillows on the pallet.

Salmon put his arms around Rahab and as he kissed her, she met his ardor with her own. She had waited and the Lord God had allowed her heart's desire.

Her tunic dropped and Salmon bent down to blow out the lamp.

29

As with her first marriage to Radames, there was no time for a seven-day wedding celebration. Salmon was anxious to return to Bethlehem to take care of his family.

Donkeys were packed with the wedding gifts and Rahab's possessions. The loom was taken apart and packed. Bahiti prepared a basket of food for the journey and when it was placed on the donkey, she stood back with tears in her eyes.

"You have endured much, Rahab. I wish you great happiness. May Jehovah go with you and your new husband and see you safely to your new home. I will remember you in my prayers."

Rahab embraced Bahiti. "Thank you, Bahiti. You have been as dear to me as a kinswoman. May the Lord God shower His blessings upon you now and always."

Bahiti took Rahab's hands in hers. "Have no worries about Akim. I will care for him as I would for my own father." She smiled. "Though I do think our ages are not that far apart."

Rahab's entire family came again to wish them well and say good-bye. She turned to her siblings. "You will watch over Abba for me?"

Isaac smiled at her. "Little sister, you worry too much! We are right here."

She embraced her father and wept. "I don't know when I will see you again, Abba. Thank you for everything you have done for me over the years."

Akim, tears running down his cheeks, could only nod.

Looking toward the entrance to town, Rahab spotted mounted men riding in. *Soldiers? Were they in danger?*

Salmon lifted a hand in greeting as the men approached. "They are friends. A week ago, I arranged for them to come here at this time. They will escort us home. It still may not be safe for a man and a woman to travel alone."

Rahab tilted her head and raised her eyebrows. "You were that sure of me?"

He grinned. "I took a chance. It was a journey of hope."

The men dismounted and clapped hands on Salmon's shoulders.

"You won her!"

"So this is your bride?"

"Good work, captain!"

Salmon turned to Rahab's assembled family. "These men fought by my side and they too have made their homes in Bethlehem." He gestured at the six men, one by one. "Eamon, Dado, Zacharias, Tacitus, Joel, and Amos."

Each man nodded to the group as his name was spoken. Rahab was relieved that they would not be traveling alone. She had been fearful of bandits, but Salmon had already seen to their safety.

The men remounted and waited. Rahab embraced each of her family members, then turned to look at her father. *Why did he suddenly seem old as he stood there, his eyes moist?* She went to him again and he gathered her in his arms. "Be safe, daughter. May this marriage bring you happiness at last. And children."

Rahab felt tears come to her eyes, but she brushed them away. *When would she see Abba again, if at all?* She went to Salmon, who helped her up on her donkey. Then she turned her face toward the town gates as they started off, moving at the donkeys' pace. *Back on a donkey.* Now with a new husband, a new home, and a new life to look forward to, she smiled to herself.

⌣

They rode steadily and finally stopped to let the animals rest and graze on the rich grassland. The men had brought their own food, packed by their families, so she opened up the basket for herself and Salmon. Bahiti had packed unleavened bread, some fruit, a round of cheese, date cakes, and a skin of wine, along with a small leather pouch full of salt, another containing savory spices, and jar of olive oil to dip the bread in.

Within the hour, the group was on their way again. The donkey's steady rocking almost made her dozy, but Rahab vowed not to sleep and fall off and thus be a burden to Salmon. In fact, riding did not seem so difficult this time. She kept herself occupied by looking around at the scenery as they passed. And thinking.

How would she fit in Salmon's household with his mother and grandmother? She felt at home with Meira, but she didn't know Deborah well; she had been so shy when Rahab had visited their camp. *Would she and Salmon have a room to themselves, or did the family have shared sleeping quarters? How much privacy would they have?* Salmon said his house was "of average size," whereas Akim's house was large by most standards. A common sleeping area was common in smaller homes in some towns, but Rahab was used to having her own room. She sighed. It would be a change....

30

That morning, they had passed through Gibeon and Ramah, where other families were settling, and followed the road to a crossing at the narrow part of the Jordan River. The waters were low and they were able to lead the pack animals across safely. They spent the night at Gibeah, left early the next day, and traveled through the small village of Jebus and on to En-rogel. Salmon was patient and watched Rahab for signs of weariness, but she did not want to slow them down. She knew Salmon's army friends were anxious to get back to their families. Amos galloped ahead and rode back to tell them Bethlehem was in sight.

Rahab looked up and marveled. The town was set on an oblong ridge, several hundred feet above the sea. She could imagine seeing the entire countryside from the town's walls. All around were terraces with fig, almond, and olive trees in abundance, as well as grapevines. Rich fields of grain waved in the breeze in the valley they were passing through. Nearby, she saw many date palms and fig trees and workers busy harvesting the fruits.

They rode up into Bethlehem and people stopped to smile and wave as they recognized Salmon and his men. Their eyes turned with curiosity to Rahab and the men laughed and poked each other.

"What's that all about?" she asked Salmon, who rode beside her.

He grinned sheepishly. "Oh, I might have said a thing or two."

Rahab recognized some of the women from the Gilgal camp and they waved to each other.

Salmon thanked his friends and they rode off to their own homes. *This is a beautiful town*, she thought, *but what type of a home would she be living in?* They continued up a narrow street and finally came to a halt at a large stone house that was obviously the home of a prominent citizen. Meira stood in the courtyard, beaming at her.

Rahab slipped off her donkey and Salmon's grandmother rushed over to envelope her in loving arms. "We are so glad for you and Salmon!" Meira cried. "He was so impatient to get to Upper Beth-horon, hoping he would find you. We could hardly contain him!"

"Oh, Meira, I am so glad to see you! I will have at least one friend to start my new life with."

Rahab looked at the house behind her. "This is your home? It looks larger than my father's."

Meira patted her on the arm. "Salmon is chief of our tribe, my dear, and though he isn't that old, he's actually the leader of the elders who govern this town." She glanced over at her grandson, her eyes full of pride. "He's a war hero, you know, so he was given this house. It was owned by a Canaanite chieftain."

While they were talking, Salmon had told his servants where to put the various burdens the donkeys were carrying and turned the animals over to a stable hand.

"Savta, I am glad to see you looking so well." He looked toward the house and saw his mother standing quietly in the entryway. He went over and embraced her. "I have brought my bride to you, Imah."

Deborah smiled her shy smile. "She is welcome, my son. It is good to see you happy." She came over and embraced Rahab. "I am glad to have a daughter at last."

A young man nearly exploded out of the house. "Salmon, you are here!" he cried, love and admiration in his eyes.

Salmon turned to Rahab. "You remember my young brother, Samuel?"

Rahab laughed. "I hardly recognized you, Samuel! You are not a boy anymore. It has been seven years since I've seen you and you're a man now." He beamed at her.

Meira took Rahab's arm and led her toward the house. "Where are our manners? Your bride has had a long journey and I'm sure she could use some rest."

Deborah spoke quietly. "I must see to the evening meal. My mother will show you the house." As she moved away, Rahab wondered at her bashful manner. *Was Deborah merely shy?* Rahab resolved to make an effort to get to know her mother-in-law better.

As they entered the house, two servants began bringing in Rahab's belongings and Salmon directed them up some stairs.

Samuel called out. "I will give your horse a good brush-down, Salmon."

"Thank you, Samuel. He needs it."

With a smile for Rahab, the young man hurried away.

Rahab marveled at the large open stone corridor. To her left was a small sleeping room, perhaps Meira's, for it held a woman's things. Meira pointed to her right, across the entry, and Rahab saw a workroom with a loom and baskets of yarn, along with several spindles for turning the wool into yarn. Pots for dying the yarn were along the wall. As they stood there, a servant was placing Rahab's own loom and yarn in a corner of the room.

Meira pointed to some steps. "These go up to the roof, where we dry the flax, figs, and grapes. It also goes to a sleeping room."

Salmon, who was following behind them, spoke up, his breath warm on her ear. "That will be the room you and I will share," he whispered.

Rahab breathed a small sigh of relief.

On her left, they came to a large kitchen and storeroom with shelves holding grain, crocks of olives, dried dates and raisins, and flour among other things, including wineskins. There was a large clay oven and a grinding stone for flour. Meira waited while Rahab took a brief look around and they continued down the stone entry. There were more steps. "These lead up to two other sleeping rooms."

At the end of the stone entry was a dining area with a low, U-shaped table and cushions for the family's meals together. Pottery dishes and wooden platters lined the shelves. Meira pointed to a small side room. "This is where we make cheese."

They turned again to Rahab's right and there was a hallway with an alcove holding stacks of wood for the kitchen fires. Past that, Salmon opened a door that lead into an enclosed stable area, where a donkey and several goats were housed.

She wondered where the other donkeys went. Perhaps Salmon had borrowed them from friends. She counted six chickens scratching through the dirt, hunting for bugs. Hay and feed were piled up in an alcove. In the far side of the stable, in his own stall, was Salmon's horse. The gelding was rubbing his head against Samuel as he was being brushed.

Beyond the stable area, an open doorway gave her a glimpse of a kitchen garden and she made a note to herself to check later to see what was growing there.

Salmon went over to pet his horse and Rahab turned to Meira. "I am amazed at the size of this house. There are places for everything. It is similar to the home I had in Jericho."

Meira put her hand to her chest and she puffed up with pride. "My dear, you have married a very smart man. Salmon used the spoils he saved from the years of war to set this house in order after the siege of Bethlehem."

Rahab put her arm around Meira. "I suspect you had a lot to do with that."

Salmon returned to them. "You have been most gracious to show my bride her new home, grandmother, and I thank you. I will show her our quarters and let her get her things settled."

He took Rahab's hand and led her away, up the steps to the sleeping quarters they would share. He closed the wooden door, took her in his arms, and kissed her. "We will have the night to ourselves, beloved, but for now, do what you need to do with your things." He indicated some pegs on the wall and a wooden cupboard.

Some of Salmon's clothes hung from the pegs and there were shelves where he had placed some of his items that could just be folded. Next to the shelves, she saw an extra pair of sandals.

She was weary and grateful for a time to rest. As he held her, the longing for him rose up and she knew it would take little to draw him to the bed, yet they both recognized how weary she was.

"The night will be ours, beloved, but for now, rest." He kissed her again and left, closing the door behind him. Leaving her things to put away later, she lay down on the bed and sank into an exhausted sleep.

31

The light from the one window was fading and shadows filled the room as Rahab woke with a start. Salmon was looking down at her, his eyes warm.

"Time to eat, beloved." Taking her hand, he helped her to her feet.

She followed him down the steps to the dining area, where Samuel was already seated. Meira and Deborah were placing dishes of food on the table and the fragrance made Rahab realize how hungry she was. There was a lentil salad with watercress and chunks of goat cheese, along with a familiar dish: squash with capers and mint, no doubt from the garden. There was a bowl of lamb stew with fava beans and fresh flat bread.

Salmon sat on one of the cushions and indicated she was to sit by him.

"I should help with the serving."

He grinned. "Not this first night. You will have plenty of time to do your share. My Savta and Imah will also join us. Our family is not large, so we eat together."

When the other two women sat down, Salmon said the blessing and then looked around the table. "I am grateful to our Lord God, for protecting me during the times of battle, for giving me the desire of my heart"—he smiled at Rahab—"and for bringing us safely to our home."

As she ate the fragrant lamb stew with chunks of bread, Samuel asked her about their journey.

"Oh, it wasn't very long," she said with an ironic smile. "Your brother has had much more experience traveling great distances than I have."

Salmon paused with a chunk of bread in one hand. "She traveled well, little brother, and never once complained."

Rahab looked at her mother-in-law and Salmon's grand-mother, who smiled knowingly. It was obvious who ran the household.

"I would like to be useful in any way I can," Rahab said firmly. "After tonight, you must not treat me like a guest."

Meira chuckled. "Well, then, tomorrow we will go over the household duties and divide them up."

Salmon's eyes twinkled and Rahab knew he was pleased. This was a loving household and she felt fortunate to have not only found a husband she could truly love, but also be welcomed by his family.

The meal passed with pleasant conversation about the crops that were being harvested and Meira shared the news of a couple they knew who were going to be married. Rahab listened carefully, gleaning everything she could. This was now her home and she needed to learn about Bethlehem and its people, particularly since her husband was the chief. *The chief! Perhaps her marriage to an Egyptian paka had helped to prepare her for this.*

When the meal was over, Rahab rose to help clear the table, but a young girl, rather plain and with a substantial figure, appeared and began to take everything away. Rahab's brows knit. *Who was this?*

Seeing her questioning look, Meira spoke up. "Levana helps us in the house. She will clean up from the meal."

Levana gave Rahab a shy smile and continued on with her task.

Nodding to his family, Salmon held a hand out to Rahab. "We will see you in the morning."

Rahab took his hand and rose to her feet. "Good night. The meal was wonderful."

Salmon led her up the stairs to their quarters and when they entered, he closed the wooden door and took her in his arms. "I don't think you will ever know how much I missed you, my beautiful bride," he whispered into her ear, his voice low and throaty.

She leaned against him, savoring his presence and basking in his love. At last, the night was theirs.

32

*I*t was not very long before Rahab knew she was with child and she was filled with joy that she would finally become a mother. When she told Salmon, he picked her up and swung her around their room. "It is what I hoped for, beloved!"

"Put me down, you wild man! You will not help things this way."

He set her back down on her feet and grinned broadly. "When is the child due?"

"I believe around the month of Silvan and the wheat harvest."

He kissed her exuberantly and they went down to tell his family. They were all delighted with the news—even Samuel, who was already planning to teach his future nephew how to use a sling. Of course, Salmon expected a boy.

"I shall be a grandmother at last," Deborah said with her shy smile.

Meira raised her eyebrows. "I was wondering when you were going to tell me that I would finally be a great-grandmother!"

Rahab blinked, astonished. "You knew?"

"Child, I have been around expectant mothers long enough to know the signs. Your face glowed."

Rahab shook her head. *There were no secrets in this household!*

The people of Bethlehem were friendly and Rahab cultivated friendships with two mothers who lived nearby: Tamar, who had a son, and Rebeckah, who had a daughter. Rebeckah was with child again and hoping for a boy this time. Rahab was happy to have someone to share her pregnancy with, to compare symptoms and ask questions.

All of the women in the town worked together when it was time for the almond harvest. They dumped the almonds, still in their split hulls, on cloths they had spread under the trees. If the trees were tall, they used poles to knock down the ripe fruit at the top. Each family was assigned certain trees to nurture, tend, and harvest for their families. After carrying their bundles of almonds home, they removed the hulls and spread the shelled almonds out to dry for a few days. The hulls were fed to the livestock, while the shells were added to firewood in the oven. The almond shells burned hot and often sparked, but they gave off a pleasant aroma.

The men of Bethlehem built a synagogue where the people gathered on the Sabbath and holy days. Salmon often had to meet with the other town elders or sit at the gate to settle a dispute. Everywhere he went, the people deferred to him and treated him with respect.

As the citizens of Bethlehem came to know Rahab, they were gracious to her as well. She made it a point to help wherever she was needed, whether stomping grapes in the winepress, gathering dates in season, or bringing a meal for a family that was suffering from a sickness.

Rahab was thankful that she finally discovered all of the holy days, festivals, and ceremonies of the Shabbat commanded by the Lord God that her family had not learned from Moses.

The three women of her household worked well together in whatever had to be done, whether it was weaving, preparing the meals, or working in the kitchen garden. Samuel's task, along with running errands, was to oversee the animals' care, help the stable hand, or take a turn shepherding.

Salmon often took his brother along when he had tribal matters to attend to. If Rahab produced a son, he would one day follow Salmon as chief, but if she had only daughters, Samuel would become chief at Salmon's death. Rahab prayed earnestly for a son, knowing Salmon longed for a male heir.

A messenger traveling through the towns of Judah brought word from Akim that all was well with her family in Upper Beth-horon. Her sister Jael had given birth to another boy, her third child, while Josiah and his wife Hannah also had a newborn son. Rahab had hoped to visit them every six months or so, but now, that was impossible. She sent word back to them that she was happy, well, and expecting a child.

∽

Months later, Rahab paused, put a protective hand on her swollen belly, and leaned against a wall. The baby kicked and even though it was uncomfortable, she laughed with delight. *With such a mighty kick, surely it was a boy!*

It had become difficult for her to do some of her chores around the house. When she tried, Meira waved a hand at her. "Let *us* do this, Rahab. Growing a baby in the womb takes all your energy."

Now, she sat on a bench in the sun and contemplated her life. The Lord God had been good to her and given her more than she ever hoped for. Her life with Radames was a distant memory; the grief had long since melted into the shadows of the past. She bowed her head and felt the warmth of the Lord's presence once again.

                                                     ~

Lying in bed before the sun had risen, Rahab was sleeping on her side when she was awakened by pain that shot up her spine and seemed to encompass her. She moaned.

Salmon was instantly awake. "Beloved, what is wrong?"

"I believe my time has come. I need your mother and grandmother."

He jumped up and dressed quickly, not bothering to put on his sandals as he rushed out the door.

Meira and Deborah appeared shortly and told Salmon to go down to the courtyard and find something to do. They placed the birthing stool in the center of the room and Deborah began to massage Rahab's back, while Meira gave Rahab a small pillow to squeeze and gently rubbed her sides and her thighs.

"The pains are coming quickly," Meira announced. "You will not be in labor long." She checked Rahab then. "I can see the crown of the head. Bear down and push, as hard as you can."

Rahab pushed and strained as they held her over the birthing stool. The pain was almost unbearable. With a scream she pushed one more time and the child slid from her body into Meira's waiting hands.

"It's a boy! You have a son!" Meira was elated and Deborah beamed. Meira tended to the rest of the labor as Deborah cleaned the baby with a cloth, rubbed him with salt, and wrapped him in swaddling clothes as his lusty cries filled the room. Deborah then put the newborn in Rahab's arms and she guided his mouth to her breast. His sucking caused more pain and she winced.

"It is expected," Deborah assured her softly. "The nursing will draw the womb back."

Salmon was called at last and as he was given the baby to hold, his face was alight with wonderment. He bent down and kissed Rahab on the forehead. "Thank you, beloved, for my son."

Weary from her ordeal, she looked up at her husband. "What shall his name be?"

"He shall be called Boaz. He will be a great chief of our people one day."

"Boaz," she murmured, "strength within him. A good name."

⁓

Boaz lived up to his name. He was a sturdy child, learned quickly, and brought joy to his parents and family. As soon as he was old enough to speak, Salmon taught his son their people's most important prayer, the *Shema*: "Hear, O Israel: the Lord our God, the Lord is one." Boaz loved learning at the Hebrew school in the synagogue and as he grew, he was already a leader among the other children.

As she learned more about Moses and how he brought God's laws to the Israelites in the desert, Rahab understood why they revered this leader who had actually spoken with their God. She marveled at the story of Moses coming down from Mount Sinai with the stone tablets of commandments inscribed directly by the hand of God.

Rahab studied all of the laws and prayers so that she knew them by heart. For the Sabbath, she covered her head with a mantle, passed her hands over the Sabbath candles, and prayed, "Blessed are You, Lord our God, King of the universe, who has sanctified us with His commandment and commanded us to light the candles of holy Shabbat." Her heart soared when she realized that all over Bethlehem—indeed, all over Israel— her kinswomen were passing their hands over the candles and saying this prayer at the same time.

At the time of the grape harvest, Meira came to the end of her long life. Rahab mourned as much as Salmon and his family did. Salmon's grandmother had been a true friend. Yet Rahab and Deborah grew close and she came to appreciate her mother-in-law's quiet, gentle spirit. Deborah had a calming effect when Rahab felt overwhelmed.

Although they tried mightily, Rahab was not able to give Salmon any more children. It grieved her, but she was gratified that she had at least given him a son to carry on his lineage.

⌒

Holding the hands of five-year-old Boaz, Rahab and Salmon stood on a hill overlooking the town of Bethlehem, with its surrounding fields and orchards.

Boaz looked up at his father. "Will I be a chief like you, Abba?"

"Yes, my son. And when I am gathered to my ancestors, you will take my place and sit among the elders. You will help to settle quarrels and decide on matters of our town."

"I will, Abba," Boaz said confidently. "You will teach me how."

EPILOGUE

Boaz became a great chief at the death of his father. As a wealthy land owner and a kinsman redeemer, he married the beautiful Ruth, who came to Bethlehem with her widowed mother-in-law, Naomi, from what was still called the Fields of Moab in the territory allotted to the Reubenites. Ruth gave birth to Obed, who in turn fathered Jesse, who was the father of David, the future king of Israel.

THE AUTHOR'S NOTES ON RAHAB

When Joseph was elevated to prime minister of Egypt, he was given the daughter of the high priest of On as his wife. They had two sons, Manasseh and Ephraim. Manasseh, the older son, was passed over by the Patriarch Jacob and the princely line was given to Ephraim.

Ephraim had three sons and six grandsons. Knowing their heritage, these men boldly entered Canaan and, for whatever reason, stole some cattle. They were all killed by the men of Gath. Ephraim despaired that the princely line was lost. Then Ephraim had another son, Beriah, who in turn had a daughter he named Sherah. (See 1 Chronicles 7:20–24.)

Sherah became a great chieftainess and eventually moved her family and household to Canaan, where she founded three towns: Upper and Lower Beth-horon, and Beth-Sherah. The generations of her family line did not experience the slavery of their kinsmen in Egypt. They did not meet Moses and travel with him for forty years in the desert, nor did they hear the Lord's law that Moses gave to the people. Sherah's descendants were only reunited with their kinsmen when Joshua led the army into Canaan to take the Promised Land.

Rahab's name is Hebrew and while it means "wide and large," the poetic meaning is "remembering Egypt." This is not a name that a Canaanite mother would give to her daughter, for that would be like a woman who had experienced Nazi terror during World War II naming her child "remembering Germany." The Canaanites were under the authority and oppression of the Egyptians.

The house in Jericho where Rahab lived was part of the wall (see Joshua 2:15) and an embassy would be placed at this location. There was an Egyptian governor, called a paka, placed in every major town in Canaan and these men collected tribute for pharaoh. Perhaps you might call them glorified tax collectors.

Since Rahab is alone and in the Urdu language and some of the other eastern languages, the word for *harlot* and *widow* are interchangeable, I made her the widow of the late governor of Jericho. I did not see her as a prostitute, since I believe she was Hebrew and if she had a family to return to after being widowed, she had no need to turn to prostitution. This "profession" was the only recourse for a woman totally alone with no family to support her. Rahab had family. (See Joshua 2:12–13.) If she was a prostitute, her family could not only disown her, but also have her stoned to death for her sin.

Because it was an embassy and officially Egyptian territory, the city's soldiers who were seeking the Israeli messengers could not enter the building. As you will read in the Scriptures, they stood outside the door and asked Rahab to send the men out to them.

Another factor I kept in mind when designating Rahab as an Ephraimite and not a Canaanite was Deuteronomy 7:1–5, in which the Lord God named seven nations that the Jewish people were *never* to intermarry with or the anger of the Lord would be against them. He wanted these nations to be destroyed. The Lord never rescinded that commandment. One of the nations named was Canaan. While it was not encouraged, the Jewish people *were* permitted to marry Egyptians due to their heritage through Ephraim. It did not therefore figure that the Lord would allow a Canaanite woman—especially a prostitute—to be included in the pure lineage of Christ. Neither would the Lord save a whole family of pagan Canaanites in defiance of His own law.

When I began writing books, I felt the Lord commissioned me to take women of the Bible who had been portrayed in a negative way and show them in a different light. This is the theme of all my books. This is the way I felt led to portray Rahab.